crash

A WILLOWBROOK NOVEL
BOOK 1

LILY ANH NAM

*This book is dedicated to all of those who give so much to others
that you forget to take care of yourself.
You deserve to be taken care of, too.
Reading this book is a form of self-care.
I hope you find your Griffin.*

blurb

A driven young woman loses her direction...

Quynh Le always puts work first and is used to being alone. She has no social life, no family, no relationship... unless you count her cranky cat. When she's unexpectedly fired from her job as a nurse practitioner, she feels lost and adrift. A cryptic text from her stepsister about her estranged father's failing health has her returning to the small town of Willowbrook—the place that tore her family apart twenty-six years ago.

A grumpy mechanic finds more than he bargained for...

Griffin Kennedy likes his life the way it is—no drama, no complications, definitely no women. He doesn't want anybody messing with the stability he's found, especially not the naïve, cheerful woman whose car breaks down just outside of town. But when he realizes Quynh has no place to stay, he strikes a deal to let her stay in the studio apartment above his shop in exchange for her help as his secretary while she's visiting her father.

When convenience gives way to craving, the spark

between these two opposites develops into a fiery affair. Can two very independent people let down their walls long enough to fall in love?

Opposites attract in this small town grumpy/sunshine romance from author Lily Anh Nam. Sweet and spicy— CRASH is all about healing old wounds and finding new direction.

content warning

This book is a contemporary romance for 18+ readers only. This is not intended to be a comprehensive list of the contents. Please read responsibly and mind your triggers.

Crash: A Willowbrook Novel (book 1) contains explicit language, sexually explicit scenes, mental health issues, history of drug and alcohol abuse, burnout, compassion fatigue, cancer and terminally ill parent, estranged family, death of a friend (in the past). It also contains brief mention of toxic parents.

For a full list, please visit my website: www.lilyanhnam.com

smut guide

For those looking for a good time. Or for those who wish to avoid it. You will find sexually explicit content in the following chapters.

Chapter 13, 19, 20, 22, 24, 36, 37

foreword

One more thing before you start, the female main character's name is Quynh. She is Vietnamese and goes by "Quinn." The Vietnamese pronunciation is "kwin" or "gun-wing."

Thank you so, so much for your time. I truly appreciate your support.

1

Quynh tried to fight back the tears pressing incessantly at the back of her eyes the entire drive to Willowbrook. She turned up the radio, blasting the catchy pop song through the sound system of her dilapidated car. Unfortunately, as she belted out the emotional lyrics, she lost the battle, and the dam burst open. It was a valiant effort, though.

She was not a superstitious person, unlike her mother, but even she knew bad news on New Year's Day was a bad omen. Quynh couldn't understand why the universe decided to slap her with a termination letter on Chinese New Year. Out of all of the days in the year, the news happened on the most important one.

Her life had taken a steep nosedive into the shitter over the past twenty-four hours. Instead of buckling under the weight of her world falling apart so spectacularly, she held her head high, packed a small bag containing her meager belongings, and high-tailed it out of town. There was nothing left for her in the city except her broken dreams.

Until this moment, Quynh kept herself together by sheer will and determination. The frayed edges of her pride barely held on to her sanity as the miles stretched on, moving her away from grim reality and into the unknown.

Quynh promised herself she would not let the past twenty-four hours break her, but here she was. As sobs racked her petite frame, she reasoned some promises were meant to be broken.

She tried not to dwell on the what-ifs and focused on the future. What used to be a clear picture in her mind was now a murky puddle, at best. No matter what her future might look like, Quynh knew she would be fine once she overcame this giant speed bump in her life. Because that's all this was. A giant speed bump. When she was on the other side of said speed bump, she would look back and think things needed to happen this way in order for her to have a better and brighter future.

It didn't mean she couldn't wallow in self-pity for at least a little while as she licked her wounds.

She passed the state's welcome sign a few hours ago, which meant there were only a few more hours left until she reached her destination. Quynh never thought she'd ever return to Willowbrook. Especially not after how she left the picturesque mountain town years ago, but here she was, speeding down the highway toward the last place she wanted to be. If her mother were still alive, she'd give Quynh a stern lecture about responsibilities and *not running away from your problems*. The thought of her mother sent Quynh into another round of racking sobs. It had been a while since she thought about her mother.

Everything had to happen for a reason, right?

As the song came to a dramatic end, she took a deep inhale to center herself. Her phone pinged in the cupholder, alerting her to a new message. Shuddering, Quynh refused to look at another email for as long as she lived. The last time she got an email, it had been the match that set her world on fire.

For the past few years, Quynh worked as a nurse practitioner. Last night, her phone had pinged with a new email. She forgot to turn it on silent for the night. Just as she got settled into bed, her phone pinged with an alert. Curious, Quynh unplugged her phone from the charger and saw a new email notification flash across her screen.

Unlocking her phone, she'd rolled her eyes at the message preview, which showed her name was misspelled. Though it was pronounced 'Quinn', it was frustrating after years of working with Jared, he still didn't know how to spell her name correctly. Annoyance quickly changed to confusion at receiving a message so late on a Friday night. She should have listened to her gut and not opened it until the next day, but the red alert beckoned her.

Her finger trembled as she opened up the email. It was an unusually long message from her employer. A cold wave of dread washed over her as she read the opening sentence, each word like a chilling premonition. Frantically, she'd scrolled to the bottom of the message.

To her horror, the last paragraph stated her employment with the company was terminated effective immediately because of "budget cuts and low funding." Donations and grants from the federal government were necessary to keep the non-profit organization running, and apparently, the well dried up.

The news hit her like a ton of bricks, leaving her in stunned silence. She'd stared slack-jawed at her phone for what seemed like hours, although it was probably only a couple of minutes. She'd snapped out of it when Pickles, her oversized Maine Coon, meowed in irritation at her lack of attention. Giving him a quick pat on the head with a shaky hand, she'd tried to go back to sleep, but thoughts of her future raced through her mind. After tossing and turning for hours, Quynh finally fell into a fitful sleep.

When she finally woke earlier that morning, she was determined to soldier on.

Quynh was a professional with a master's degree and

many years of experience under her belt. She was marketable and employable. There was no need to panic.

Empowered by her pep talk, Quynh leaped out of bed, accidentally bumping Pickles, who let out a disgruntled huff and thump of his fluffy tail. She gave the cranky old cat a loving pat on his head as she bounded to her bathroom. Dressed in jeans and a loose sweater, she skipped putting any makeup on.

She needed to head into the office to gather her belongings. Since it was a Saturday, the office was closed, and she'd rather be alone for this than have an audience. She shuddered to think about the pitying looks on their faces if she waited for Monday.

No, thank you. I do not need to be a spectacle or the added humiliation.

Marching into her living room, Quynh located a cardboard box. She had been too lazy to take it down to the other side of her apartment complex for recycling. In this case, her laziness worked out in her favor. Besides, Pickles had been enjoying hiding inside the box for the past couple of weeks. She flipped the box upside down to rid it of the fur balls Pickles left behind.

She'd clean up the mess when she got back.

Box in one hand, Quynh grabbed her purse and keys from the table by the door. She found her favorite pair of sneakers and headed out of her small apartment.

She couldn't think about her future yet. First things

first. She needed to get her stuff from her office. Then, she'd figure out her next steps.

Quynh drove the short distance to the clinic, where she spent more time than at home. As she pulled into the parking lot, she noticed a slew of police cars in front of the building.

Frowning, Quynh parked her car at the edge of the parking lot before slowly getting out of her car with the box in one hand. Bright yellow crime scene tape, stark against the building's aged brick, created a chilling and foreboding atmosphere. Quynh suppressed the rising panic at the scenarios flashing through her mind.

Why are the police here?

Hesitantly, she approached the police officer standing guard at the entrance of the building. He looked her over disdainfully when she was a few feet away.

"What's going on?" she asked.

The police officer placed his hands on his belt and waited for a beat before responding.

"Can I help you?"

"I work—worked here…I was coming by to get my belongings."

His expression shifted from disinterest to curiosity at her response.

"What's your name?" He pulled out a notepad from his breast pocket, clicked his pen, and poised it as if to take notes. When she didn't immediately answer, he glanced up at her with an eyebrow raised.

"Um…Quynh Le. Can I go inside? I'll be really quick." She gestured with her empty cardboard box as if that would convince him.

"You can't enter the premises. This building is a crime scene."

Her head reared back in surprise.

"Did something happen here?"

Was someone hurt after I left last night?

She was usually the last person to leave, but the night before, Jared had still been in his office when she left.

"I can't discuss the details."

The main doors creaked open just as she was about to ask more questions. She watched in horror as someone wheeled a gurney out with a black body bag.

The blood drained from her face as she stared in shock. Her ears rang as her attention focused on the obviously dead body being wheeled into the ambulance.

"Ma'am, are you okay?"

She snapped back to attention when a hand gripped her upper arm.

"I'm f-fine," she lied as the earth tilted beneath her feet.

"You should sit down." He guided her to the curb and gently pushed her to sit.

With her butt firmly on the curb, she inhaled deeply as the dizziness subsided. A dozen different scenarios flitted through her mind. The officer stood beside her as she caught her bearings. When she glanced up, she realized he was studying her.

"What do you do for work?"

"I'm a nurse practitioner for the clinic."

"Why do you need to get your things?"

"I-I got an email late last night from Jared that I was terminated." A flush crawled up her neck, and her cheeks heated with embarrassment.

The officer paused before tucking his notepad away into his breast pocket.

"Can you show me the email, please, miss?"

"Oh, uh, yeah, sure." She fumbled to grab her cell phone tucked in her back pocket. Her hands were trembling, and it took several attempts before she could unlock her phone and pull up the email.

"Here."

The officer grabbed her phone out of her hands. She bit down on her lip and tucked her hands between her thighs to stop them from trembling. A prickle of unease rolled down her spine. She forced herself to remain still as his eyes scanned the email. Voices trickled into her awareness as she waited with bated breath. Her eyes roamed the mill of people bustling around the building. A quick glance around confirmed she was the subject of several people's attention. The noises from the crime scene on the otherwise quiet street amplified her anxiety. The officer's face furrowed in concentration when he reached the bottom of the email. She didn't want to focus on how embarrassing it was to have your most shameful moment shared so candidly.

After a tense moment, he finally looked up from her phone and requested a copy of the email. At her nod, he typed on her phone. She assumed he forwarded the email to his own as evidence.

"Thank you. You've been very helpful," the officer finally said. "I'm afraid I can't let you into the building until we clear it."

"What happened?"

"The cleaning service called us this morning to report that they found a man dead in his office."

She stared wide-eyed at the officer, covering her mouth with a hand as the shock of the news hit her.

"Was it...?"

"I'm afraid the details are confidential."

She nodded along as if everything he said made sense

when, in reality, she couldn't figure out which way was up or down anymore. He handed her his business card, got her information, and assured her he would be in contact if necessary.

She vaguely recalled getting into her car and driving back to her apartment. She'd sat on the couch in a daze until an alert pinged through her phone.

Frowning, she pulled her phone out to check the message from an unknown number.

UNKNOWN

Dad's in the hospital. Doc said he won't have much longer. Thought you should know.

Only one person could be texting her.

2

The sounds of the shop closing for the evening were like music to his ears. Griffin watched as Julio and Sean left for the evening. It was just past five in the evening, and the sun was setting beyond the horizon. The daylight hours were getting shorter as summer slowly came to an end. He was not looking forward to the impending days when the sunlight disappeared even earlier. He didn't enjoy working in the dark. The cold weather didn't bother him too much, but the dark days were rough.

There were a few things that still needed to be done around the office before he could retire for the evening. Griffin stifled a groan at the work waiting for him. He was looking forward to putting his feet up and relaxing with a cold beer. It had been another long week. He missed the days when he didn't have to do the bullshit paperwork, but since he'd fired Delilah a couple of months ago, the paperwork just kept piling up.

Thankfully, Julio and Sean were both competent mechanics, able to keep the shop running smoothly and complete orders on time so he could handle the administrative tasks, but, dammit, he missed the hands-on work.

Griffin wasn't cut out for office work. He'd known from the start. Firing Delilah had been a long time coming, though. Griffin first hired her when he was desperate for some help around the office. She had been young and enthusiastic and came with a great recommendation from his long-term client, Henderson. And, begrudgingly, she was good at her job for a while.

Unfortunately, Delilah got it into her head he was interested in her romantically and wanted to pursue a more intimate relationship than one he was comfortable with.

At first, the flirting was irritating, but when it didn't seem to work, she doubled her efforts by dressing provocatively at work. The guys all noticed—of course they did. They'd even given him a hard time about it, too. They made jokes about an illicit office affair between him and his secretary. None of which was true.

Despite his efforts to set clear professional boundaries as her boss, Delilah was frustratingly persistent. A couple of months ago, he let Julio and Sean leave work early. It had been a slow week for them, and he could finish the rest of the job by himself. He thought he'd heard Delilah leaving earlier, but the rhythmic thump of his wrench against the underside of the car and the music blaring through the radio masked what he'd thought was her departure.

Imagine his surprise when someone climbed onto his lap. He'd barely resisted the urge to bolt upright and bang his head against the car.

Fingers crawled up his abdomen as Griffin quickly rolled himself out from under the car. He'd known who it was before seeing her face. He could barely suppress the rage at her audacity. He should have fired her a long time ago, but he gave her the benefit of the doubt. He could no longer ignore her advances.

"Delilah. What do you think you're doing?" he'd bit out through a clenched jaw, forcibly removing her from his lap.

She'd pouted when he plopped her unceremoniously onto the dirty cement floor.

"I thought you sent the guys home so we could be alone together."

Brows furrowed in confusion, he'd noticed she'd changed from what she'd been wearing earlier. Instead of the low-cut shirt and skirt she'd often wear around the office, she was now wearing a shirt so sheer that he could see the red lace of her bra.

He stood up to put some distance between them.

"You thought wrong." Heat crawled up his neck with his repressed fury.

She scrambled to stand up, straightening her outfit and fixing her hair. He'd never once let his eyes stray. Griffin was man enough to admit she was an attractive woman, but he'd never been interested in Delilah sexually.

He'd been patient with her, hoping she'd get the clue he would never sleep with her.

"Delilah, this has gone too far. You're fired." The harsh words left his mouth and hung in the air between them.

Griffin had watched, unmoved, as tears filled her blue eyes.

"You-you're f-firing me?" Her tears spilled over as she crossed her arms over her chest. "You can't do that!"

Griffin tried not to flinch at her shrill voice. Hands braced on his hips, he stepped away from her. He knew exactly where the security cameras were in the garage. In the event things went south, he needed irrefutable proof that he was not the aggressor.

"I'll leave so you can pack up your things in peace." Giving her a curt nod, he'd turned and exited through the open garage bay doors.

That was the last time he'd seen Delilah.

The paperwork could wait until tomorrow. Decision made, he turned off the computer and hoisted himself out of the chair with a groan.

Griffin made his way to the back lot. He pursed his lips, let out a sharp whistle, and waited impatiently for the sound of Rover's giant paws on the packed dirt as he bounded from the woods. When Rover was not by his side in the shop, he liked to go into the woods to hunt for bunnies and squirrels. Hunting was probably a strong word for what he really did with the forest animals. More like rolling in the grass and frolicking like the big buffoon he was.

"Come on, buddy, let's go home."

They walked side-by-side across the street to the two-story house he'd built across from the auto body shop about five years ago. His property bordered Crystal Hollow Lake, a large lake that offered him stunning sunrises and sunsets daily. He'd loved watching the boats coming back to the dock in the evenings as Rover ran around the backyard.

For years, he lived in the apartment above the shop, and when the opportunity came for him to buy the lakefront property across the street, he'd pounced on it. It had taken over a year before he could move into his home, but it was well worth the wait to have his own sanctuary.

Opening the front door, he stripped out of his coveralls in the hallway. He normally kept it at the shop, but he did not want to stick around for another minute with Delilah there. The last thing he needed was to be caught in a precarious situation with him being partially undressed.

Griffin dragged his feet into the shower after hanging

up his coveralls in the hallway closet. His home was small, but it had everything he needed. Normally, he'd cook dinner for himself and Rover, but tonight, he just wanted to relax. Hair damp from the shower, Griffin trekked to the kitchen to heat up some leftovers in the microwave. While he waited for his food to get nuked, he grabbed an IPA out of the fridge. The beer made a satisfying fizz when he cracked it open with the bottle opener attached to his fridge. The bitter taste exploded across his taste buds. He let out a sigh as his tensed muscles loosened. Rover was already waiting for him in the living room for their evening routine, which consisted of watching the news before bedtime.

The microwave chimed. He carried his dinner and beer to the living room. He'd just turned on the TV and put his feet up before he heard the unmistakable sound of his phone ringing.

"Fucking Christ, can't a guy catch a damn break?" A rhetorical question as Rover glanced up from his spot with furrowed brows.

He didn't look at who was calling him before barking into the offending object in his hand.

"Hello?" The sound of static filled his ears as he waited for whoever dared to interrupt his evening to answer. After a moment of silence, the static cleared as a woman's soft voice came on the line.

"Oh. Hi! I didn't expect anyone to answer so quickly. The service out here is terrible."

"What do you want?" Griffin winced at his harsh words.

"Oh, um, I need help." Her voice seemed to crack on the last word. "My car broke down, and I'm about ten miles from town."

Griffin bit back a curse. He dragged in a deep, calming breath before he said anything else he'd regret later. He couldn't let her be stranded on the side of the road. Besides, he knew Ricky was out of town for the weekend and wouldn't be back for a few more days.

"Yeah, alright. Give me a few minutes." His heavy sigh hung between them.

"Oh, thank—" Her phone cut off before she could finish her statement.

Groaning, Griffin took his beer back to the kitchen and watched as it went down the drain. It was his favorite IPA, but there were plenty in the fridge.

Maybe tomorrow he'd have better luck on a relaxing evening, but now, he needed to rescue a damsel in distress.

Griffin scoffed at the idea of being someone's knight in shining armor.

3

"No, no, no, Shelly, don't do this to me. Please," Quynh cried as she tried to convince her car, named after its eggshell color, to give her at least a few more miles. Her destination was only ten miles away based on the navigation of her dying phone. But, as she pulled a sputtering and jerking Shelly to the side of the road, she knew she was out of luck.

The smoke coming from the hood of her car was also not a good omen. She stopped in the emergency lane on the nearly abandoned road, putting Shelly in park before turning the ignition off. Quynh took some deep, calming breaths, but the death rattle beneath Shelly's hood and a giant puff of dark smoke billowing out broke her composure.

She smacked her head on the steering wheel a few times and let out a scream of frustration. The last thing she needed was another disaster. She knew bad things happened in threes, so at least she'd gotten them all over with at this point. There was nowhere left to go but up. God, she hoped so.

After another moment of wallowing, Quynh lifted her head off the steering wheel, wiped her tears away, and took a few calming breaths. Leaning over, she rooted around her glove compartment for some drive-through napkins she hoarded. She needed to collect herself.

Get your shit together, Quynh.

As far as pep talks go, it was all she could muster, but it seemed to help wrangle her composure back under control.

Quynh had fallen in love with the rusted VW Beetle when she first saw it sitting alone in the back lot of the dealership. Her previous car expelled its last rattling breath on the very same highway she was currently traveling after working a brutal fourteen-hour shift at the hospital.

She couldn't afford a new car at the time since she'd decided to go back to school to get her master's degree. It seemed like a great idea at the time. Her first job as a nurse practitioner wouldn't start for at least another couple of months. Unfortunately, her student loans would be crippling until she started her new job.

The salesman, Jimmy, pounced on her as soon as she set foot on the lot. Jimmy tried to get her to look at all of their brand-new vehicles, but she'd been adamant about buying a used one. Reluctantly, Jimmy brought her to the back, where a lot of their used cars were sitting, collecting dust. This lot resembled more like a ghost town, each car appearing worse for wear.

She'd perused the options, and just when she was about to admit defeat, she spotted Shelly in the back. Shelly was a faded yellow Volkswagen buggy with rusted rims and a pale pink flower on its hood. Honestly, she was cute but completely impractical. The price tag sold her. She'd taken joy out of the look of horror that crossed over Jimmy's face when she'd pointed at Shelly.

He probably thought no one would ever actually be interested in the disaster of a car, but after taking the buggy for a test drive, Quynh couldn't find any reason she shouldn't buy Shelly right then and there. Once back inside the showroom of the dealership, she'd sat down with Jimmy, who continued to subtly push her toward the cars in the showroom.

Once Jimmy realized how futile it was to continue trying to dissuade her, he led her to his office. Quynh knew that because she was a woman, sales agents were more likely to take advantage of her. So, she was ready when Jimmy extended the price tag. Quynh met his gaze unflinchingly with her arms folded defensively across her chest. Her eyes held a silent challenge. Jimmy squirmed in his seat under her intense stare.

"I'll give you $2500 for that piece of junk."

Jimmy balked at her boldness before collecting himself.

"I'm afraid I can't do that, but for the current price tag, I can add on some free oil changes for the next year."

"Fine." She watched as he'd sagged in relief. Sitting back in her seat, she inspected her nails. "I'll give you $1500. Final offer. Oh, and the free oil changes stay."

Poor Jimmy. He'd probably thought he had an easy sale, but what Jimmy didn't know was that she had years of experience with haggling. It was in her blood. Her mother was the best haggler known in the history of haggling. She'd learned from the best.

The moment Jimmy capitulated, she knew by his defeated posture. He'd let out a sigh and pinched the bridge of his nose. Jimmy gave her an appraising glance before turning to his computer to draw up the contract for the sale. She'd driven off the lot with Shelly that same day.

Shelly had been a faithful servant to her for years. She'd driven her through all the ever-changing New England weather, always reliably getting her from point A to point B with only a few shudders and screeches when she turned the engine over.

Until today.

After pulling her phone down from its stand, she checked for any messages or missed calls. Ruth didn't even bother to reply to any of the messages Quynh sent, leaving her on read. Nor did Ruth answer when she tried to call. Instead, she was sent straight to voicemail. The last attempt at calling didn't even ring before getting Ruth's voicemail. Ruth probably blocked her number. Quynh and Ruth had a contentious relationship. She didn't blame Ruth for hating her. After all, it was technically her fault for Ruth's complex relationship with their father.

The navigation app showed she was stuck right outside of Willowbrook. She could make out the peaks of the snowcapped mountains. She was so close to reaching her destination, but the universe was working against her this week. Quynh sighed as she opened her internet browser to search for the nearest auto body shop to tow her car to.

The last time she was in Willowbrook, she was about nine years old. She never thought she would ever step foot back into this small town, not after what sent her mother packing in the middle of the night. Thoughts of her mother threatened to drag her back down. She forcefully shoved them away. She needed to focus on the task at hand.

With the sun setting behind her, she did not want to be stuck on the side of the road when it got dark. The thought of hitchhiking her way into town didn't appeal to her either. Considering there were no other cars on the road for the past few miles, it didn't bode well for her. She would have to spend the night sleeping in her car. Unfortunately, Shelly lacked a full back seat. It would be cramped despite her petite frame.

No, thank you.

Quynh pulled up the contact information for the first towing company that came up and clicked 'call.' She held the phone to her ear as it rang. And rang. And rang. Finally, the phone clicked on.

"Hi! I need he—."

"Hello, you've reached Ricky's Auto and Towing. Unfortunately, we are closed. If you need emergency services, please contact Griffin's Auto Body."

The sound of the recording ended as the phone number to Griffin's Auto Body was rattled off. Quynh hung up and called again to catch the phone number. She dialed the new number and lamented her misfortune when the phone rang again.

Just as she thought she was out of luck, she heard the phone click on. Holding her breath, she waited for a beat. After a pause, a gruff voice answered the line.

"Hello?"

"Oh. Hi! I didn't expect anyone to answer so quickly. The service out here is terrible." Excitement was clear in her voice.

"What do you want?" Quynh deflated at the abrasive tone. Guess today won't be getting better anytime soon.

"Oh, um, I need help. My car broke down, and I'm

about ten miles from town." She bit her lip, fingers tapping against the steering wheel to distract herself from breaking down in tears again.

"Yeah, alright. Give me a few minutes."

"Oh, thank-"

Quynh pulled her phone away from her ear as the tell-tale tone of her phone shutting itself off echoed in her ears.

"Wow, that was...rude."

She blew her bangs out of her face and rested her head against the headrest.

What a day today had been.

She tried not to let her thoughts spiral, but the events of the last twenty-four hours had finally caught up to her. Tears welled in her eyes as the crushing sensation of being lost threatened to consume her. She fought so hard to get to where she was today. She'd undergone years of therapy and worked through her insecurities to help her move forward with her life and her career. It was all for nothing. She knew she was being dramatic, but she was allowed to be.

I can't believe I was fired.

Never in her life did she imagine she would be fired from a job. Even more astounding was shortly after, she watched her boss wheel away in a body bag. After her embarrassing encounter with the detective at the crime scene, they asked her to go down to the precinct to answer some questions.

With her options limited to driving herself or a ride in his police car, Quynh reluctantly agreed. She opted to drive herself to the police station instead of being transported in the back of his police car like a suspect. Quynh wanted to get it over with quickly so she could move on with her life. Besides, it wasn't like she had anything useful to report.

As she sat in the cold, sterile examination room, she reflected on the absurdity of the moment. At the direction of the detective, she gave a statement that was recorded for evidence. Following her statement, the detectives informed her Jared was under investigation, but refused to answer her when she pressed for more details. After what seemed like hours, the detectives wrapped up their questioning and told her they'd stay in touch if there were any fresh developments. Until then, she could not get her belongings from the office until the investigation was complete.

In those awful moments, she was trapped like some damsel in distress stuck inside a horror movie or a living nightmare.

She fought back more tears as the setting sun cast a kaleidoscope of colors in her rearview mirror. Streams of pink, purple, and orange stretched across the horizon. It would be a magnificent sight if she weren't so distraught.

She reached over the glove compartment for more napkins and blew her nose. A loud knock at her window made her jump.

Her heart leapt in her chest at the man looking down at her. A very large, but handsome man. Her nerves calmed slightly when she caught sight of his name patch, Griffin, embroidered on his thick coat.

At his gesture, she rolled her car window down. Shelly did not have automatic windows, and she squawked noisily at being mishandled. Quynh pressed her lips together as she continued to roll the window down.

"You called for help?"

"Yes, my car broke down. I can't get it to start up again." She winced at how hoarse her voice sounded from crying.

Griffin grunted as if annoyed with the situation.

Me too, buddy.

She watched as Griffin walked to the front of her car. The look of disappointment as he stared down at Shelly made her want to cringe. Hands on his hips, he brought his assessing gaze up to meet hers through the dirty window.

"You're going to need to tow it back to the shop."

Her brow furrowed in confusion. She got out of Shelly and slowly approached Griffin.

Isn't that why he was here?

"I didn't think Shelly would make it into town, so I called for a tow truck," she stated slowly.

"No, you called an auto body shop. I don't tow. That's Ricky's gig. And who the fuck is Shelly?"

Her mouth parted in surprise.

"But the message on Ricky's voicemail said to call Griffin's Auto Body in case of emergencies. Well, I would consider this an emergency." She gestured toward her broken-down car. "And Shelly is my car." At that moment, Shelly let out a puff of black smoke as if she were saying hello.

He whipped his head to glare at her. She was unprepared for the intensity of his ire and flinched backwards. His facial expression softened slightly as he placed his hands on his hips. Quynh watched in fascination as he threw his head back with a groan.

He's so tall.

It was hard to judge, but she guessed he was probably at least 6'4".

"That fucking bastard." Griffin covered his mouth with a giant hand. She watched the muscles of his biceps flex as he rubbed his hand across his five o'clock shadow.

Quynh crossed her arms as she tried to make sense of what was happening.

"Umm...can you tell me what's happening here?"

At her words, he turned to face her, so they stood toe to toe.

"Yeah, Ricky's a dumb bastard trying to get me back for something."

"So…he…pranked you?"

She tried not to shrink as he looked her up and down. When their eyes met again, his anger dissipated. In the retreating light of the sun, she saw flecks of green in his eyes.

"Listen, I don't have a tow truck. That's Ricky's job. He tows it, and I fix it. I'll give you a ride into town and come back for your car later."

She turned to look behind Shelly, finally noticing the big truck parked right behind hers.

"Yeah, ok. Let me just grab my things from the trunk."

Making her way to the back of her car, she popped the trunk and grabbed the single bag she'd packed. She didn't plan to stay in town for long. Honestly, Quynh didn't think much beyond the next couple of days.

She left her suitcase and rounded to the passenger side door. Leaning in, she grabbed the heavy cat carrier from the back seat. Pickles was still snoozing inside without a care in the world. He normally hated car rides, but she'd given him some extra catnip to keep him comfortable for the ride. She might have given him just a little too much catnip in her rush to get out of her apartment. He had not made a peep in a couple of hours.

She rounded Shelly and noticed her suitcase was gone. Griffin approached her warily.

"What is that?"

He waved his hand at the cat carrier.

"Oh, this?" She flipped the oversized carrier to show a still snoozing Pickles lying on his side. "This is Pickles, my emotional support cat."

She could see the skeptical look in his eyes. He probably thought she was crazy, but she didn't care. Pickles was her constant companion for the past decade. He'd been there for her through nursing school and then later when she went back for her master's degree. Not to mention, he helped her through her failed relationships.

"Well, Pickles is not getting in my truck."

"What?" she sputtered in surprise.

"He is not getting in my truck."

Her jaw dropped in shock and anger. She would not leave her cat behind, even for just a few minutes. She hugged the carrier to her chest.

"I am not leaving him behind." She balked at the suggestion.

Quynh glared at him. Making sure he knew how ridiculous his suggestion was. Judging by the muscle clenching in his jaw, he was not happy with the idea, but too fucking bad. She'd wait in the car and call for another tow truck if it came down to it.

She knew the moment he relented as the tension bled from his shoulders. Griffin dropped his hands to his sides and gave her a curt nod before turning back to the truck.

The passenger door was left open for her, and she gently placed Pickles down in the seat before climbing into the truck. At her height of 4'11", it was a little difficult, but she made it inside the cab of the truck without falling on her face. She saw it as a win, considering how her life turned upside down in such a short time period.

She placed Pickles in the middle of the bench and reached for the seatbelt. Only then did she realize she'd left something important behind.

"Oh, shoot. I forgot my purse!"

Griffin let out a frustrated sigh. He stood poised with his door open, but before she said anything else, he stomped back to her car. She watched him as he opened Shelly's driver's side door and grabbed her purse from the passenger seat. He also grabbed her car keys, which she'd left in the ignition. She flushed in embarrassment at her oversight. He even locked her car up for her before stalking back to the truck.

The overhead light illuminated his thunderous expression as he climbed into the truck and handed her purse to her. She accepted it graciously and murmured a soft thanks under her breath. She stayed quiet as he started up the truck and set off down the road leading to Willowbrook.

The silence in the truck was taut with tension. Neither one of them spoke as the miles passed. The only sounds in the truck were Pickles's soft snores. As far as emotional support animals go, Pickles was not the best at his job at the moment. If not for the extra catnip, he'd likely be yowling and howling at the injustice. He hated car rides with a passion. She couldn't blame him. The only few times she'd taken him on a car ride were to go to the vet for his annual vaccines. After the first time she brought Pickles to the vet, she'd been instructed to give him sedatives before his next appointment. Apparently, he got extra feisty with the vet when they tried to give him his shots.

"I'm Quynh, by the way. Thank you for helping me." Her voice echoed loudly in the truck. He merely grunted in response.

A minute of silence passed before his gravelly voice broke the quiet. "Where ya headed?"

"Um, I'm not sure. I was going to see if there was a hotel with availability tonight."

His hands gripped the steering wheel in an unforgiving grip. Knuckles white, he turned to glare at her.

"There are no hotels in Willowbrook," he said through gritted teeth.

No hotels? There are hotels everywhere.

"Willowbrook Inn is undergoing renovations. The nearest hotel is about twenty-five miles past town."

"Oh." Well, that put a damper on her plan. "Can you just drop me off somewhere, and I can get an Uber to the hotel?"

She swore she saw steam coming out of his ears as he took in a fortifying breath.

"There are no Uber drivers in Willowbrook."

Despite knowing Willowbrook was a small town, she would have thought it would have the basic amenities by now. Silence filled the truck bed as she tried to figure out her options. She didn't really have much of a plan other than getting here as quickly as she could. She still needed to visit her father, but she got little information from the single text message Ruth sent her. So, she'd still have to track Ruth down later and figure out the next step.

Griffin let out a long sigh and ran a hand through his dark curls that were longer on top. The sides of his head was cropped short giving him a dangerous appeal. One she shouldn't be noticing.

"I can set you up in the extra bedroom above my garage. You'll have your own space and a bathroom. The kitchen is small, though."

Taken aback by his kind offer, she was quiet for a moment. When he dared to look at her, she gave him a shy smile and nodded.

"If you don't mind, that would be great. Thank you. I can pay you for the room."

"No bother. I'll send Ricky to get your car in the morning."

Well, looks like she had a place to stay, after all.

4

The rest of the drive was quiet as Griffin drove them into Willowbrook. Pressed against the car door, she watched as the streetlights turned on in the sleepy town while the sky darkened behind them. The sunset was nearly complete, though the last rays of light still stretched longingly across the sky. She'd have to admire the magnificent colors another day when she had the time to appreciate them. It would also be nice if her world weren't collapsing so quickly around her. Hopefully, someday soon.

The streets were mostly empty except for a few cars and pedestrians. When she was last in Willowbrook, she was just a child. This place held fond memories before it was ripped away from her.

Quynh pushed thoughts of her past back into the corners of her mind. There was enough on her plate as it was. There was no use dredging up the past. Besides, she was only here for one thing, and once the task was completed, she would be gone. The quicker she could wrap up loose ends from her past, the sooner she could move on and figure out her future.

At least, she wished it were that easy, but given her recent luck, she was bound to hit a few speed bumps along the way.

Griffin glanced at her from his corner of the truck bed when she let out a melodramatic sigh, but remained quiet. The car ride was thick with tension as he made his way into town. The air in the cabin crackled and pulsed with a strange energy, a tangible hum vibrated through the floorboards and up into her feet. Though it was difficult with Griffin's larger-than-life presence in the small space, she tried to ignore the sensation.

She risked a small peek at Griffin, who didn't seem to be bothered in the slightest. Quynh resisted the urge to fidget in her seat. She definitely ignored the slow warmth spreading through her center at the proximity of such an obvious alpha male.

The cabin smelled like him, a warm, rich, and woodsy scent with hints of leather and sandalwood. He didn't smell like he wore cologne, though she could smell traces of motor oil. Quynh pressed her thighs together to relieve the small ache.

What the hell is wrong with me? How am I even aroused right now? I must be seriously fucked up in the head.

The past twenty-four hours were traumatic enough

without adding *inappropriately turned on by a stranger* to her list of grievances.

God, she was definitely going to need to find a therapist to sort through her issues, something she was pushing off for a while, but she needed to prioritize once she got out of Willowbrook. There was no way she wouldn't have echoes of the trauma, which would probably show up later in her life, and knowing her history, at completely inappropriate times.

She was mature enough to recognize when asking for help was necessary. Besides, having a therapist was like having a nonjudgmental best friend who also gave great advice, unlike a real best friend who may encourage more self-destructive behaviors.

Speaking of best friends, she had not talked to Megan in a while. They'd been best friends since college, but it's difficult to still keep in touch with how busy their lives are. It's no excuse, but she'd have to call Megan soon to let her know she was out of town.

Quynh grimaced at the thought. She was definitely not looking forward to the conversation. Thoughts of the impending conversation with Megan made her inwardly groan. This is probably not going to go over well.

Megan was an incredible friend, but she sometimes went over the top. She didn't put it past Megan to hop on a plane and fly all the way from across the country just to be here with Quynh as she sorted through the mess. The sentiment made her smile.

It would be nice to have someone in her corner right now, but Megan was a busy woman with her own business she built from the ground up. She now has multiple franchises, and her success would have been enviable if Quynh possessed a jealous bone in her body. It had been amazing to watch the shy and quiet college girl grow into the strong powerhouse she is today. Megan never let the success get to her head, though. She'd stayed humble to her roots and never left Quynh in the dust of her success.

They lived on opposite sides of the country with busy lives. It made for conflicting schedules, but they always tried to talk at least once a month. She should definitely call Megan tonight.

After a couple more minutes of shallow mouth breathing to avoid Griffin's captivating scent, Griffin finally turns into the auto body shop off Main Street. Quynh glanced around at the building. It was smaller than the ones she was used to from Emerald Heights. The two-car garage was attached to the two-story main building. She assumed it acted as the office or reception area.

Quynh looked up at the upper level. The small, curtained windows were drawn shut. She assumed it was where she'd be staying the night.

Griffin parked the truck and got out without saying a word. She waited a beat before slowly opening her door and hopping down. Turning around, she reached back into the cabin to pull a still-drooling Pickles out.

At the sound of a throat clearing, Quynh whirled around, and Pickles let out a meow in protest of the quick movement. She found Griffin glaring at her as if he were offended by her mere presence, her bag gripped in one hand. After a moment, he led the way to the front door of the shop.

"The main entrance is through the main lobby, behind the office. There's a rear entrance, but I don't have the key on me. I'll give you a copy of the key later." Griffin tossed the words over his shoulders as she scrambled to follow closely behind him.

He opened the door and gestured for her to step in ahead of him.

What a gentleman, she thought sarcastically.

She stopped in the middle of the lobby with both hands on the handle of Pickles's cat carrier, waiting for his direction. The bell above the front door rang as Griffin pulled the door shut behind him. He led the way to a narrow hallway and rounded the corner.

Quynh followed a few paces behind him as he entered a door-marked office and came back with a key ring. He handed it to her, and she scrambled to grab it from his hands without jostling Pickles too much.

Griffin didn't wait for a response as he led the way to

another doorway. Using the key on his key ring, Griffin opened the door to reveal a staircase.

Quynh watched in amazement as Griffin pushed the handle of her suitcase down and bent to lift the case over his head. He practically sprinted up the stairs while she gingerly cradled the carrier containing the giant Maine coon in her arms. By the time she made it to the top of the stairs, the door was left ajar for her.

Griffin was nowhere in sight when she walked in and looked at her temporary home. The open floor plan boasted a quaint living room equipped with a couch and TV. A small island separated the space into the kitchenette with a small refrigerator and stove. A narrow hallway led to the back, where she assumed the bedroom and the bathroom were located. It was small, but it was exactly what she needed for the night.

She set Pickles down on the coffee table and leaned down to peer into his crate. He was still asleep, but she expected the catnip would likely wear off soon. A night of the zoomies was probably in her future. She loved it when Pickles acted like a wild cat. He always got super affectionate after his bursts of energy, and she always welcomed the extra attention.

She reached a finger in and pet Pickles's fluffy tail.

The sounds of Griffin's footsteps made her straighten up. When she turned around, he was standing at the entrance of the hallway with his hands on his hips, a frown marring his otherwise handsome face.

"Your bags are in your room." He gestures behind him with a thumb. "I turned up the thermostat, but it will take a few minutes to warm up."

Quynh wiped her hands on the front of her wrinkled sundress nervously. She didn't know why she was nervous, but her heart raced as she looked at her unsuspecting hero.

"Thank you," she finally murmured.

An intense silence filled the space between them. Just like when trapped in the truck, the atmosphere thrummed with intensity.

Her eyes dropped to his thick neck as his Adam's apple bobbed. She chewed on her lower lip, captivated by the sensual curve of his neck. With a sudden jerk, Griffin bolted for the door, desperate to escape her presence.

"If you need anything, I'm just across the street. Get some rest. I'll call Ricky in the morning."

She jumped when he slammed the door shut as he left, his footsteps fading as he descended the stairs. She ran to the window and pulled the curtain aside, watching as he jumped into his truck.

He seemed tense, almost angry, though she couldn't figure out why. He'd left like his ass was on fire.

She watched as he left the parking lot, only to drive to the charming home across the street. He wasn't joking when he said he was just across the street. Quynh ducked behind the curtain when he glanced up at her window and waited a moment before pulling the curtain aside again. He went inside, judging by the lights that were now on in his house.

Dropping the curtain, she went to make sure the front door was locked and slid her shoes off her feet. Her toes curled as they buried themselves in the plush carpet. Pickles was going to love destroying this carpet once he woke up.

She unlocked the carrier and placed it on the ground. Running to the kitchen to find two bowls, she poured water into one and placed the empty one next to it. She brought some of Pickles' dry food with her in the suitcase.

The bedroom was furnished with a queen-size bed and a dresser. There were fresh sheets on top of the unmade bed. Her suitcase lay on its side in the corner of the small room. Kneeling on the floor, she opened her suitcase and took out a few items she'd needed for tonight before closing it back up.

First things first, she needed to set up Pickles' food and litter box. Once the task was completed, Quynh went to the bathroom and turned on the shower. As the water warmed up, she made her bed with the salmon-colored sheets.

She was looking forward to a relaxing shower to wash off the grime of the last twenty-four hours and sinking into the fresh sheets. The thought revitalized her as she started stripping her clothes off and made her way back into the shower.

Finally, the hot water slid over her body, taking the clingy film of sweat and grime with it. Her tense muscles relaxed under the almost too-hot spray of the shower. Quynh braced her hands against the warm tiles as the tears she had held back since she met Griffin fell.

She finally let go. She imagined the tight ropes holding her sanity together, snapping as the dam burst open. She allowed herself the space to unload the emotional turmoil of her unexpected job loss. She cried for the loss of a colleague whom she had known for years, and about the poor health of her birth father, whom she never really got to know but would have to say goodbye to shortly.

Life was unfair.

The cooling water brought her back from her wallowing. When she was freshly washed and showered, she shut the water off and sniffed as the tears dried along with her shower. Sometimes, all a woman needs is a cathartic crying session to reset. Or, in her case, multiple crying sessions.

Tomorrow will be a better day. It has to be.

She couldn't have been more wrong.

5

Quynh's eyes snapped open as she became aware of three things at once. The first was that she was not in her apartment. The second, she was naked under the sheets.

She didn't normally sleep in the nude, but she was so exhausted after the events of the past couple of days, and coupled with letting all of her emotions out in the shower, she was completely wrung out. She must have just crawled into bed and passed out.

The third thing was the loud and angry knocking at the front door. The knocking sounded again as she bolted upright in bed, tits perky in the morning's chill air. She scanned the room and found the oversized shirt she'd left on top of her suitcase with the full intention of putting it on before bed. Scrambling out of bed, she ran to get the shirt and put it on as she raced toward the front door.

There could only be one person knocking at this hour. She yanked the door open just as the knocking resumed again and met the angry glare head-on. Squaring her shoulders and clearing her throat, she glared right back at the hot-tempered mechanic.

"Yes?" She leaned into the edge of the door and tried to ignore the way her skin pebbled underneath her shirt.

Quynh didn't think it was possible, but she swore Griffin's glare intensified as if the mere sight of her incensed him.

"Do you always answer the door in just a shirt?"

His growl sent shivers through her body, and she knew he could probably see her nipples pebble in response to his tone.

"Of course I do." She couldn't resist pushing his buttons.

He glowered at her for another moment, the muscle in his jaw feathering, and his nostrils flared.

"Was there something you needed…? I was having a really good dream before you woke me up."

"Your car is downstairs."

"Oh." She straightened up as she was reminded of the reason she was here in the first place.

"I have an order to finish up first, but I'll take a look under the hood to see what's happening."

"Oh, thank you." A blush crept up her neck at his generosity. Here she was, being ungrateful when all he'd done was help her when she didn't even deserve it.

She fought the urge to fidget. She had on just the T-shirt. Belatedly, she wished she'd at least put on a bra or panties. Hell, even a bathrobe would have her less exposed than she was at that moment.

Griffin cleared his throat, and she glanced up from beneath her lashes. He no longer looked as angry, but the frown was still present on his handsome face.

"I didn't have your number. Otherwise, I would have texted instead of waking you up."

She offered him a small smile at the concession.

"I really appreciate it. Thank you."

At her words, his eyes softened. His green eyes were especially striking in the early morning light. She tried to ignore the way his tightly fitted Henley clung to his muscled chest. His hair still looked damp from his shower this morning, and he'd trimmed his beard. She should not have noticed how his dark jeans and boots made him look absolutely delicious, like a wet dream standing on her doorstep.

It would be so easy to jump into his arms and demand he take her to bed. Right now. It wouldn't take much since she wasn't wearing any panties. All he needed to do was take his cock out of his tight jeans and...

Quynh jumped when Griffin coughed. Fuck, she must be tired if she was imagining climbing the grumpy man like a tree and mounting him like a cat in heat.

Her libido was out of control.

She stepped back involuntarily as if the small distance

would keep her from acting on her impulsive thoughts. She watched as Griffin raised an arm and ran his hand through his hair, muscles flexing with the movement.

"If you need me, I'll be downstairs."

He left without waiting for her response.

She realized belatedly he probably caught her checking him out. Shutting the door a little more forcefully than necessary, Quynh stood with her forehead pressed to the hard surface. Groaning, she smacked her head against the wooden door a few times and prayed it would knock some sense into her.

She needed coffee.

And pants would probably help.

The sun was fully out by the time Quynh found suitable pants to venture out of her temporary lodging in search of life's essence: coffee. She'd done a quick search on her phone and found a small cafe just a few minutes away on foot. Quynh found the nerve to text Ruth to see if she'd be up to meet her there for the day.

The coffee shop was located right on Main Street. Quynh smiled at the catchy name, Sip Happens. The tantalizing aromas of freshly brewed coffee beckoned her to enter. Bells chimed as she walked into the small but homey space. The shop boasted modern decor with Art Déco vibes throughout. The colors were a muted blend of neutral and earthy tones. And there, shining like a beacon, were the multiple, no doubt expensive, coffee brewing contraptions which kept her sustained throughout most of her adult life.

Quynh before coffee and Quynh after coffee were two very different people. Many people have not had the misfortune of meeting the former. Usually, by the time she'd stepped foot out of her apartment, she'd consumed at least two cups of coffee and was well on to her third. It's what kept her awake and alert as she powered through her workday.

But today, she did not have work to worry about. No, something far worse awaited her. A potential meeting with her estranged stepsister, whom she'd only ever met a couple of times before. Unfortunately, none of those instances were on good terms.

Quynh didn't blame Ruth for disliking her. Hell, she'd probably hate herself, too, if she were in Ruth's shoes. The scandal rocked the neighborhood when the truth came out was enough to send her to therapy for several years. Thankfully, she learned some healthy coping mechanisms. Well, healthy according to her own scale.

Sure, she was probably a workaholic who buried

herself in work and caring for others instead of caring for herself. Quynh did not kid herself into thinking she was unique. Many healthcare workers often experience compassion fatigue when they spend their whole lives and careers caring for other people. It left little time or energy to ensure self-care.

She would never change a single thing about the past few years. She had plenty of regrets, though. Devoting her entire life to her career and caring for her ailing mother in her final years of life meant little time for dating. She couldn't even remember the last time she had sex. It wouldn't surprise her if there were actual cobwebs sealing her shut with its years of neglect.

But, first, coffee.

She'd realized she'd been standing in the coffee shop's doorway, staring longingly at the menu for an inappropriately long time, judging by the uncomfortable look on the young barista's face. Shaking herself out of her reverie, Quynh approached the counter with a bright smile she hoped didn't make her look deranged at this hour and before coffee.

"What can I get you?" Jodie said, her name tag displaying her name.

"Can I please have a large quadruple shot caramel latte with extra pumps of caramel, please?" She almost sighed at the thought of the rejuvenating nectar as it was about to enter her bloodstream. She really should see if they made caffeine in intravenous form and just have the damn thing injected straight into her body instead of having to drink a large coffee multiple times a day.

"Sure thing." Quynh paid for her coffee and left a generous tip. "Have a seat, and I'll bring it to you."

Quynh ambled off and found a seat just outside of the sun's reach by the window. She loved to people-watch but didn't care to be in direct sunlight. At her age, the sun's damage to her skin would be irreversible. Besides, she rarely even needed to try for her brown skin to tan. Her body loved the sun, and she loved sunscreen. It was a win-win.

When Jodie came over with her coffee, Quynh wrapped her cold hands around the hot cup and relaxed. This was her favorite part of the day. The quiet moments between getting her day started were precious to her. All too soon, she'd have to hit the road running. Most days, she barely had time to eat, choosing to work through her lunches so she could fit in more patients, but also because the administrative tasks never seemed to end. There never seems to be a stop to the amount of notes to sign, prescriptions to refill, phone calls to return, results to review, etc.

If she hadn't loved what she did day in and day out, Quynh probably would have found a different job a long time ago. But helping people who live in chronic pain gave her a sense of satisfaction no other specialty would, even if it was emotionally and mentally draining. It was worth it.

Or, at least, it was what she told herself.

Quynh checked her phone after a few fortifying sips of her coffee. The sweet flavor of the caramel danced across her taste buds. She imagined the caffeine as it flowed through her body and woke up all of her sleepy brain cells. She was already more awake in the short time she sat there.

No new messages on her phone, but it looked like Ruth saw her text, judging by the read receipt. She wished she'd brought a book with her. There was no rush to do anything today, considering her car would not be ready until later, anyway. She'd have to take a walk down the strip and find the bookstore she'd seen when they drove in last night.

The cafe was relatively quiet as people came and went as they started off their day. It seemed to be a pretty popular spot, with friendly locals. She stuck out like a sore thumb. She didn't recognize anyone who came in and didn't expect to. It had been so long since she was last here, and she was just a kid.

The bell above the door chimed again as a woman entered. Quynh didn't pay it any mind until she noticed the scowling woman approaching her table. She straightened up as the woman hovered over her.

"Quynh?" the stranger said.

"Um, yes, that's me."

"You don't recognize me, do you?"

Taken aback by her haughty and angry tone, Quynh looked over at the woman carefully. Dark blonde hair hung around her face in curls. Her blue eyes glared at her, though she thought the shape seemed familiar.

"Ruth?" she hazarded a guess.

"Yeah, Ruth. Jesus Christ. You don't even recognize your own sister." With a huff, Ruth pulled out the chair across the table and plopped down.

"I'm sorry. It's been a really long time..." she stammered. And they were *stepsisters*.

"Yeah. It has."

Quynh straightened and tried not to fidget under Ruth's assessing gaze.

"How are you?"

Instead of answering, Ruth furrowed her eyebrows in anger.

"How am I? Oh, I'm just great. Shouldn't you be asking how our father's doing? Do you even care?"

Ruth's loud voice seemed to echo in the otherwise quiet cafe, and Quynh tried not to shrink at her accusation.

"Of course I care. I came as soon as you texted."

Ruth let out a disbelieving sound.

After another tense moment, Quynh broached the topic.

"How...how is...how is he doing?"

It was so weird to think of her father, a man she only knew for a short period of her life.

"He's still dying, last I checked."

Ruth's callous response was a shock to her. It made her wonder what her relationship with their father was like.

"Where is he?"

"At home. He's on hospice. Old bastard wanted to die in his own bed."

"Oh."

Quynh had some experience with hospice patients. Mainly when she worked as a bedside nurse. She understood the sensitive situation surrounding death. Everyone coped differently, and it was a delicate balance of providing dignity to the dying while being respectful of the living, who were in varying stages of mourning. Grief made people do strange things sometimes.

Clearing her throat, Quynh asked cautiously, "Can I see him?"

Ruth didn't respond for a few moments, using the time to look around the cafe as she contemplated the question. Then, quietly, as if another person sat in front of her, she finally said, "I think he'd like that."

Quynh thought she saw tears glistening in Ruth's eyes, but by the time she brought her gaze back, they were gone.

"Okay. Let me know when a good time is."

A quiet moment passed. Both women were lost in their thoughts before the whirring of the coffee machine grinding beans shook them out of their stupor.

Quynh inspected Ruth. Really looked at her and past the angry demeanor. She saw the strain bracketing the corners of her lips, the wrinkles at the corners of her eyes, and the pinched expression of an exhausted woman. Quynh saw past the barriers which stood between them and their potential.

"How are you really doing?"

The hard glint in Ruth's eyes returned almost instantly, a defensive mechanism, one Quynh herself was all too familiar with.

"Fine. Just dandy. I'll text you his address and let his home care nurse and housekeeper know to expect you sometime soon."

Before Quynh could utter another word, Ruth got up and left through the front door. She watched as Ruth's figure disappeared down the street. Her hunched shoulders seemed out of place in the otherwise idyllic town and happy townspeople.

Grief does that to people. It didn't matter that their father was still alive. His prognosis was terminal. He did not have much time left on this Earth. Quynh didn't know what Ruth's relationship with their father was, but it didn't take a genius to guess it was likely complicated.

Her phone pinged a moment later with a new text message. Ruth sent her the address to their father's home. She inputted the address into her navigation app. Her father lived on the other side of town, which would require a car to get there.

She'd have to talk to Griffin and find out how long it would take to get her car back on the road.

A problem for another day, but not right now.

Right now, her only concern was to enjoy her cup of coffee and explore the town she could get to on foot.

She could pretend she was on vacation.

If only for just one day.

6

The phones would not stop ringing. Griffin was at his wit's end. It was impossible to do the work that needed to be done and also manage the office. This was why he needed a secretary. It's too bad he fired Delilah, but he did not need the complication in his life right now.

There was no denying it. He needed help. His orders were already delayed by a couple weeks. At the rate he was going, it would take working all day and night for the next month to make up for the delays. Something he was more than willing to do.

If it came down to it, Griffin knew Julio and Sean would help him play catch-up if necessary. He didn't want it to come down to it, though. They worked hard enough to help him keep the business afloat. They deserved to enjoy their time off. He just needed to find some temporary help with managing the office.

If Jacob Henderson called one more time to ask for an update on his car, Griffin was going to toss the phone through the window. He'd have to pay someone to fix the window, but it might just be worth the added expense to stop the incessant ringing which interrupted him from doing what needed to be done under the hood of the Impala he currently had in the garage.

Henderson dropped off his vintage Mustang several weeks ago. They talked about doing some basic modifications to the engine a while back, but Griffin didn't hear from Henderson since giving him a quote for the work requested until he showed up with his shiny car. Instead of calling ahead to ask if Griffin was available to fit in the work, Henderson just dropped off his keys at the front desk and hitched a ride with his new girlfriend of the month before Griffin was even aware he had come and gone.

When he pulled his head out from under the car, he'd seen the shiny red Mustang sitting in his parking lot and cursed. Griffin stomped into the reception to find Delilah painting her nails. She hadn't seemed too concerned about Henderson's unannounced visit, nor did she seem to understand what it meant for his timeline. This time of year was busy for the shop, and he didn't need a surprise order on his case. A low growl rumbled in his chest, but he forced it down. His voice was tight as he told Delilah she needed to leave early. His jaw was clenched so tightly he could have cracked a walnut. Her retort died on her lips when she saw how angry he was, for which he was thankful. He was in no mood to handle her mood swings.

After Delilah made her dramatic exit, Griffin stalked into his office to clean up the mess. Henderson was blasé about the whole affair, not understanding it would be weeks before Griffin could even look at his car. Though he seemed uncaring at the time, the multiple phone calls he received each week were a different story.

Unfortunately, he'd fired Delilah shortly after. One of her main responsibilities, besides answering the phones, was to take inventory and order the necessary parts for the job. Which meant he'd have to do those menial tasks himself, taking time away from fixing the cars sitting in the shop.

What a mess.

Despite the added responsibilities, he had no regrets about firing Delilah. She worked with him for a year and still needed frequent reminders. She always showed up late to work. Delilah was good with the customers, though, which was a skill he appreciated when he could barely tolerate talking to most people.

If he didn't get help soon, he'd have to stop taking

new orders, which meant income would slow down. He needed to at least pay Julio and Sean or risk losing them to the auto body chain that opened up across town and boasted better pay and benefits than his small shop could offer. They were both loyal and hard workers. He'd have a hard time replacing them.

Slamming the phone down on his desk, Griffin ran his hands through his hair. The sounds of music floated through the bay windows. His office was otherwise quiet as he tapped his fingers on his desk.

He could probably post a 'help wanted' sign in the window and ask around town if anyone was looking for work the next time he went into town. The busy season would be over in a few months, then he could pretty much handle the rest of the year alone.

His thoughts drifted to the woman temporarily residing just above his head.

She was a temptress. The worst part was that she had no idea.

The moment she'd looked up at him through her dusty car window, her dark brown eyes, magnified by the grime, locked onto his, and he knew he was in trouble. Her red-rimmed eyes, swollen and puffy from crying, combined with her tear-stained face, tugged at the dark corners of his heart. A deep-seated, overwhelming need to protect her seized him, overriding all other rational thoughts. It was jarring and disorienting. He hated it.

Her soulful eyes trapped him, held him in his place, making the breath catch in his lungs.

Is my heart racing?

She looked so magnificent with the fading rays of the sun streaming through the dark strands of her hair. He was gripped with an urge to find out if her hair was as soft as it looked.

Is she soft everywhere?

He wondered what brought her to Willowbrook. There was not much to this side of town. It was mostly quiet with some mom-and-pop shops. The trendier part of town most people frequented was on the opposite end, closer to the city, which is now known for its up-and-coming hipster bars and shops. That was the side of town Griffin avoided at all costs. If he ever needed to get anything, he'd send Delilah, who loved to spend her day and his hard-earned money picking up supplies.

The entire trip into town was agonizing. He concentrated on thoughts of his deadbeat father to avoid his body reacting to the temptress in his truck. His breaths were shallow as he tried not to inhale her intoxicating vanilla scent. A scent which was both tantalizing and torturous.

Known as the town grump, Griffin admitted he was rougher with her than others to mask his discomfiting reaction to her.

He'd never been so affected by the mere presence of

another person before. Even with his last relationship, he'd never had the urge to rip off her clothes and have his way with her on the side of the road. It took a great deal of effort and thoughts of his delinquent parents to keep his cock from rising to the challenge.

After dropping her off, he'd hightailed it into his bathroom and jerked off in the shower. He'd come to thoughts of her on her knees, looking up at him through those dark lashes on the side of the road, her face tear-stained from choking on his cock as he fed it to her hungry mouth until he spilled himself down her throat. A dangerous fantasy he never knew existed until he met her.

He'd gone to bed slightly satisfied and fought off the urge to beat off again in bed as the thought of her sleeping just mere feet from him tried to invade his mind. He'd fallen asleep with a semi and woken up to a raging hard-on which was impossible to ignore.

The loud alarm yanked him out of his dreams just as he was about to plunge his aching cock into her willing pussy. He'd nearly ripped the alarm out of the wall and thrown it across the room for its rude awakening.

Fuck. He should not be this fixated on a stranger. His cock wouldn't listen, even as he'd gripped it under the covers. Another cold shower failed to calm his libido. Instead, his mind conjured up how her brown eyes looked, wide and innocent, as she'd looked up at him last evening.

When he'd knocked on her door later that morning, he knew the universe was working against him. He was not prepared to see her barely dressed and her long legs on display. The shirt she'd been wearing was barely long enough to reach her upper thighs. All she needed to do was bend over a little, and he'd glimpse her panties. If she even wore panties.

It took a Herculean amount of effort not to shove her against the wall and take her right then and there. He had to keep his fists clenched and lock all his muscles in his body so he would not act on the impulse.

He was mortified when his voice came out deeper than normal. It was like he was a damn horny teenager all over again, with no control over his thoughts or his cock.

He didn't like how he acted when she was near. Griffin did not need the distraction.

The bell above the front door chimed as someone entered the main office. Griffin bit back a groan as he heaved himself up out of the chair to meet the guest. He'd only taken a couple of steps out into the hallway when a soft body ran right into him.

"Oof."

Griffin reached out instinctively to catch his assailant before they fell backward. It was a mistake. As soon as his hands made contact, he knew exactly who was in his arms. The heat of her body burned his hands. Instinctively, he dropped them and took a large step back to create distance between them.

"Sorry. Didn't see you there." She let out a small chuckle. "I was just heading back to the apartment."

She looked up at him through dark lashes, and he fought the urge to take another step back. She could bring him to his knees with just her eyes. The thought terrified him.

Griffin only managed to grunt in response.

"I wanted to talk to you anyway, so I'm glad I ran into you. Literally. I mean, I'm sorry I ran into you. I hope I didn't hurt you. Are you okay? You look like you should sit down."

"I'm fine." If his voice sounded deeper than usual, it was probably because all of his blood flow went straight to his dick since she'd run into him. He got a taste of what it was like to have her body pressed against his.

"Oh. Okay. That's good."

She seemed nervous. He noticed the stack of books in her hands and reached out to take them from her.

"Oh, that's okay. I can get those..." Her voice trailed off as he motioned for her to lead the way to her apartment.

After a moment, she stepped past him, making sure not to touch him in the too-narrow hallway. He probably could have stepped back to give her more room to maneuver, but a part of him wanted to feel her body against his, even for a second.

As he followed closely behind her, he realized the terrible mistake he had made. With her mounting the stairs ahead of him, it put her ass in the direct path of his treacherous and gluttonous eyes. Her perky bottom was temptingly swaying and beckoning more than just his eyes to appreciate it.

Griffin almost dropped the books and ran back into the office. Instead, he averted his eyes to distract himself from thoughts of her bent over the staircase as he fucked her from behind and watched as her ass bounced with each of his thrusts.

This was a bad idea. He shouldn't be staring at her ass like this, but he couldn't help himself. Even worse, the knowledge that he was following her upstairs, where she'd slept the previous night, made his cock stir with attention. He glanced down at the stack of books cradled in his arms to distract himself. There was a shirtless man on the cover with some neon font displaying the title of the book.

Griffin clenched his jaw at the unexpected stirring of jealousy in his gut. He had no right to be jealous if she was ogling another man. They barely even knew each other, but it didn't stop the possessiveness from rearing its ugly head. He knew she wasn't married by the lack of a wedding band on her ring finger, nor was she recently divorced, since her smooth hands lacked a tan line where a ring would have been.

It didn't mean he could assume she was single. For all he knew, she could be in a serious relationship and came this way by herself. The thought only angered him more.

What kind of idiot would let his woman travel miles alone? What if something happened to her?

Before his thoughts could continue to spiral down its dark path, she stopped abruptly at the front door and turned around to face him. He kept his distance, stopping at the top of the stairs a few feet away from her.

She shifted her weight on her feet as her hands played with the hem of her top.

A strand of hair escaped her bun and partially covered her face from his view. He resisted the urge to push it back so he could look his fill.

"Um, thank you for helping me with the books." She slowly raised her hands up as if she was scared he'd bite her.

Griffin carefully handed the stack of books back to her, making sure their skin did not make contact. Every time they touched, he experienced a rush of heat which made a beeline straight towards his traitorous cock. He did not need to get a boner in the hallway right now. There were still a lot of hours left in the workday.

"You're welcome."

If his voice sounded too gruff, he blamed it on all the attention it took to keep his cock from stirring. The hallway was oppressive as her scent drifted to his nose.

Before he could take his next breath, he was already backing away.

"Oh, Griffin?"

Her soft voice made him pause in his escape.

"Yeah?" Was she going to ask him to go inside? He shouldn't want that.

"When do you think my car will be ready? I don't want to be in your way any more than I am…" Her voice trailed off, no doubt unsure why he was glowering at her. The thought of her leaving so soon suddenly made him want to commit a crime.

He would not, could not, intentionally delay fixing her car so she was forced to stay a little longer.

Right? Right.

"I'll take a look at it tonight."

The distant sound of his phone ringing filled the silence between them.

Groaning, Griffin rubbed his hands over his face.

"Fucking Christ."

Hands on his hips, Griffin made to leave again when her soft hand on his biceps stopped him.

"Do you…Do you need some help? You know, with the office stuff?"

The sight of her small, tanned skin on his pale arm was a sight he wished he could forget. Images of her hands on other parts of his body flashed through his mind.

"No. I'm fine."

"Are you sure? I don't mind helping. Besides, I'm kind of stuck here anyway until you fix my car, so...put me to work. I know how to do the basics, at least."

Griffin knew it was a bad idea. He should say no. He definitely should not entertain the idea of her in his office.

"Yeah, fine. Come down when you're ready."

With that, he stomped down the stairs before he made any more terrible decisions.

Like fuck her against the door.

7

"Yes, Henderson, I am actually really busy and have not gotten to your car yet." Griffin was about to rip the hair out of his head.

What did the entitled prick expect when he dropped by unannounced? Does he not understand I need to finish all the overdue jobs before getting to his car?

He briefly considered making Henderson a top priority to avoid further contact, but decided it would reinforce bad behavior. If Henderson called him one more time today, he would set the Mustang on fire and call it a day. Chalk it up to faulty wiring.

A soft knock prevented him from following through with his dark thoughts.

Quynh stood at the entrance to his office, her petite frame outlined by the soft morning light.

"Tough customer?" A small smile teased at her lips.

The taunting lilt to her lips made him pause. It was

the first time he had seen her really smile since she came crashing into town.

He wondered what she would look like with a genuine smile gracing her face.

Would her eyes crinkle in the corners?

He imagined she probably looked radiant, especially with her skin glowing like it was.

Griffin shook himself out of his runaway thoughts. He shouldn't be imagining what she'd look like smiling. They were still strangers.

"Yeah. Won't stop calling," Griffin finally responded, his tone conveying his annoyance about the entire ordeal.

"Just show me what I need to do, and I can take care of it for you."

There wasn't much to his office other than his desk, an outdated computer, and an office phone. He didn't even have any other chairs besides his own. The only item on display in the otherwise empty auto body shop was a simple, slightly tarnished frame holding his first hard-earned dollar a decade ago when he was granted owner-ship of the business. The significance of the fateful day was etched into the building.

Heaving himself out of his creaky office chair, Griffin rounded the desk and gestured for her to make herself comfortable. The wave of vanilla from her perfume hit him as she passed by. The sweet scent was subtle, but still, his body reacted involuntarily. His muscles tensed, and his breath caught in his throat as she rounded his desk. The silence in the room was thick with tension.

As he watched her settle into his chair, the metallic clang of the garage doors opening echoed loudly in the otherwise quiet office. She looked so small in his space.

"I got this, boss. Go get some work done." A teasing smile played on her lips as she made a shooing motion with her hand, her eyes sparkling with laughter. Reluctantly, he backed away without a word. In the quiet hallway, a small, involuntary smile tugged at his lips. A phenomenon entirely foreign to him.

Boss?

He liked the sound of her calling him boss. His fantasies about what he wanted to do to her on the desk were far from professional, though.

Fuck. There went his cock again.

He walked out into the garage just as Julio and Sean entered through the giant doors.

"Mornin'." Julio was always peppy in the morning, while Sean took a couple of hours and about three cups of coffee to wake up. By lunchtime, they would all be begging him to stop talking.

They quietly put their coveralls on and got to work. The hours moved quickly, and before he knew it, there was a tapping on his leg. He was underneath a car, fixing the engine from beneath, when he slid out from under the hood to see who it was.

He wasn't expecting to see Quynh standing there with a couple of boxes of pizza.

"I didn't know if you were hungry, but I ordered pizza."

The heat of Julio and Sean's interested stares bored into the side of his face as he moved to stand up. Wiping his hand on the rag he kept in his back pocket, he tugged down the zipper to his overalls and slid the top off so it hung off of his muscular frame.

A sense of satisfaction filled him as her gaze tracked his movements. When she looked at him again, her cheeks were tinted a delicate pink.

When Sean coughed, Griffin's attention was pulled away from the alluring blush spreading across her cheeks.

"Did you hire a new secretary, boss?" The fierce scowl he directed at Sean was met with a mischievous smirk. The bastard was not scared of him.

"Yeah, uh, this is..."

"Quynh. Your new temporary secretary." She offered Julio and Sean a wave before turning back to meet his eyes. "My car broke down, and Griffin's letting me stay in the apartment upstairs while he's fixing it." Her hand dropped back down to her side, and he offered her a sheepish smile, thankful she stepped in.

"Thanks for lunch."

"Oh, it's no problem. You boys have been working all morning. I figured you could all use a break."

"Hell yeah!" Julio's enthusiasm was infectious.

"Thanks, doll." Sean flashed a flirtatious smirk at Quynh. His smirk widened into a grin at Griffin's glare. It was infuriating.

"You boys wash up, and I'll set this up inside the office for you. I'll run upstairs and grab some plates and cups."

True to her words, the pizza boxes were laid out in the main reception area by the time they washed their hands of the grease and grime of motor oil. Quynh was nowhere in sight, but it didn't stop Julio from pulling a slice out of the pizza box. Julio's groan of appreciation made his own stomach rumble with hunger. Griffin didn't have enough time to eat breakfast this morning.

Normally, he'd run back to his house to whip up leftovers from the night before, but they were so behind already. He still needed to look at Quynh's car. She must be getting eager to get going.

He never asked why she was in town.

Griffin was about to grab a slice when Quynh reentered the room, balancing some paper plates and cups in one hand.

She moved with the fluid grace of a dancer, her footsteps barely disturbing the stillness of the room. Time seemed to slow to a crawl as he watched her graceful movements. Each move she made was deliberate and precise. The low, indistinct hum of voices echoed in his ears.

"Griff!"

Startled from his trance, Griffin glanced over at Sean to see he sported a shit-eating grin on his face.

Fuck, did Sean catch me staring at Quynh?

"What?"

Sean was not intimidated by his glower. Instead, his grin became impossibly wider.

"I said, can we keep Quynh?"

Sean waggled his eyebrows over Quynh's head as she turned to look up at him.

"She's just helping out while she's in town."

"I don't mind helping. I can't really do much without my car, and apparently, Uber doesn't exist around here." A dramatic gasp escaped her lips.

Quynh handed him a plate with two slices of pizza. He slowly took the plate from her hands and moved to sit on the desk. Griffin watched as Quynh picked out a small slice of veggie pizza and sat down next to Sean.

Sean was a nice guy. He talked too much sometimes, but the ladies found him charming. Griffin had never been threatened by him before, but watching the two of them engage in conversation made his skin itch. He fought the urge to jump up and physically force the two of them apart. He briefly entertained the idea of sitting on Sean's much lankier frame. Sean wouldn't be able to flirt if he sat on him.

Griffin wanted to punch Sean in the face at the way he

looked at Quynh. A look he recognized as one of male interest. Punching Sean in the face felt like the appropriate response. He'd have to examine these urges later.

The shrill sound of a phone ringing filled the air. Quynh jumped up to grab the phone she had left sitting by the pizza box. Griffin watched as she unlocked her phone and read whatever was on the screen. Quynh's facial expression went from unbothered to upset at whatever she saw. Her eyes were pinched in the corners as her lips pursed.

"What's wrong?"

Startled, she looked up from her phone, brows furrowed.

"Oh, it's nothing."

She turned her phone screen off and tucked it into her back pocket.

"You boys enjoy the rest of your lunch."

With her parting words, she headed to his office. Griffin wanted to march back there and demand she tell him what caused her distress. He didn't like the way it made him feel to see her upset. This insane urge to set the world on fire for anyone or anything that upset her.

It was ridiculous. He was a stranger to her.

Griffin tried to ignore the impulse to go to her. He really did. He distracted himself by eating two more slices of pizza than he normally would have. He even cleaned up the office and brought the trash out back.

Both Julio and Sean returned to work when he took out the trash.

Standing in the lobby, he debated what he should do. He couldn't hear anything coming from the office. He lasted maybe another moment before his body directed him where his mind told him not to go.

Griffin slowly approached the open doorway of his office. He didn't want to startle her again. Quynh's nerves seemed frayed. The last thing he wanted to do was add stress to her day.

The sounds of muffled sniffling made his decision for him. He shoved the door the rest of the way open and barreled into the room like a freight train.

To his horror, she was crying at his desk. A pile of tissues in front of her as she stared up at him with those wide brown eyes of hers. Twice in the past twenty-four hours, he saw her tear-stained face, and both times, it drove a shard of pain deep in his gut. The sight of her crying made him sick.

She tried to wipe her tears away as if he wouldn't have noticed.

"Oh, um, hi. Did you need help with something?"

Her voice was thick with emotion as tears still strangled her voice. She fought valiantly to keep the tears brimming her eyelids from streaming down her face.

Griffin slowly approached her like she was a wounded animal. Her apprehension at his approach made him even more cautious. He wasn't very good at dealing with emotions, but he sure as hell did not know what to do with a crying woman in his office.

All he knew was he wanted it to stop. The only tears she should have were tears of pleasure instead of whatever was haunting her.

Griffin's cautious footsteps brought him around the desk until she was looking up at him. Slowly, he crouched down so they were eye-to-eye.

"Tell me what's wrong."

It wasn't a question. Rather, it was an order. He was determined to know what troubled her. As irrational as it was, he knew he would move heaven and earth to protect her.

Her lips parted as she stared at him in disbelief. After a moment, she must have seen the determination set in his features. She sniffled once more.

"It's my father."

He waited for her to continue talking, allowing her the time and space she needed to unpack her issues.

"He's dying."

The silence between them pulsed as he waited to hear more.

Griffin grabbed the tissue box and handed her another tissue. She smiled gratefully as she blew her nose.

"I don't even really know him, but apparently, he doesn't have much time left." She offered him a watery smile as he placed the tissue box back on his desk. "That's why I'm here. I was supposed to see him, but my car broke down. Obviously." She gestured vaguely to the office.

"Where is he?"

"Ruth, my stepsister, texted me his address earlier this morning. She just texted me again not too long ago. His condition seems to be deteriorating at a rapid pace. I still haven't been able to get over there to see him."

He watched in horror as another fresh round of tears pooled in her eyes and fell over. He gripped the armrest of her chair so hard he heard a squeak of protest.

Relaxing his hold on the chair, he gingerly raised his arm to brush away an errant strand of her dark hair. The softness was permanently branded in his mind. He resisted the urge to cup her face, just barely.

"Give me the address. Let me finish one last thing here, and we can get going. Fifteen minutes."

With the command, he got up and left the office before she could protest.

He would not be the reason she couldn't see her dying father. Especially since he still needed to look at her car, much less fix the damn thing.

A wave of guilt threatened to overwhelm him, but he pushed it down. Walking back into the garage bay, he told the guys he'd be heading out shortly to a round of head nods. If Sean gave him a knowing look, he ignored it.

Instead, he focused on finishing the task he was working on when Quynh interrupted with lunch.

He would take her to see her father and fix her car so she wouldn't need to rely on him for car rides. No wonder she needed an Uber. He should have asked her why she needed a ride instead of caging her on this side of town.

The taste of regret over the past twenty-four hours was bitter on his tongue.

8

Quynh sat with her body pressed against the passenger door as Griffin drove them to the address she showed him. He took one look at the address and gave a curt nod. It seemed like he knew where he was going, which was a reprieve since she didn't know her way around town anymore.

The town has changed so much from what she recalled. Her memories were fuzzy, like trying to look through a dirty window, but she didn't remember there being so many shops on Main Street. Modern progress didn't erase Willowbrook's small-town appeal.

They drove past Sip Happens, which was on the corner of Main Street. The bookstore she visited earlier was across the street. Small boutique shops lined the streets with mom-and-pop restaurants offering a variety of food options. Down an alleyway, she saw signs for vintage jewelry and even a comic book store.

It was odd to her that a practical stranger dropped everything to help her. Quynh wasn't used to the kindness of strangers. She had always been fiercely independent, a trait born from losing everyone in her life. Instead of focusing on how alone she was in the world, she made it her mission to help others. It became second nature to be the caretaker. It was nice to be taken care of for once, to let someone else take the reins, even if it was just for a moment.

She'd already protested about the necessity of Griffin stopping his work to take her to see her estranged father when he was clearly so busy. But one look at his unforgiving face had her biting back any further protestations. She knew he wouldn't budge, and though she was embarrassed he saw her blubbering in his office earlier, she was also thankful for how he handled the situation.

He didn't make her feel stupid for being emotional, nor did he make it seem like she was being overly dramatic for crying over a man she hadn't seen in well over a couple of decades.

The last time she remembered seeing her father was right before her mother moved them across the country. She was nine years old. Her birthday was right around the corner. They had been planning her tenth birthday party, and she made all of her invitations by herself to give to her classmates.

Quynh never got to hand out the cards.

The night before she planned to pass out her birthday invitations, her mother woke her up in the middle of the night and carried her out to the car, which was already packed with their meager belongings. Quynh had been disoriented from being woken up, but her mother reassured her and told her they were going to stay with her sister. Her mother drove them far away from the only life she ever knew. Throughout the car ride, her mother remained silent and unresponsive. English was her mother's second language, though she preferred speaking in her native tongue. Quynh knew her mother wouldn't open until she was ready. If she were ever ready.

It took just about three whole days of driving with minimal bathroom breaks before her mother pulled the car to a stop in front of a colonial-style home in Washington state. They arrived in the middle of the night, but when they turned off the car, Quynh was surprised to see the front door open.

Her mother drove them to her older sister's house. She sat in the car while the sisters greeted each other in hushed silence. They didn't hug, but there was respect between the two women. Her aunt, whom she later learned was from a different father, peered in the car and offered a small smile.

They stayed with her aunt and extended family for most of her life until Quynh finally went off to college in the great state of California. Unfortunately, her aunt died while she was a sophomore in college, and she never got to see her graduate.

Living with her was like having two mothers. Her aunt never had kids of her own, so she treated Quynh as if she were her own daughter. She had nothing but fond memories of growing up. Her aunt's presence was sorely missed.

When her mother became ill a few years ago, Quynh dedicated her life to making sure her mother wanted for nothing, often at the expense of her own well-being. But it was what was expected of her. So, while also attending graduate school, she spent every waking moment caring for her mother in her last years of life.

Her mother passed a couple of years ago in the comfort of her own home. She left behind journals Quynh wasn't quite ready to read yet. It was mostly written in Vietnamese, a language Quynh regrettably could not read fluently. She needed someone to translate her journal, but she wasn't sure how to navigate the situation. The idea of sharing her mother's private thoughts with a stranger was too invasive. So, it sat in a box with a few other trinkets and jewelry her mother left behind for her.

Her mother had been a hardworking woman, and the only thing that stopped her was the terminal stages of cancer. Even when she was receiving chemotherapy and radiation, her mother still showed up to work. She continued to work at a much slower pace, but she had built up a loyal clientele who were willing to wait for her. It was wonderful to see, even if Quynh tried to convince her mother she needed to rest and not work.

It made her mother happy though. She couldn't deny anything that made her mother happy.

From the brief conversations she overheard between her mother and aunt, her mother never found love again, at least not that she was aware of.

The scenery outside changed from suburban homes to dense trees as Griffin drove them to the remote address. He pulled onto a long, winding driveway that stretched on for what seemed like miles before revealing a large mansion at the top of the hill. The circular driveway in front of the home boasted a gleaming fountain of a naked woman and two small girls playing at her ankles.

Griffin pulled to a stop at the main doors. She glanced over at Griffin and gave him a smile of thanks before unbuckling her seatbelt. She was just about to reach for the door handle when the front doors opened to reveal an older woman.

Griffin jumped out of the truck and rounded the hood to open her car door. He gave her a hand as she hopped out of the truck. Walking side-by-side up the front steps, they approached the waiting woman.

Quynh wasn't really sure what to expect when she came here. It certainly wasn't this giant mansion. She didn't remember this home from any of her memories.

"You must be Quynh."

She nodded as the woman stepped aside and gestured for them to come inside.

"He will be so happy to see you again. My, how you've grown up." Quynh resisted the urge to frown. She didn't remember this woman, but maybe she knew her when she was a child. "You probably don't remember me. I'm Cynthia. Arthur's housekeeper. You can call me Cindy. You were so young when you left."

Cindy led them into the sitting room and gestured for them to make themselves comfortable.

"Let me check with his nurse and see if now's a good time for a visit."

Cindy disappeared back into the foyer. Quynh glanced nervously at Griffin, who sat stiffly on the uncomfortable bench. She chose the armchair across from him, though it wasn't much more comfortable than his bench. On the coffee table was a tray with a pitcher of pink lemonade. Her hands were shaking as she poured two glasses and took a small sip, though her stomach was churning with anxiety. Griffin took the glass she offered him, but didn't drink from it. They waited in stilted silence until Cindy returned a few moments later.

"He'll see you now."

Quynh slowly stood up and straightened her pink sundress as she followed closely behind Cindy. Griffin stayed put on the bench as she walked by him. The scent of his cologne wafted toward her in a comforting embrace. She squared her shoulders to prepare herself for the impending encounter.

Cindy led her up a set of stairs until they were on the second floor. The hallway was long, but they stopped in front of the closest set of doors to the stairs. Cindy's soft knock echoed loudly in the dim hallway. She didn't wait for a response before opening the door.

She expected to see her father lying in bed with tubes and beeping machines, but the sight that greeted her was more shocking. An elderly man sat upright in an armchair with a distinct robe covering his slim frame. Besides the oxygen tube wrapped around his nostrils to hide behind his ears, leading to a portable oxygen tank, she did not spot any other medical equipment in the room.

At the sight of her in the doorway, his eyes seemed to gleam with hope and excitement. He sat up straighter and tried to stand up. Cindy picked up her pace and admonished him for overexerting himself. Quynh watched the disgruntled man be chastised by the much older woman and almost smiled.

When he was back in his armchair, he gestured vaguely for Quynh to have a seat across from him. After a moment's hesitation, she sat perched on the edge of the seat. A tray of tea and biscuits sat on the table between them.

"Quynh. It's so good to see you again."

His voice was raspy from misuse, and she could tell the short sentences caused him a great deal of effort. He was already looking winded. She guessed he probably suffered from chronic lung disease. Perhaps even cancer, given his gaunt cheeks and sallow skin.

She tried to find the man she used to call her daddy in the aged man sitting across from her. The shape of his eyes, though now wrinkled, was the same. So was the earnest look in his eyes, as if he truly was happy to see her.

"Hi," she offered lamely as she sat on her hands. She didn't really know what there was to say. There was a giant elephant sitting in the room with them in the shape of her deceased mother.

"I heard..."

He didn't even need to finish the sentence. Quynh knew what he was going to say.

She nodded, "Yeah, she passed a couple of years ago. Breast cancer."

She watched as the man seemed to deflate, sinking deeper into his armchair as his lips thinned. He blinked back tears and offered a small smile.

"She was a wonderful woman." His heavy breathing filled the air as she nodded. Her mother was a wonderful woman. She didn't deserve to be humiliated like she was.

Quynh's thoughts bolstered her. He didn't get to talk about her mother when he clearly broke her heart. Her mother changed after she left town. She became quieter and more withdrawn, almost as if she were walking around with a heavy boulder weighing her down. Quynh recalled a time when her mother easily smiled and laughed a lot, but it all changed that fateful night.

She bit back what she wanted to really say to him. In his dying days, he didn't need to hear about how he broke her mother's spirit. He didn't deserve to know anything about her mother or her life. She was here to pay her respects so the memories of what could have been would stop haunting her.

She deserved some closure. There was no use in torturing a dying man.

"How have you been?" His simple question was laced with layers of complexity.

Oh, just great. Peachy. Really. Not like my entire life was literally collapsing around me.

"Fine."

She didn't think it was possible, but he seemed to deflate even further, shrinking into his body at her curt response. Quynh wasn't sure what he was hoping for from the encounter. He was practically a stranger to her, but the least she could do was to be polite. She'd worry about her feelings later.

"I'm doing fine. I'm between jobs right now as a nurse practitioner." It wasn't exactly the truth, but it wasn't a lie either. Besides, he did not need to know she was recently unemployed or how her boss killed himself shortly after. It was depressing enough. Better to keep the information to herself.

He perked up at her willingness to share about her life. It gave her the courage to share minor details: where she lived, why she was in town, and her terrible emotional support cat. He seemed to soak up any information she shared as if it would sustain his soul. They sat there for maybe close to an hour before he wilted again. The strain was back at the corners of his eyes, though he fought hard to pretend he was fine. His breathing seemed to get heavier the longer she talked.

She paused and rubbed her sweaty hands across the fabric of her dress.

"Well, I have to get going now. I don't want to keep my ride waiting any longer."

He nodded reluctantly as she stood up. When he tried to push himself off the chair, his arms collapsed underneath him. She rushed over to help him sit upright just as a nurse came rushing in from the hallway. She must have been keeping watch from outside the door.

"Now, now, Mr. Jones. It's time for you to rest. Wasn't it lovely to have a guest for a while?" The home care nurse offered her a tight smile before dismissing her completely.

Quynh left the room and found her way back to the sitting room, where she found Griffin still seated on the uncomfortable bench. He glanced up from his phone when she entered and stood up. Phone tucked into his back pocket, he approached her.

They stood toe-to-toe, unspoken words passing between them before he opened his arms up. She didn't even hesitate; she leapt into his arms and let out a deep breath as his arms came around her to cradle him to his chest.

He seemed to know what she needed without her having to say a single word. Quynh wasn't much for hugging strangers, but Griffin's tight bear hug made her feel anchored in a way nothing seemed to lately. For the first time in days, she took a deep, fortifying breath. Her muscles relaxed in his tight grip. The stress of the world practically melted away beneath his touch. Unfortunately, when he loosened his grip, it all came rushing back.

"Ready to get out of here?"

She looked up into his green eyes filled with concern and nodded. He let go of her, letting his fingertips glide down her arms, making her flesh pebble from the soft contact.

The drive back to his shop was quiet, though it wasn't uncomfortable. She appreciated that he didn't need to fill the silence with inane small talk. It allowed her the time to process her thoughts and the emotional rollercoaster she couldn't seem to get off of.

When they pulled into the parking lot, Griffin turned

to look at her, one arm braced across the bench of the seat. His fingertips were just a hairsbreadth away from touching her shoulders. Turning in her seat, she looked at him questioningly.

"Are you okay?" Concern etched itself into the lines around his worried eyes.

She opened her mouth instinctively to respond with the socially acceptable answer, but one look at his hard expression, and she knew he wouldn't appreciate it if she lied to him.

"I'll be okay." It was all she could offer. She knew, eventually, she would feel the warmth of the sun on her skin again, once the numbness ebbed away and allowed her to fully process how her life had taken a dramatic and traumatic turn in such a short time. There were so many unanswered questions, but for today, she relished the feeling of having Griffin's warm gaze on her.

For a brief moment, she wondered what it would be like to have a man like Griffin in her corner. She imagined he'd be caring in the ways he'd unknowingly taken care of her. He offered a virtual stranger a ride, put her up in his apartment, and drove her to see her dying father. Not to mention the way he'd opened his arms to her when he'd taken one look at her face as if he knew exactly what she needed, even when she didn't have a clue.

What would it be like to be Griffin's woman?

Oh God, was he seeing other women?

This whole time, she just assumed he was single. He probably had a woman waiting for him. There was no way a man like him was not attached.

With that thought, she scrambled to get out of the truck. She was already halfway inside the lobby by the time Griffin made it out of the truck.

Thankfully, he didn't follow her as she hightailed it past the office and into the back stairwell. She needed a moment to herself before coming back down. There were still a couple of hours left before the shop closed, and the guys would head home.

Quynh was no coward, but she knew whatever she was feeling toward her gracious stranger was not strictly platonic.

A dangerous notion when she was only in town temporarily.

9

The rest of the day crawled as the minutes inched toward closing time. He heard Julio and Sean wrapping things up and saying their farewells before leaving him alone in the garage bay. Judging by the sounds of the phones ringing in the office and the soft murmurs he heard, he knew Quynh would eventually come back downstairs to help in the office like she said she would.

He pretended he was too busy to notice when she showed her face downstairs again. His body was fully aware of her every move despite his attempts to ignore her. It made little sense to him why he seemed to hang on to her every movement. He couldn't deny the relief rolling through him at seeing her come back down, fresh-faced with resolve in her eyes.

Whatever happened in the time she disappeared upstairs, tail tucked between her legs and trying to escape him as if he was the plague, to when she came back downstairs must have revitalized her.

Griffin was never one for many words. He preferred silence over dull conversations, though he wished he possessed at least some skills to lean on in order to extract whatever was bothering her so he could try to fix it. Apparently, Quynh made him want to be a fixer. His work, where he literally fixed cars for a living, and his romantic relationships were always separate. With Quynh, though, he had an irresistible urge to fix whatever was bothering her.

It occupied his thoughts as he finished up the last task for the evening. He swapped cars to bring Quynh's into the bay. Popping the hood, he looked for any visible problems. Not seeing anything obvious, he slid underneath the car and cursed at what he saw. The splash guard was missing, which left the underbelly of her car completely exposed. Any number of things could cause a car to stop running, but it would take a lot longer than one hour to figure out what was wrong.

After troubleshooting common issues, he finally figured out the culprit. It was good news on one hand, but likely not the news Quynh was looking for.

Sighing, he started cleaning up. The sun set a couple of hours ago. The office was quiet. He assumed Quynh probably retreated into the apartment once the workday was over.

He shut the garage bay doors and locked the front door. Running across the street to his house, Griffin started undressing in the doorway. It was late, and he still needed to cook dinner. He'd left the chicken to thaw in the sink, and it should be ready by now. He normally cooked enough leftovers for lunch the next day, but tonight, he decided to share his meal with Quynh. No doubt she had little else to eat besides the single slice of pizza she ate at lunch.

The apartment was hardly stocked with any fresh food. Only canned goods and some snacks. She could probably make it work if necessary.

He hurriedly prepped the chicken and boiled water. As the stove was warming up, he ran upstairs to change out of his sweaty clothes. He'd shower after dinner.

It didn't take him long to prepare dinner. He had a plate wrapped in aluminum foil and was running across the street before he knew it. Unlocking the front door, the bell above it chimed at his entrance. He made sure it was locked behind him before making his way to the back. Climbing the steps two at a time, he stood on the welcome mat, suddenly unsure.

Taking a deep breath, he knocked once. The sound of her shuffling footsteps preceded the door slowly creeping open. When she realized who was at the door, she opened it wider. She was dressed in the same damn shirt from the other night, but underneath it, he saw a pair of shorts peeking out. Thank god. He definitely couldn't handle the temptation right now.

"Griffin? Is everything okay?"

He held the plate in front of him as a peace offering.

"I made too much dinner."

"Oh! Thank you. It smells delicious." She tentatively reached out to grab the dish from him. Their fingertips brushed, and a surge of awareness shot to the base of his spine.

"Would you like to come in?"

He really shouldn't even entertain the idea. Besides, he still had his own dinner at his house to eat, though the thought of them both eating alone seemed silly now.

"No. I'll see you tomorrow."

Griffin turned and left before she said another word.

He'd never been a coward before, but retreat was the only thing he could do. He couldn't very well shove her up against the door and have his way with her.

He was in for another long, sleepless night.

10

Quynh stretched her aching muscles, groaning softly as the incessant blare of her phone alarm finally pulled her away from her dreams. Mornings always involved a symphony of buzzing alarms, each one ignored for at least a few snooze cycles before she could muster the energy to open her eyes. Getting out of bed was a different story.

To say she wasn't a morning person was an understatement of the year. Yawning, Quynh rolled over in bed, her sleepy brain slowly realizing she was not in her own apartment. The events of the past couple of days flooded her mind. With a groan of annoyance, Quynh heaved herself into a sitting position.

She had high hopes today would be a better day. A person can only endure so much negativity before they eventually break. Unfortunately, she was on the verge of a breakdown.

My god, she was utterly exhausted. It wasn't the type of exhaustion that a few cups of coffee could fix. This was a heavy, leaden feeling, like a physical weight pressing down on her, leaving her utterly drained. She moved as though weighed down by countless burdens. A wave of melancholy washed over Quynh as she wondered if her mother experienced this same sense of loss and grief in the years after leaving this town. The irony of her situation was not lost on her. She was back in the town that broke her mother's heart. And, if she wasn't careful, it would leave her broken, too.

The wooden floor was chilly beneath her bare feet as she rushed into the bathroom to take care of her full bladder. It was still early enough in the morning for her to take a walk and grab a cup of coffee before Griffin opened up the shop. With the promise of her favorite drug, caffeine, in her near future, Quynh washed up and got dressed in a green dress and a light eggshell sweater with floral beading. She didn't bother doing her makeup. It was too early for her to care. She would probably regret the choice later, but it was a problem for future Quynh and not present Quynh to worry about.

By the time she made it back from her early morning coffee stroll, Griffin and the gang were already busy working in the garage bay. She yelled a greeting from the parking lot and made her way into the office.

Her first call came from Mr. Henderson, whom she got

to know pretty well yesterday when he called. She soothed his ruffled feathers and let him vent his frustrations about not having his "precious baby" under the same roof as him, even though he begrudgingly admitted dropping by unannounced was not his best idea.

Mr. Henderson seemed placated by her platitudes, and they spent a few minutes chatting before he promised not to call again until tomorrow. She reassured him she'd call him the first moment before anything changed, and if his car was miraculously ready for him.

The rest of the phone calls were simple questions she could answer. In between phone calls, she started organizing the messy office. There was something to be said about having to work in a clean space to help ease anxieties. Once Griffin's desk looked like it could be featured in a magazine, she stood at the doorway and admired her work. She was pleased with herself.

"Looks great in here."

Griffin's deep voice startled her as she whirled around, hand against her heart as it raced. She pretended it was the shock of his unannounced visit that sent her heart racing.

"Oh, geez, you scared me. Do you like it?" Suddenly, she was nervous that she overstepped. They hadn't exactly talked about what was expected of her.

"It looks much better than when I had an actual secretary I paid to do the work." He gave her a grateful glance.

"Thank you." His soft green eyes, like moss after a spring rain, held a warmth that made her weak in the knees.

Quynh basked in his attention. She couldn't help preening from his praise. Though she was normally unaffected by male attention, being the center of Griffin's attention made her heart race. His presence sparked an electric tingling throughout her body as warmth spread through her like a wildfire. When he spoke, a dull ache began in her core. The throbbing intensified until she became hyper-aware of it. Her face heated with an awareness of her physical reaction to him.

Could he tell she was blushing?

She clenched her thighs together to ease the incessant ache. It did nothing though, and she flushed even further when his eyes tracked her movements.

He can't possibly know what I'm thinking.

A slow burn ignited in his eyes as they found their way back to her face, smoldering with unspoken desire. She gulped at the intensity of his gaze. Her breaths hitched in her throat, rapid and shallow, as the air crackled with tension. Griffin's nostrils flared, jaw clenched, as if he was physically restraining himself from moving forward to snatch her up. Or, even better, bend her over the desk and fuck her senseless.

Oh, god. Here she was, having sexual fantasies about a stranger. She lamented her circumstances just as the telltale signs of wetness pooled in her panties. Her pussy was desperate to be stretched and filled.

Down, girl.

She'd never had such an intense reaction to any man before. Not even to her ex-boyfriend of three years. Though, to be fair, it had been years since she had sex. Despite owning a vibrator, she did not have the desire or energy to take care of her needs.

The office phone rang, making them both jump apart as if caught doing something wrong.

How did I get so close to him?

Quynh took the chance to run to the phone, putting the desk between their bodies. Though it wouldn't be much of a real barrier, it gave her a sense of control over the situation.

"Hello, Griffin's Auto Body. Can I help you?" She listened as the person asked for a status update on their vehicle, to which she responded any updates would be relayed to them as soon as there were changes. As in, we'll call you when it's ready.

She hung up the phone and glanced up to see Griffin still in the doorway. He leaned casually against the door-jamb, arms and ankles crossed, as if he didn't have a single care in the world.

"Are the children behaving themselves?"

She chuckled when she realized he was referring to his customers.

"Oh, them? It's nothing." He didn't seem to believe her. "Trust me, I can handle irate customers."

"What do you do for work?"

Her face fell at his question, memories of her termination and current unemployment flooding her. She chewed on her bottom lip as she contemplated what to say.

He seemed tense, waiting for her answer. His muscles bunched and braced to jump or run at a moment's notice. She took in a deep breath and offered him a small smile.

"I'm a nurse practitioner. Pain management, actually. But...uh...I just lost my job the other day..." Her voice trailed off as she stared at the ground. It was the first time she'd said the words out loud. The reality of her situation hit her hard.

A warm hand gripped her chin and raised her face so they met with his green eyes. His brows were furrowed in confusion as he took her in. He moved his hand to cup her face as his other hand moved around her back to pull her into a tight hug.

She melted into his embrace, tension leaking out of her as he held her in his arms for the second time in the past twenty-four hours. Quynh took a deep breath, letting his musky scent and the faint smells of motor oil fill her senses. She gripped the back of his shirt tightly in her fists as she held onto him.

He smoothed the strands of her hair as she let him hold her. Quynh did not know how much time had passed before they pulled away. Hands gripping her upper arms, Griffin surprised her with his next words.

"I'm looking for a secretary. If you're willing to work, I can pay you for your time."

Quynh didn't have to think about it. She was jobless and planned on staying in town for at least the next week. She nodded and made to break their contact just as the phone rang again.

"I guess I start now?" She smiled and answered the phone.

11

The rest of the day passed by in a blur. Griffin offered to take her to see her father again after lunch. She texted Ruth to let her know of her plans. Cindy let her in as soon as Griffin put the car in park. She surprised Quynh by giving her a large hug and said she was excited to see her again.

Even though she did not have much of a relationship with her father, she would not waste what little time they had left. She wanted to get to know him as much as possible. Quynh would deal with the consequences later.

She didn't see the harm in appeasing a dying man's wishes. He seemed just as eager to see her, though they were careful to avoid any conversation that might involve her mother or her childhood.

It was a pleasant visit, and when he started to wilt, Quynh made her exit. She asked Griffin to drop her off this time so he could get some work done. She waited in the sitting room while Cindy chittered on about the weather this time of year.

At the rumble of Griffin's truck approaching, Cindy escorted Quynh through the lobby to the front door. This time, when Cindy gave Quynh a hug, she was prepared for it and returned the gesture. When she turned away, she could have sworn she saw tears in the elderly woman's eyes.

By the time Quynh made it to the porch, Griffin was already standing by the passenger door, waiting for her. As she approached, he opened the door for her and helped her climb into the truck with a firm grip on her hand. He waited until she was settled into the seat before shutting the door and rounding the hood of the truck.

In the short time she sat alone in the truck, she tried to hold her breath to avoid breathing in his intoxicating scent. It was a pathetic effort since she'd obviously need to breathe at some point or pass out from sheer stubbornness. As soon as he settled into the driver's seat, she could have sworn the heat inside the otherwise chilled cabin of the truck ratcheted up. Or maybe it was just her heart rate at the close proximity of someone she clearly found attractive.

Not just physically attractive, because any woman with good eyesight could tell Griffin was a handsome man. His chiseled jawline underneath his neatly trimmed beard was enough to melt many panties. Coupled with his piercing green gaze and soft, kissable lips, she didn't know why there wasn't a line of women banging on his door.

Or, she supposed, it was possible it was happening. She had only been in town for a short time. He hadn't mentioned anything about having a girlfriend or a lover, but she never asked either.

The questions were bubbling up inside her, making her feel like she would burst.

"Griffin?"

"Hmm?" He glanced at her from the corner of his eye briefly.

"Can I ask you a question?"

"You just did."

She huffed. "I mean, can I ask you a personal question?"

He paused before answering.

"Sure."

"Are you…Are you seeing anyone else?"

The silence stretched between them as she waited anxiously for an answer.

This couldn't be a good thing, right?

It wasn't a complicated question. A simple yes or no answer would suffice.

God, she wished she could take back the last thirty

seconds. This was humiliating. Maybe she was better off just jumping out of the truck now.

"No."

"No?"

"No. There's no one else."

No one else? Does that mean I was someone to him?

Probably just wishful thinking. They hardly knew each other, though one thing was for certain.

There was an undeniable attraction between them.

Her body never felt so alive until she met him. Now, she was uncomfortably hyper-aware of the way her skin was stretched too tight. Or how empty her core was, desperate to be filled. Never mind how she suddenly became unnervingly aroused in close proximity to him.

His scent was intoxicating.

She wondered if he smelled better up close. Suddenly, she had an urge to shove her face into the meaty crook of his neck and take a big whiff.

Yeah, totally normal.

Snap out of it, you hussy!

"That's good."

The sounds of the passing highway settled in around them.

She relaxed against the seat. The truck coming to a stop jarred her awake. She hadn't realized she'd fallen asleep.

Oh, god, was that drool on my chin? Just kill me now.

Can the universe stop fucking with my life, please?

"I'm making dinner. I always make too much. Come over in an hour."

Before she could make sense of his words, Griffin was already out of the truck. He came around to open the door for her. She unbuckled her seatbelt and took his hand. She loved that he always helped her get in and out of his truck. The rough touch of his hand on hers was something she could get used to. His grip was always steady and firm. It was a sense of safety she hadn't known she was missing.

They stood in the open doorway of the truck, toe to toe, so close only a hand span separated their bodies. The heat emanating from his body sent a delicious shiver down her spine, causing goosebumps to erupt across her arms.

Staring up at him, she had a reckless thought.

What would happen if I kissed him right now?

The idea of a hot and torrid affair seemed extremely tempting. No strings attached sex.

"See you in an hour."

Griffin pivoted on his heel and stomped across the street. She watched him as he entered his house. He never seemed to lock the door.

Quynh dropped her head back with a frustrated groan.

Well, that was embarrassing.

She hoped he hadn't been able to read where her thoughts led her. He saw so much and said so little. She'd never been more exposed in all of her life.

It was embarrassing enough that she couldn't seem to control her reactions around him. He disrupted her equilibrium yet, paradoxically, kept her grounded in the present moment. His penetrating gaze made time seem to slow down, like a bunny caught in the sight of a menacing wolf, completely at the mercy of the predator.

Shutting the truck door, she made her way slowly into her temporary home. What started as a matter of convenience turned into a place of comfort for her. The small but functional apartment was a safe haven she didn't know she needed. Distance separated her from her past. The added benefit of being so close to her father during his last days made her even more grateful for the space.

She'd have to figure out a better way to repay Griffin for his generosity. Sure, she was helping out at the office, but he never once asked for money. And, if she were being honest, she actually didn't mind working for him. It was actually a nice reprieve from the backbreaking work of her bedside nursing days. When she moved to outpatient as a nurse practitioner, the volume of patients she needed to see was wild. She often took her work home with her. At first, it didn't bother her since she didn't have much of a social life. Over the months and, now, five years into her job, it grew tiresome.

Is this what burnout feels like?

Very likely.

The hours were unsustainable. She saw patients all day without stopping for any lunch breaks. It was exhausting work, and she liked to think it was rewarding. Some of her patients were loyal to her. It wasn't something she ever took for granted.

So, working for Griffin around the office was a welcome reprieve.

Quynh undressed and hopped in the shower. She was nervous about dinner with Griffin.

It wasn't dinner *with* Griffin, like a date or anything.

No, he just invited her over for dinner because he's a nice guy. Griffin seemed the type to help people around him, though he'd deny it if confronted. She didn't mind. It wasn't like she had much of an appetite lately. Besides, most nights, she'd order dinner to be delivered or pick up fast food on her way home from work. She often worked well into the evening, so there was little time to cook.

It was a terrible habit, but she didn't know where she could find the time. She spent the weekends resting or recuperating from the work week, only to repeat the same routine the following week.

She rarely took time off for vacations and had a good chunk of time off saved. Thankfully, as part of her unexpected termination, she would be given her paid time off, paid in a lump sum, which would allow her the luxury of buying time. It would be at least a few months before she needed to find a new job.

The prospect of finding another job was daunting.

A problem for another day.

12

Dressed in a pastel pink dress, Quynh checked her reflection in the mirror by the door. She rubbed all of her makeup off in the shower. Her hair was still wet, but she didn't see the point in getting all dolled up for dinner. He'd already seen her at her worst. She doubted he would care that she had bypassed makeup for the night.

On second thought, she ran to grab her purse and pulled out her tinted lip gloss. Maybe just a touch of lip gloss to boost her confidence.

Running her hands through her drying hair, Quynh blew herself a kiss in the mirror.

The walk to Griffin's only took less than a minute. It wasn't enough time for her to gather her courage. No, by the time she stood on the porch of his home, she was sick to her stomach.

He made her nervous. She didn't know how to handle

herself around him. Her body's reactions were foreign to her.

Dating was not really a priority for her. She went on a few dates over the years. She even had some less than memorable relationships. At her age, most people were already having their second baby. The dating pool for single men without red flags was woefully small. Sure, red flags in her romance books were acceptable, but in real life? It was a terrifying prospect.

She didn't need the drama of being in a toxic relationship. Frankly, she was just too tired and overworked to care. It's why none of her relationships made it past the second or third date. She hadn't gotten laid in years.

She didn't really miss sex. It was not usually worth her time to allow someone in her body who couldn't even last much longer than a few minutes. There didn't seem to be any point when she could get more pleasure out of her vibrators.

Quynh owned many different vibrators to choose from. Unfortunately, none of which she brought with her, so she needed to make use of her fingers.

Last night, she tossed and turned in bed. The memory of Griffin's strong, tanned body ignited a deep ache inside of her. She pictured how he would look on top of her. Her imagination was so vivid, it was like he was in the room with her.

She found she was fantasizing about her generous

neighbor/boss all too often. She was so worked up, she brought herself to an orgasm with her fingers in order to sleep.

Teenage Quynh was never this horny.

She needed to get herself together, or dinner tonight would be torture.

Just as she was about to knock on the door, it swung open. She was eye to muscled chest, his pecs pressing against the white fabric of his shirt obscenely. She glimpsed gray sweatpants and nearly swallowed her tongue. Her gaze slowly drifted upwards to find him staring at her intently.

He always seemed to do that. Stare at her with so much intensity that it made her nervous.

Instead of asking her to come in, he stepped aside so she could enter. The narrow entryway made it difficult for her to move without accidentally grazing him with her breast. She could have sworn she heard him take in a sharp inhale.

"You don't need to take your shoes off."

She didn't realize she slipped her sandals off. It was second nature to her. She bent to move them to place them near the door when he placed a hand on her arm. Quynh watched as Griffin grabbed her sandals in his large paw and placed them by the door.

"Thank you."

"Dinner's about ready. Make yourself at home."

She followed a few paces behind him as he led her into his home. It was furnished with the bare essentials. He gestured to the living room, where the TV was turned on to the local news channel.

"I'll be in the kitchen for a few more minutes."

"Do you need any help?"

"No."

She paused. It was probably rude to sit in the living room while he cooked for her. He didn't need to serve her.

He noticed her hesitation and turned to look at her.

"You can keep Rover and me company in the kitchen if you want."

She nodded, grateful for the suggestion. Quynh didn't watch much TV anyway. A perverse side of her wanted to see how he moved in the kitchen.

Griffin the mechanic was a fantasy all on its own, but Griffin the cook was swoon-worthy.

Whoa, girl, get a hold of yourself.

If her mother were alive, she'd admonish her for acting unladylike in public. Thoughts of her mother were like being splashed with a bucket of cold water. Her posture straightened as she fought to control her facial expressions.

Stoic. I have to be stoic.

Griffin showed her to the center island with bar-top seating.

"You can dice the tomatoes if you want."

She gave him a curt nod and went to the sink to wash her hands. By the time she dried her hands, he had set up a cutting board with the tomatoes in question for her. She sat down and lifted the sleek knife, admiring how lightweight it was in her hand. She was no cook, but she could figure out how to dice up tomatoes.

Griffin returned to the stove as he continued to prep dinner. They worked in comfortable silence. The only sounds were the muffled voices coming from the news channel in the living room. Rover lay in the corner, chewing on his bone while his tail thumped against the linoleum happily.

Her tense posture relaxed as she cut up the tomatoes. When she was done, she placed them into the small bowl on the counter.

Since dinner wasn't quite ready, she cleaned up the counter and washed up. She wasn't sure where they were going to sit for dinner, but at the very least, she could set the table.

It was all so very domestic, helping Griffin prepare for dinner. She could get used to this.

It's too bad she wouldn't be around for much longer.

13

This was a terrible idea.

He never should have invited her over for dinner. He didn't mind cooking for someone else, but having her tantalizing presence in his home was wreaking havoc on his senses.

Her vanilla scent hit him like a Mack truck when he opened the door to find her on his porch. He tried to ignore the way she'd looked at him, dusky lips parted with a teasing peek of her pink tongue. It took him a great deal of effort to step aside to allow her to walk past him. He held his breath to avoid breathing in more of her alluring scent and was caught off guard when her breast grazed his chest.

There was no mistaking the sharp inhale as he tried to control his body's reactions. His cock, which had been an annoying presence all day, rose to the occasion, taking her brief touch as an invitation for more.

Down, boy.

His cock refused to listen. The traitor.

He'd hoped if she was hidden away in the living room while he cooked, he'd have some more time to wrangle his cock under control. Unfortunately, luck was not on his side, and she'd opted to help him in the kitchen.

He made sure to keep his back toward her while he cooked so she wouldn't spot the very obvious hard-on in his sweats. Griffin only typically wore boxers when he left the house. He hadn't even thought about putting on a pair of boxers for his guest when he'd hopped out of the shower earlier. He might have jerked off to thoughts of bending Quynh over in the open doorway of his truck. It was necessary to get his libido under control before she got here, so he didn't mount her as soon as he saw her like a feral beast scenting a woman in heat.

Griffin couldn't recall a time when he'd felt this way about a woman. He'd had his fair share of flings over the years. He was no monk and often had a willing woman to take care of his basic needs if he wanted it. Mostly, they were transactional with no strings attached. He'd make sure his women were satisfied before he was finished. Then, once the awkward cleanup of the used condoms was over, he'd say his farewells and head home.

It had always been a hard line for him. He never took the women home with him. The cliche of not wanting a woman to become attached and think there was more to it than just sex was his primary concern. He had no desire to be in a relationship.

Frankly, he'd probably make a terrible boyfriend. Griffin almost chuckled out loud at the idea of being called someone's boyfriend. The last time he'd been referred to as such was in his twenties. A younger and wilder Griffin who had been reckless with his life until he almost lost everything.

He never wanted to go back to the dark place in his life. Being single suited his lifestyle just fine. He put the finishing touches to the chicken piccata with penne pasta, drizzling the lemon sauce he made from scratch over the pate before topping it off with some more capers. It wasn't anything fancy, but it was one of his favorite meals to make.

A sudden wave of anxiety washed over him.

What if she doesn't like it?

He had some microwavable meals he could offer her if she hated it. He turned to grab plates and realized she'd set the table up for the two of them.

Grunting out a thanks, he brought the hot pan over and served the hot meal on each plate. He poured the excess lemon sauce from the pan over the meals before placing the pan in the sink.

By the time he came back around to the table, she was already seated, waiting for him. He flushed as he realized she'd been waiting for him to eat. It had been a long time since he'd shared a meal with someone.

"Thank you for making dinner. It smells delicious." Her pink tongue made a reappearance as she licked her lower lip. His traitorous cock stirred at the sight. He finally was able to get his cock to stand down when he'd been distracted with making dinner, but now sitting across from her would test his resolve.

"Eat."

Griffin knew he likely came off as rude with his blunt words. He wasn't responsible for his conversational skills when all the blood was rushing from his head to his cock. The very act of breathing was difficult with her so close to him. Thankfully, the aromas of the freshly cooked meal overpowered her sweet scent.

He pretended to focus all of his attention on the meal in front of him, but really, he was gripping his utensils tightly at all the sounds of pleasure she emitted.

Griffin bet Quynh was not aware she moaned when she ate. He doubted she knew she groaned with pleasure whenever she bit into the capers, and the salty flavors burst across her taste buds. Judging by her innocent expression as she devoured her dinner, he would guess she had no idea what she was doing to him.

Is she always like this with food?

He imagined her moans as he ate her pussy like she was a hot meal served on a platter for him.

Suddenly, a rush of irrational rage surged as he thought of her making the same sounds with other men.

"Oh my god, this is so good," she moaned.

His grip on the knife was too tight. He tried to distract himself by eating his dinner, which tasted like ash in his mouth. He had a sudden craving for something else. Or, more appropriately, *someone* else.

The thought of laying her on this table and tasting her sweet pussy was driving him insane.

Rover's wet nose nudging into his thigh broke him out of his thoughts. He'd almost forgotten all about Rover's dinner.

"Excuse me." He got up and grabbed the freshly shredded chicken he'd made for Rover's dinner.

"Sit." Rover sat obediently as Griffin placed his dinner in his food tray. "Stay." Griffin refreshed the water dish and brought it back before giving the command for Rover to eat.

He chuckled to himself as Rover ate voraciously. It never got old watching him devour his food.

When he came back to the table, he was pleased to find her plate was empty. She ate every last drop.

"Good?"

"Hmm. It was delicious. You're an amazing cook!"

He tried not to preen with her compliments, but he'd be lying if it didn't make his chest swell with pride. He sat down quickly so she wouldn't see another part of his anatomy was also swelling under her attention.

"Thanks."

His response came out more like a grunt than actual words as he hunched over his plate and finished his dinner. She didn't fill the silence with vapid conversation. Instead, he saw her give Rover attention when he snuck under the table. Rover was not used to having guests in the house, and the thumping of his tail signaled his enthusiasm for the extra attention.

As soon as he finished the last bite, she stood up and grabbed their plates. He tried to protest, but she'd shushed him and brought the dirty dishes to the sink. Washing the dishes was one of his least favorite chores, but being a single man meant he needed to take care of his own dishes. Griffin would be lying if he didn't appreciate her for clearing the table, though when she started washing it, he'd already moved to stand.

"You don't need to do that." He stood behind her as she soaped up the dish brush and washed the plates.

She turned to look at him over her shoulder with a smile.

"I don't mind. I appreciate the hot meal. It's been a while since someone has cooked for me."

He fought the urge to box her in against the sink. If she had any idea how hard he was for her, she'd probably run away screaming.

They were still practically strangers.

Strangers with an undeniable connection, which was getting harder to resist the more time he spent with her. He didn't know her story yet, but he wanted to know. For the first time in forever, Griffin wanted to know everything about a woman. Not just any woman. This woman.

Wanted was putting it lightly. He needed to know everything about her. The things that made her unique. Her life story. Her likes or dislikes

Griffin knew she was a kind woman with a huge heart, not only by the way she'd stepped up and taken care of him and the guys but also by making space in her life for her estranged father. Griffin didn't know much about what happened between them, but old man Jones was well known on this side of town. He was one of the richest men here. Griffin recalled some drama that made the rounds, but he had been too young to care. He wondered if it had anything to do with Quynh and her reappearance.

He'd grown up in Willowbrook all of his life. The only child he'd known Jones to have was Ruth. They didn't run in the same social circles, but she seemed to be the apple of her father's eye.

Realizing he was still standing a little too closely behind her, Griffin stomped away before he acted on his impulse to bend her over the counter and strip her out of her pink dress. Her dainty feet were encased in matching pink socks, and he wanted to take them off with his teeth.

Griffin seemed to have developed a foot fetish in the time he'd seen her tiny feet. He'd certainly like to see those toes of hers curl in pleasure.

He was flipping through Netflix when he heard her soft footsteps approaching, followed closely behind by the clacking of Rover's claws on the wooden floors. She stood on the precipice of the doorway and shifted on her feet.

"Want to stay and watch a movie with me?"

Griffin surprised himself with the words that came out of his mouth. It was probably a bad idea to sit next to her for so long, but he didn't want her to go back to her place where she'd be alone. Well, alone with her cat. When he was also sitting alone with his dog.

What was the harm in keeping each other company?

The shy smile she offered him cemented his decision to invite her to stay. It made him wonder if he had ever asked a woman to stay longer than was necessary. Come to think of it, he'd never cooked for any other woman, either. She was his first of so many things.

He made room on the couch for her. Rover typically liked to lie with his head on his lap as they relaxed before bed. It was a nightly ritual for them.

"Any requests?" he asked as he continued flipping through the options.

"Just no horror." Her body shifted on the couch to get comfortable. She sat with her feet curled up under her, and he bit back a curse. She was probably cold. Unfortunately, he didn't keep any blankets in the living room.

After flipping through a few more options, he saw her perk up when he scrolled onto *Suits*. He knew he had made the right choice when she offered him a smile and settled into the couch.

He rarely watched legal drama, but he admitted the show was actually pretty good. Though Griffin attempted to concentrate on the TV, he increasingly found himself enthralled by her responses as time went on.

He snuck glances at her as she watched the show. Judging by her rapt gaze, she seemed to enjoy the show, though he wondered if it was the show or the undeniably attractive male characters.

By the time the first episode was over, he'd worked himself up into a jealousy frenzy at the thought of her finding an actor attractive. He had no right to her or her affections. His jaw ached from clenching it so tightly for so long. A small arm touched his shoulder, making his tense muscles relax slightly.

"Hey, are you okay? You seem tense."

No kidding.

"Fine."

She let go of his shoulder. He ignored how the loss of her touch made him panic.

"I should get going. It's getting late. Thank you so much for tonight."

She was already in the hallway by the time he got his act together and followed her. Cursing himself for being a rude host, he stomped after her retreating form.

He grabbed her arm before she got to the door and whirled her around to face him.

"Hey, hey. I'm sorry." He wasn't sure exactly what he was apologizing for, but he knew he needed to apologize for his irrational response to the idea of her finding anyone else attractive.

"It's okay." She made to move out of his grip.

Acting purely on impulse, he slowly backed her up against the hallway until her back was flush against the hard surface. He maintained a couple of inches of space between their bodies.

Using a finger, he lifted her chin and looked into her amber eyes. Eyes that captivated him with her unspoken words.

"I'm sorry." This time, when he said it, he knew she believed him. Her tense shoulders dropped away from her ears, and she offered him a soft smile at his lame apology.

He leaned his head down so their foreheads were almost touching, her vanilla perfume filling his lungs as he breathed her in. It was intoxicating, and he nearly closed his eyes in pleasure at how her fragrance lit up all of his senses.

It was not clear who moved first, or maybe they both moved at the same time. One moment, they were breathing each other. The next, her body was flushed against his. Slowly, he brought her chin up with a hand. His lips slammed against hers in a sudden and possessive kiss. He groaned at her shocked gasp, but her lips softened beneath his.

Using the tip of his tongue, he coaxed her lips apart before plunging into her warm heat. When her tongue met his in a tantalizing duel, he nearly fell to his knees at her soft touch.

He could never get enough of kissing her.

Griffin needed to possess her like she possessed all of his waking thoughts lately. Honestly, this was her fault for causing him to be so out of control around her. Judging by her eager kisses and small hands tugging on his hair, she didn't have any complaints. He reached a hand down to grip her by her waist before hoisting her up under her thighs to bring her to eye level.

Breaking the kiss, they panted for breath as he kept her pinned against the wall with his hips.

"You okay?" His voice came out more like a growl. "We stop when you say stop. Understand?"

She nodded frantically as she licked her lips. This time, when their lips met, she made the first move, yanking on his hair and pulling him down to her lips as he ground into her. His cock was hard between them, and he rocked gently against her core, the warmth seeping through the layers of their clothing.

Griffin was about to come just from rubbing up against her. He pulled back before he embarrassed himself and came before giving her any orgasms. He wasn't a damn teenager anymore. He knew how to please a woman, and she deserved nothing less.

"Let's take this upstairs, yeah?"

He was already running up the stairs with her in his arms before she'd finished nodding. He braced an arm against the wall when she started kissing and nipping at his neck, the sensation of her nips and licks causing jolts of pleasure to shoot straight to his cock.

"Fuck, baby, you gotta stop that if you want to make this last." He groaned in agony.

She pulled away and gave him a cute pout.

He slammed her up against the wall as his lips wiped away her sassy pout. His dick hardened impossibly further at her moans.

Fuck. He was definitely going to come in his pants if he didn't slow this train down.

Ripping his lips away, he sprinted the rest of the way to his bedroom. He tossed her unceremoniously on the bed and smirked at her yelp of surprise as she bounced on the mattress. He reached a hand behind his head and yanked off his shirt.

He had a large tattoo of a dragon mid-flight, spanning

the right side of his chest that wrapped around his ribs and shoulder to encompass his back. The tip of its tail wrapped around his collarbone. Quynh gulped at seeing his chest.

"Like what you see, sunshine?" He gave her a cocky smirk as he closed in on her.

She moved to make more room for him on his king-size bed as he crawled over her prone body. She parted her thighs, and his hips hovered over hers. With a hand braced by her head and the other cupping her face, he stared down at her, making sure she knew it was her choice if they took this any further. He almost wept with joy when she gave him a small nod.

He brought his lips to meet hers in a gentle kiss, letting their lips and tongues do all the talking, ratcheting up their arousal to scorching levels until she was tugging at his sweatpants. He pulled away and chuckled at her soft whine.

"Shh. I'll take care of you, sunshine."

He trailed his lips over her jawline, peppering kisses down the slim column of her throat. He flicked his tongue at the juncture of her neck and bit back a groan at how she arched her body at the caress.

His fingers toyed with the hem of her dress. He took mental notes of what made her gasp or moan, taking pleasure in driving her crazy with his touch.

He lifted her dress, fingers gently grazing her smooth

skin, baring her inch by inch to the cool air. He scooted down and hovered above her as she tried to catch her breath. Griffin blew a warm breath against her skin and watched in fascination as her belly quivered from the sensation.

"Griffin," she moaned.

Hmmm, he liked the way his name sounded when she moaned it.

He teased the edge of her shorts with his fingertips, giving her a chance to stop things from progressing if she wanted to. God, he hoped she didn't stop him, though. He needed to taste her and feel her come on his tongue more than his next breath.

She sat up on her elbows, their eyes meeting as Griffin slowly hooked his fingers into the waistband of her shorts and tugged them off of her at an agonizing pace. Her tongue came out to lick at her lower lip, making her lips shine. Lifting her hips to help him get her shorts over her perky butt. She didn't look away as he pulled her shorts off. His cock ached at the sight of her lacy lavender panties. He wondered if this was her preferred style.

Did she wear it tonight hoping I would see it?

Peeling her out of her clothes was like unwrapping a present. The more her smooth, tanned skin was exposed, the more his mouth watered. He leaned down and nipped at her inner thigh, earning a shocked gasp from her. He licked the wound and was rewarded with a moan as she dropped her head back. The dress came off quickly after that. He tossed the offending garment over his shoulder and sat back on his heels. He ran an admiring look over her magnificent body.

"You look good enough to eat."

And eat, he would. He ran his palms over her calves, delighted with her skin beneath his touch. The way her thighs quivered as he got closer to her apex. He teased the edges of her panties and watched as her pussy soaked the lavender material.

"Fuck. You're so wet for me."

"Oh, god, I'm sorry."

Frowning, he tore his gaze away from her tantalizing pussy to find she had covered her face with her hands.

Is she embarrassed?

Abandoning his mission, he reached up to gently pull her hands away from her face.

"Nothing to be sorry for, sunshine."

She bit her lip. If she didn't believe him, he'd show her how much the sight of her soaked panties made him.

"Now, hold on to something 'cause you're not leaving this bed until I've made you come at least three times," he promised.

"Wh-what?"

He chuckled at her shriek.

Sitting back on his heels, he glided his calloused palms over her abdomen, gliding his rough hands down her thighs. With a firm grip, he pulled her legs until her knees were bent, giving him the perfect view of her wet panties. He scooted backwards until he was kneeling on the floor, dragging her panting body with him as he went.

"Do you have any idea what the sight of your wet pussy does to me? Hmm?"

She shook her head as her fingers gripped his duvet tightly.

"N-no."

"That's okay, sunshine. I'll show you what it does to me."

With his hands on her knees, he placed one leg over his shoulder and ran the tip of his nose along her inner thigh. By the time he reached her panties, they were completely soaked with her arousal. He tried not to stare, but he couldn't help but admire the sight. Nothing better than seeing someone so turned on they drenched through layers of cloth.

Leaning in, he rubbed the tip of his nose along the wet cloth and inhaled her sweet scent. Pulling her underwear aside, he flicked out his tongue for a taste.

Fuck. He almost came in his pants when she let out a sharp gasp. She tasted so good.

Burying his face in her pussy, he licked and teased at her slit, coaxing more of her arousal to drench his face and tongue. Her gasps and moans were like music to his ears. A symphony he'd never tire of hearing. When his searching tongue found her sensitive clit, her hips bucked as if to escape from the onslaught.

Oh, no. She would not get away that easily. He wrapped an arm around her waist and pinned her down while the other hand tugged her panties aside. Looking up from the altar between her legs, he smirked, fully aware his lips were coated with her arousal.

"Uh-uh. You're going to be a good girl and stay still for me. You hear me?" At her frantic nod, he returned his attention to her needy pussy.

His mouth watered as he leaned in and placed an open-mouthed kiss on her mound. Her groan of protest made him chuckle until her small hands tugged at his hair.

Something snapped inside of him, like a feral beast locked in a cage for too long. He unleashed his hunger, and her pussy took the brunt of the assault. He licked and sucked at her folds. The noises she elicited sounded obscene if he had been a prude.

Thankfully, he was no prude. Each moan of pleasure ratcheted his own, and he hungered for more. He discovered she loved it when he flicked and sucked at her clit while his fingers spread her open. He teased her with his fingertips, circling at her entrance and applying just enough pressure to drive her wild.

"Griffin...p-please."

"Hmmm. I love the way you beg for me, sunshine."

He pushed his finger into her core, delighted at her gasp of pleasure. He thrusted his finger in and out a few times before slowly adding a second finger. He doubled his efforts on her clit, alternating between licking and sucking. Her thighs threatened to crush his head, but if he died with her taste on his lips, he'd die a happy man.

He knew she was on the brink of an orgasm when her thighs quivered and her grip on his hair became frantic.

"Oh, oh, god!"

"Say my name when you come, sunshine."

He curled his fingers inside of her, pulsing it against her spongy G-spot and set a relentless rhythm between flicking and sucking at her clit.

"Oh, fuck, Griffin, I'm co-coming!"

He didn't let up even as her body threatened to strangle his fingers or when she suffocated him by shoving him harder against her pussy. Her body spasming from the intensity of her orgasm beneath his strong grip around her waist was worth every single car in his garage.

Her body relaxed and melted into the mattress. Her legs loosened to release his head, and still, he licked softly at her pussy. Griffin brought his fingers coated with her cum to his lips, wrapping his lips around his digits and sucking her juices off his fingers.

Gripping her hips, he continued licking and lapping at her center, tasting her sweet cream from the source.

"Ahh. Griffin...no more."

He wrapped his lips around her clit and sucked gently, letting it go with a soft pop.

"One more, sunshine. You can give me at least one more."

He returned his attention to her glistening pussy, reveling at the way her body responded to his touch. This time, when she came, his name came out in a scream before she fell limply in bed.

A double orgasm for dessert. His favorite kind.

He put her panties back, but grabbed a pair of his boxers to slide up her legs. He didn't think she'd want to squeeze back into the tight shorts when her pussy was probably oversensitive. He grabbed his discarded shirt off the ground and helped her into the garment.

Picking her up gently, he maneuvered her into the center of his bed and covered her with his blanket. She left out a sleepy sigh, her eyes fluttering open. The soft smile on her face made something in his chest squeeze. A foreign sensation. One he was determined to ignore.

"Rest." He placed a soft kiss on her forehead and went in search of a glass of water for her.

She'd probably be dehydrated with the amount of fluids that leaked out of her from her orgasms, so hydration was important.

Normally, he'd be pushing to leave once the deed was done. But tonight, he'd thought only of her pleasure and ignored his still-aching cock. He almost came with her the second time she'd convulsed and screamed his name, barely holding back on spilling into his sweatpants.

Admittedly, it was the first time he'd enjoyed someone else's pleasure so much that it threatened his otherwise iron-clad control of his own desires. He'd wanted to plunge into her tight pussy while she was in the middle of her orgasm and feel her come around his cock. Next time.

He'd make sure it would happen next time.

There *had* to be a next time. He wasn't done with her yet. If anything, he'd become a man obsessed with owning and possessing her, even for the short time she was in town.

When it was time for her to leave, he would let her walk away. No strings attached.

It was simply a sexual attraction, and once they got each other out of their systems, they'd be able to both move on.

No hard feelings.

Or, at least, it was what he told himself.

He ignored the small voice calling him a liar.

It had to be over when she left. There was no way to make a long-distance relationship work.

Besides, he wasn't interested in being in a relationship. He was too old to be anyone's boyfriend. Nor did he want the complications a relationship would likely bring.

No. He didn't need to be tied down to any woman

who would want more from him than he was willing to give.

He was happy with his lifestyle just the way it was.

Grabbing a clean cup from the cabinet, he filled it with water and gulped it down. Her taste still lingered on his lips. No doubt her cum was drying in his beard.

He should probably wash it off, but the thought didn't last. He liked the idea of falling asleep with her cum on his face, having her sweet smell be the last thing he'd smell before falling asleep.

She was probably waiting for him. Griffin grabbed another cup and poured some fresh water for Quynh.

By the time he returned, she was snoring softly in his bed. He didn't have the heart or will to wake her.

Sliding between the sheets, he lay on his side and watched her as she slept. He fought the urge to trace her profile with his fingers, just barely.

The sight of her in his bed didn't bother him as much as he thought it would.

In fact, he liked the way she looked in his bed.

Maybe, a little too much.

14

Quynh was burning alive. Awareness came to her in increments. Something hot and hard was plastered to her back while a heavy weight kept her weighed down. She cracked an eye open to yet another unfamiliar room.

Where am I?

The memories from last night hit her.

Did I pass out last night?

Judging by the muscled arm coiled tightly around her middle, she must have fallen asleep. Nobody could blame her for blacking out after not just one but two intense orgasms, back to back. She'd never come from oral before. Didn't know it was possible. Griffin's skillful fingers and mouth coaxed her orgasms out of her like a magician or a snake charmer.

Speaking of snakes, something firm was poking her in her backside. Quynh's eyes widened at the python nestled between her butt cheeks. The angle probably made it seem larger than it was, but if it was close to how it felt, she probably wouldn't be able to take a cock that long and thick.

An urgent need pestered her, reminding her of her predicament. She looked around for her dress. Last time she saw it, it was tossed over Griffin's broad shoulders.

The first peeks of sunshine just rising over the horizon dimly lit the room. She tried to wiggle out from Griffin's hold, only for his arms to tighten around her as he grumbled in his sleep.

She'd smile at being used as a teddy bear if not for her bladder screaming at her. Slowly, she lifted his arm and wiggled to the edge of the bed. She turned to look over her shoulder at his sleeping form, face relaxed in sleep.

Griffin's almost permanent scowl was nowhere to be seen. He looked so handsome, with sleep softening his features.

How many women got to see Griffin like this?

The thought sobered her as she hastened her efforts to find her clothes and relieve her bladder.

Ah! There you are!

The offending garment lay folded on the bench at the foot of the bed. The thought of squeezing herself into the tight-fitting dress was less than appealing, but she couldn't do a walk of shame in Griffin's clothes, even if she was just going across the street.

Tip-toeing across the cold hardwood floor, she snagged her dress and shorts and hustled into the en suite bathroom. The sound of the lock snicking shut was loud in the otherwise quiet room. A happy sigh escaped her as she relieved the uncomfortable pressure that woke her up from an otherwise peaceful slumber.

She pulled up her panties and slid her feet into her shorts, lamenting at the tight fit against her skin. She always wore fitted shorts under her dresses to prevent chafing and keep her belly pouch contained, but having to wear them first thing in the morning was torture. Slipping on her dress, she washed her hands in the sink. Gasping at the sight that greeted her, she frantically tried to fix her bedhead and splashed warm water on her face to wash off the drool.

Jesus, she couldn't recall the last time she'd slept so soundly.

Well, this is as good as it's gonna get.

She admitted defeat and dried her face on the towel.

Careful not to make too much noise, Quynh slowly peeked her head out of the bathroom door. A sigh of relief left her at the sight of his sleeping back, his soft snores reaching her ears.

It was so tempting to crawl back into bed with him, to burrow into his heat and pretend they were just a normal couple. For a moment, they could just act like they had no worries in the world.

She wasn't a fool, though. Relationships rarely lasted longer than a few months for her. Deep down, she knew it was her inability to connect to men on an emotional level that eventually drove them away. All she'd ever known of men was... they always left her.

The only person she could count on was herself. She used to be able to depend on her career; however, it clearly blew up in her face. All those sleepless nights and hours wasted on a job that dropped her like she meant nothing.

Why did I work so hard for so long? What was the whole point of working for a system that only cared about the bottom line?

There were so many questions, and it was *way* too early to think.

Quynh left as quickly and quietly as possible. She held her breath until she shut the front door quietly behind her.

Rover slept in his bed in the hallway. He'd watched her with what seemed like judgment in his beautiful brown eyes as she did her walk of shame. A quick pet on his head rubbed the frown right off his face.

Finally, tension escaped her when she got back to her apartment as she sagged against the door. Pickles leaped off the couch where he slept to greet her. Bending down, she gave him a scratch under his chin. His food dish was nearly empty, but she could take care of it later.

What a mess!

Just because they were intimate didn't necessarily mean anything more. It certainly wouldn't be grounds to discuss having a relationship.

What they were doing was working out. For now.

It was inevitable they'd have to part ways. She needed to go back home and deal with the mess she left behind. So many things she needed to handle.

Right now, at this moment, the only thing she needed to worry about was getting back in bed. It was still a couple more hours before she'd have to eventually drag herself back out and face the music.

Quynh, you are being dramatic. So what if the man made you see stars not once but twice in a row? It didn't mean anything.

Ugh. Just the memories of the way he'd looked when he went down on her between her legs were making her achy all over again. Before her impulsive side took over and she ran back to his house to crawl back into Griffin's warm bed, Quynh made a mad dash for her bed. Burrowing into the cool sheets, she closed her eyes and ignored the tingling sensations through her body at the thought of Griffin.

She resisted the urge to touch herself as thoughts from last night filtered in. It was like she had no control over her body or reactions anymore, like a damn teenager.

One thing was for certain, if he could eat pussy like that, he was likely amazing in bed.

After what seemed like an eternity, she finally fell asleep to thoughts of the handsome, grumpy mechanic with a sinful mouth and wicked tongue.

15

ing. Ring. Ring.

Groaning, Griffin rolled over to find the offending alarm that dared to wake him up from a deep sleep. He was having pleasant dreams before being pulled out of them. Dreams about what would have happened if Quynh hadn't passed out after he made her come. Twice. Yeah, he was proud of his prowess, though he hoped to have pushed her for a third. He only stopped when he noticed her droopy and sated form. He hadn't had the heart to keep pushing for it.

In his dream, he'd strip her of the rest of her clothes, kissing and tasting every part of her body with every inch he revealed, giving the areas he didn't get to claim last night extra attention.

He needed to find out where else she liked being kissed. What made her moan or gasp in pleasure? What caused her toes to curl? Or even what would cause him to push him away, whether in pleasure or disinterest.

Would she push me away, or would she let me continue to explore her body?

Turning off the annoying alarm, he realized he was alone in his bed. This wouldn't have bothered him, except he fell asleep next to her sleeping form. She must have snuck out sometime during the early morning hours.

The idea of her leaving him while he was dreaming about her stung. She didn't even bother to wake him up to let him know she was leaving. Sure, the walk to her place was short, but anything could happen to her. Willowbrook was a relatively sleepy town with low crime rates, but it was never a good idea for a woman to be out alone at night, regardless of how safe the town was.

He pretended the sting in his chest was about worrying about her safety rather than the fact that she left without a word.

Did last night mean nothing to her?

It wasn't like he was interested in pursuing a relationship with her, but he deserved some respect.

Insecurity threatened to drag him down into their dark depths.

Was she just using me? Does she even care about me?

There was no way she could have faked her orgasm. He'd tasted it directly from the source.

Sitting up in bed jerkily, Griffin ran his hands over his face, blowing out a breath at the errant thoughts running through his tired mind. He should get his day started. No use dwelling on things he couldn't control.

If he was grumpier than normal, he blamed it on not getting his usual eight hours of sleep.

It had nothing to do with the dark-haired beauty who came on his face and then left his bed like he was a dirty old man.

His shower was colder than necessary. He reluctantly washed the traces of her off his body, rinsing out his beard thoroughly. He didn't need to smell her on him while he worked. It would be distracting as hell.

Rover followed him into the kitchen. He sat down patiently at his food dish, waiting to be served his breakfast. Rover normally slept on the bench at the foot of the bed, but he'd been in the hallway last night. Guilt pierced his gut at the thought of Rover sleeping in the cool hallway, but he'd seemed perky as ever this morning. He didn't mean to lock Rover out of the room, but it's hard to seduce a woman when there was a slobbering giant dog in the same room with him.

16

Her stomach was in knots. Quynh knew she would need to go downstairs and face the music eventually. One-night stands just weren't her style. This was a whole new experience.

Sure, she'd gone on a few promising dates in the past. At least a handful of times, there was at least an intellectual connection to them. After going on several dates, it typically led to the bedroom. Though she was curious to test their physical compatibility, the experience had always been...disappointing. Lackluster.

Despite having relatively low expectations, she was always unnerved by the experience. It probably took her longer to get undressed than it did for the entire ordeal to be over. Orgasms were always one-sided, and sometimes it hurts. She knew it wasn't normal to be in pain during intercourse, but whenever she suggested more foreplay or the use of lubrication, it made her feel inadequate.

She'd bolted to avoid the humiliating situation as

soon as the awkward cleanup was done. She'd rush home and take a long, hot shower to scrub the scent of them off her.

She ignored the uncomfortable sensation of having another person inside of her. Even if it was for a few minutes. It never felt like a welcomed intrusion. She blamed it on her low libido and older age.

Do women my age still have sex regularly?

If she had friends, she'd ask them, but her only friend was Meg, who was too busy with her thriving business to be in a relationship.

Last night, though...Heat crept through her as thoughts of how effortlessly Griffin reduced her to a writhing mess.

It was like a whole new level she'd unlocked. One she did not know she was capable of.

Being around Griffin was akin to her first teenage crush. Her feelings were intense and off-putting. Any time she thought of Griffin, her gut would bubble with what she assumed was akin to butterflies. Though it was more like nervousness churning and swirling inside of her whenever she thought about his handsome face. Like a raging tempest ready to ravage her sanity and make her act on her impulsive thoughts.

Quynh should celebrate how she was actually able to orgasm with another person. This has never happened to her before. Until last night, she didn't even know she *could* reach the precipice.

Griffin didn't just take her to the cliff's edge. He shoved her into the dark abyss; one she went over willingly when she finally relaxed under his touch. What a glorious way to go.

Is this what it feels like to let someone else have complete control over my body?

After her initial bouts of vulnerability, she'd been so at ease and safe under Griffin's touch. He paid attention to what she liked and noticed when she wasn't comfortable. Griffin toed the line of pushing her boundaries while making her feel safe enough to shatter so completely.

Never in her life had she come so hard she thought she might have blacked out. The second orgasm was almost torturous, pushing her past the brink of her comfort zone. She was so blissed out, she'd nearly passed out. Griffin cleaned her up gently and tucked her into the bed where she'd succumbed to sleep.

The walk of shame was definitely a new experience, though.

Pickles gave her the side eye when she'd finally crawled into bed. No doubt he was upset she'd got under the covers he'd spread himself all over. He'd huffed and stomped off the bed when she'd climbed under the sheets. When she woke up again, he was curled up on her hip.

Guess she was forgiven for abandoning him most of the night.

It was still early. She had plenty of time to grab a cup of coffee and breakfast at Sip Happens before her day started. Hopefully, she wouldn't run into Griffin before she'd at least fortified herself with some caffeine.

It was quickly becoming a favorite part of her new routine. The cafe was always comforting and cozy. The energy was both soothing and stimulating with the scent of freshly ground coffee beans. She didn't have time before the shop opened today to go to the nearby bookstore, but maybe this weekend, she'd see if there were any new romance books that came in. She'd been dying to read the latest romantic fantasy that had left the book world in a frenzy. Something involving dragons and a girl with a disability. It sounded so unique. She was excited to read it. Maybe she could call the bookstore and request a copy so she could pick it up for this weekend.

She wasn't sure how much longer it would take for Griffin to repair her car. Last she knew, he was still waiting for the parts to be delivered. Unfortunately, there was a manufacturing shortage. So what would normally be here in a few days could end up taking a few extra weeks.

The thought of being stuck in Willowbrook longer than she planned didn't send her into a panic frenzy like she thought it would. She didn't have a job to rush back to. In reality, Quynh welcomed the extra time in town. The delay worked out in her favor. She could use the extra time with her father while waiting for her car to be repaired, though it was probably annoying for Griffin to be her chauffeur. He seemed like he was always so busy at the shop.

She'd have to look into alternative options for rides. Maybe Julio or Sean could give her a ride on their way home. Or, she supposed she could call Cindy and ask if she could send a car to get her.

By the time she mustered up the courage to head downstairs, Griffin was nowhere in sight. She experienced a mixture of relief and disappointment at not seeing her grumpy mechanic. Her walk to and from the coffee shop was uneventful, other than the thoughts swirling inside her mind about her conflicting feelings about Griffin. By the time she came back, the garage doors were wide open, music pumping through the speakers, and voices drifted through to the parking lot.

She shouted a hello in greeting as she quickly made her way into the office, careful to avoid making eye contact with an especially grumpy pair of eyes peeking out from under the hood of the car at her.

She settled in to begin the workday. While most of the tasks were administrative: checking on orders, sending invoices, checking emails, answering the phones, and organizing around the office, she found she quite enjoyed the work. Sure, she wasn't seeing patients, prescribing medications, making medical diagnoses, or fighting with insurance companies, but it was still fulfilling to check off a task once it was completed.

Ironically, the administrative tasks were always something she dreaded at her last job. Not that she didn't enjoy the work, obviously, but there just never seemed to be enough hours in her day to be both the provider, prescriber, and her own secretary. The staff were always willing to help, but quite often, the patients would refuse to discuss anything with anyone but her. It made her job more difficult when she was doing the work of multiple people.

A few days away from work made her realize how intensely burned out she was. It did no one any good because her mental exhaustion left her too drained to care for herself. In a way, working for Griffin had a therapeutic effect on her.

In her mind, she pictured her mental and social batteries recharging like a phone that was blinking red and was finally plugged into the charger. By the time she got to Willowbrook, her battery levels were critically low. She probably should have recognized the signs earlier, but she didn't see the signs when things were at their worst.

It was only after the devastating loss of her job and, pretty soon, her father, that she realized how unhappy she was with her life.

17

The sun was setting over the horizon by the time she heard the telltale signs of the garage bay doors closing. Julio and Sean popped in occasionally throughout the day to grab water from the water station and steal some snacks Griffin left for paying customers.

She'd laugh at their antics when they'd come inside. It was always nice to have a break in the monotony of the day. Sean would grab a bag of chips and munch on them loudly, giving her a playful wink before strolling back outside. He was probably a heartbreaker with his smooth-talking tendencies, while Julio was happily married with a baby on the way.

Julio was the quietest of the duo but no less friendly. She likened him to a golden retriever with his affable personality. While Griffin, the grouch, as she'd heard both Julio and Sean refer to him, was probably the grumpy cat meme she loved.

His tendency to lean more toward irate than friendly didn't bother her. It was refreshing to meet someone who didn't fake being happy in front of other people. There was no pretense with Griffin. What you saw was pretty much what you got. Well, for the most part.

She had no clue how he felt after last night. The few times she'd seen him since, there was the same permanent scowl across his face. Quite honestly, she was too much of a coward to meet his eyes for more than a couple of seconds before she averted her gaze. Pretending to be busy with something else.

Oh, shoot! That reminded her. She needed to order the parts he'd asked for earlier this afternoon. The ones he needed to fix her car. The sooner he could get the parts, the sooner he could finish the task. She wouldn't be so dependent on him for car rides anymore. It would be a relief to gain some of her independence back, though she'd be lying if she said she wouldn't miss his calm demeanor on their rides. It helped to soothe her anxiety about the upcoming visit with her father.

The side door opened.

Her skin prickled with a familiar awareness. She didn't need to look up from her computer screen to know who walked in. She cleared her throat, pretending to be hyper-focused on the task at hand. Truth be told, it was really a simple task to order the parts. The login information was already saved. Griffin gave her a notepad with the parts he needed, so all it took was using the search function, adding to the cart, and then pressing the order button.

Voila!

The whole checkout process was made easier since the payment information was already saved to the account. Unfortunately, the shipping time frames were hardly accurate, per Griffin. So, now, it was just a waiting game.

When she was done with the order, she finally glanced up to find Griffin leaning on the high-top bar with arms crossed. A playful smirk hinted at the corner of his upturned lip. The mischievous glint in his eyes made her sit up straighter.

Gulping, she met his gaze. Heart racing, she was caught in his snare, like a lion with its sights on its next meal. There was no graceful way to escape her predicament. It was now or never.

"I'm just about done in the shop. I'm taking Rover for a walk by the lake before dinner. Care to join us?"

She glanced down at her simple blue sundress paired with ballet flats. Hardly an outfit meant for a stroll around the lake.

"Umm...I'd love to, but let me change first."

"Meet me at my place when you're ready. I'll close up the shop."

He tapped the counter twice with his fist before

pushing away. She tried not to stare at his ass in his tight coveralls, but it was hard to resist. She jumped when she heard him clear his throat, only noticing he'd caught her staring at his ass.

Oh my god! Did he just catch me checking him out?

He threw her a knowing smirk over his shoulder before walking back out to the garage bay. If Quynh could melt into the earth, she would have. She smacked her head on the table.

Of course, he did. How embarrassing!

She needed to be on her best behavior. There's no use falling for someone when there was no future for her here. There weren't any health clinics nearby she could even work at if she wanted to find a job.

Not that she was entertaining the idea or anything, but she needed a new job. Her bank account would run dry, eventually. She might as well explore all of her available options. For the first time in her life, she was at a crossroads. The next choices she made would determine what the next few years of her life would look like.

Do I want to find a new job and stay in the same city? Or venture outside of my comfort zone and move to a new town? What was really keeping me in the city?

Quynh was no city girl, but she'd taken the job right after getting her degree. It seemed like the deal of a lifetime when she received the job offer. She always dreamt of working in the city and having an equally active social life, hoping to find a place where she belonged. Plus, there were countless lonely people looking to connect in the city, so she was bound to find at least one friend. Or so she hoped.

However, things didn't exactly work out the way she imagined. She ended up working too much to have a social life. Most of her classmates relocated far from their university, which made it hard to stay in touch. Most days, though, she rarely had the energy to go out to the local bars. Instead, she preferred to spend her downtime curled up on the couch with a spicy romance while Pickles kept her company.

The most important question she needed to ask herself, though, was also the most difficult to answer.

Am I happy with my life? My career choices? Am I too old to change? Or am I capable of having a fresh start?

So many questions. So many variables.

Quynh knew with absolute certainty that being around Griffin sparked something new inside of her. The exhilarating feeling of being alive. For most of her life, she was treading water. Just barely holding her head above the surface to keep her from drowning under the impossible expectations she'd set for herself. And waiting for something amazing to happen to her.

She was always waiting.

Maybe it was time she stopped waiting for life to happen.

Is this my opportunity? Or am I being naïve? What if Griffin was only interested in sex? What if things didn't work out between us? Am I putting all of my eggs in one basket?

Get yourself together, Quynh.

She didn't need to answer anything right now. All she wanted to do was enjoy whatever this was.

One thrilling step at a time.

18

Quynh was out of breath by the time she made it to Griffin's house. She ran upstairs to change into leggings and a loose sweatshirt, but Pickles demanded to be fed immediately. She'd stopped to feed the dramatic Maine Coon and tried to freshen up in the bathroom, but her hair was looking rather limp, so up her hair went in a messy bun. This was the best it was gonna get. She didn't want to keep the boys waiting on her.

The front door opened by the time she was on the porch. Rover's excited barking probably alerted Griffin to her arrival.

Griffin looked her up and down before stepping aside to let her in. Giving him a small smile, she went to walk inside and was almost knocked over by the giant dog.

"Oof!" Rover's giant paws landed on her abdomen.

"Down, boy!"

Rover sat down at Griffin's command.

"You're a big boy, aren't you?" she said as she kneeled down, petting the drooling animal behind his ears.

Rover's excitement was contagious. She never had a dog in all of her life. Her mother and aunt worked a lot, and there wasn't any room for pets. When she graduated from nursing school, she thought about getting a pet, but the idea of leaving it to itself for long days didn't sit right with her.

Pickles sort of fell into her lap. She just moved into her apartment, and the loneliness was oppressive. She overheard a coworker, Joe, lamenting about having to get rid of the giant Maine Coon as he was moving for a job and could not take the cat with him.

It was barely a fully formed thought before she'd whirled around and told Joe she'd take the cat. She hadn't even asked for any pictures. She'd rather take in the cat than have Joe put the poor cat up for adoption. Or worse, leave the cat behind.

Joe was so relieved to find a new home for Pickles. Several weeks later, she was a mother to a grumpy Maine Coone cat who wanted nothing to do with her. It wasn't exactly what she had envisioned when she volunteered to adopt the cat, but she had no regrets. He was relatively low maintenance, though the litter box was an unpleasant experience. Thankfully, he came completely litter-trained, neutered, and vaccinated.

In the weeks leading up to the adoption, she'd done a little research on the process to make the transition as comfortable as possible. It couldn't be easy to be uprooted from the only home he'd ever known. She even went out and bought a new cat bed, toys, and anything else she could find at the pet store. She'd set it all up in her bathroom prior to picking Pickles up.

It took months for Pickles to warm up to her enough to sit next to her. He kept his distance and refused to allow her to pet him for the longest time. Now, though, he was always getting in the way and demanding attention from her.

"No need to take off your shoes. We can go out the back door."

She followed Griffin and Rover as they led the way to the back of the house. The hallway was a straight shot toward the sliding glass doors, which faced the lake. She could see a small walking path at the edge of the well-maintained lawn.

When Griffin slid the door open, Rover took off like a torpedo, bounding off into the grass and frolicking like the happy puppy he was. She smiled fondly at his antics as they made their way to the walking path.

Rover found a giant stick and brought his prize back to Griffin with a joy that was unrivaled. Griffin took the stick clenched tightly in Rover's jaw. He didn't toss the stick immediately. Instead, he seemed to be testing

Rover's patience and obedience. Quynh watched in fascination as the giant puppy sat as still as his giant body allowed, tail thumping wildly against the grass.

When Griffin raised his arm to toss the stick, she was no longer looking at Rover. No, she suddenly became aware of his flexing biceps beneath his dark henley and the way his back muscles rippled with the movement. She tried to rip her gaze away as the telltale heat pooled in her abdomen.

They both watched as Rover took off to retrieve his prize. After a few moments, Griffin led the way along the path, and she fell into step with him.

"It's so beautiful here." She looked around at the tranquil setting. The sun was setting. The magnificent sky was alight with bright colors ranging from pinks, purples, and oranges. The lake gleamed as it mirrored the sky, making the effect even more ethereal. She had never seen such a beautiful sight before. It truly was breathtaking.

The temperature cooled, making her shiver beneath her sweatshirt. Though there was a slight chill in the air, it was the perfect temperature for an evening stroll. She wouldn't have wanted it to be anywhere else at this moment.

The fresh lake air was rejuvenating, so much different from the congestion of city life. The air pollution would probably catch up to her, eventually. A problem for future

Quynh. Today, she was breathing in fresh, clean air, and it was wonderful.

Another thing she noticed was how quiet Willowbrook was compared to the city. At first, it was difficult for her to fall asleep without the usual noises of the city, which normally consisted of a symphony of passing cars, wailing sirens, or sometimes drunk and disorderly pedestrians.

"Definitely beautiful."

She stopped to admire the view, not realizing she'd been lost in thought. She'd been doing that a lot lately.

I'm losing my damn mind.

When she turned to look at Griffin, he was looking at her.

Was he calling me beautiful? Or am I imagining things?

Was she pretending there was something between them when there was nothing?

She couldn't help the blush blooming across her cheeks. Hopefully, it was too dark for him to see it. She crossed her arms across her chest, not used to being the center of attention.

"How are you liking Willowbrook?" Griffin broke their silence after a few minutes of following Rover. The walk was otherwise leisurely, pausing occasionally when Rover would run back with his stick before running off to retrieve it when Griffin tossed it.

"It's...unexpected."

At his questioning glance, she shrugged her shoulders.

"I didn't expect to ever come back here. It sorta never crossed my mind. It's like I've blocked all memories of ever being here when I was a kid."

"When did you move away?"

"I was maybe nine or ten years old. Too young to really understand what was happening."

"Where did you move to?"

"My mom and I stayed with my aunt until she passed."

The sounds of their footsteps through the dirt path and the gentle lapping of the lake were soothing. Griffin didn't push her for more information, which she appreciated. She had fond memories of her aunt, though it was still difficult to think about all the people in her life who were no longer with her.

Her aunt passed. Her mother followed suit not too long after. And now, she was about to lose a father she barely remembered. It was like she was always in varying stages of grief.

Was she always destined to lose the people around her? Was she cursed to live alone for the rest of her life?

"Where'd you go?"

"Hmm?" She turned to look at Griffin, who paused in the path.

He angled his body to face hers, his back to the lake as his eyes roamed her features.

"You went somewhere. In your head."

"Oh."

How did he know that?

"Tell me."

The command in his voice would have normally made her bristle if it were anyone else, but coming from Griffin, it sounded more like a plea. She knew he'd be respectful if she decided not to respond. He was always respectful to her during the time they'd known each other.

"I was just thinking about my family. Pretty soon, there won't be anyone left. I'll be alone."

She shot him a melancholy smile and continued walking. A hand gripping her arm softly halted her.

She turned to look at him, the setting sun behind him casting his face in shadows. His green eyes were almost glowing in the dim lighting as he stared down at her, one hand reaching up to cup her chin. Then, slowly, as if he didn't want to spook her, he lowered his face. He hovered mere inches from her lips, giving her the option to make the last move.

She gripped the hand holding her and stood on tiptoes as their lips met in a sweet kiss. It differed from their other kisses, seeming to communicate he understood how it felt to be alone in life.

The kiss was brief, but it ignited her nerve endings,

nonetheless. She was dizzy with the intensity of her reaction to him.

She wondered if kissing him would always make her feel like she was coming alive.

It was disconcerting how her body responded to his caresses, as if it were vital to her existence. As if she were a zombie and he injected her with a life-giving serum.

She could get addicted to this. The way her body responded to him was like magic. It was hard to imagine being this way with someone other than Griffin.

All too soon, Griffin pulled away from their kiss. He didn't go far, bending to touch his forehead to hers. Her hands found their way into his hair while his hand cradled her head, fingers wound in her messy bun.

It probably needed to be fixed, but it was the least of her worries at this moment. Standing nose to nose, breathing in the same air, the rest of the world faded away.

"You are never alone."

It took her a moment to realize he was responding to what she said before he kissed her. Well, technically, she kissed him, but nobody was keeping track.

Standing in his arms, locked in the intimate embrace beneath the oak tree, she could believe him. She let herself believe she wasn't alone in this life. It felt nice.

Is this what it was like to have someone on my side? To know there was always someone there for me?

"Thank you."

His eyes bounced between hers. It was like he was trying to see if she believed him. Griffin must have been satisfied with what he saw in her eyes as he took a step back and grabbed her hand.

They continued walking hand in hand until the sun was nearly gone from the horizon.

19

He needed to get away from her.

Right now.

Before he crossed the line and things got complicated. Before they did something they both would regret.

He would never forget the way she looked, with the last remaining rays of sunlight caressing her beautiful face, as if the sunbeam bent itself around her to illuminate all of her to him, revealing the delicate curve of her neck and the sparkle in her eyes. He'd never been more in awe of her than when she showed her vulnerability to him.

Who am I to her but a complete stranger?

Never mind how he knew the way she tasted when she came apart on his tongue. It was nothing compared to how she'd let him peek inside her fragile heart. A heart she kept protected behind walls built by life's harsh lessons to protect its most tender parts.

He could tell she'd been through so much in her short life, too much, in his opinion. Her eyes held a guarded look. Or how she always seemed to hold herself at a proverbial distance from everyone, as if she didn't want to get close for fear of losing them.

How he got so lucky to break down her walls, he'd never know.

Was she even aware she'd let me in just a little?

Which brought him to the problem at hand. He couldn't afford to get close to anyone. Things never ended well. He didn't have the time for the complications that came with relationships. He was content with his life. He didn't need anything more than what he had: his shop, his dog, and his house.

Anything else was unnecessary. Frivolous. A slippery slope he'd dare not risk.

Why am I fighting this urge to claim Quynh as mine?

He hadn't meant to kiss her. He only invited her out for a walk because the thought of her being alone made something inside of him ache.

He hated the idea of her being alone. The grumpy old cat of hers was probably shit for company. Pickles didn't count.

So, he'd asked her to join him on his evening walk with Rover. He didn't think anything could go wrong. It wasn't like it was a date or anything.

It was clearly a terrible idea.

As they made their way back, having walked about half a mile around the lake, he fought the urge to shove her against a tree and kiss her senseless again, to show her what it's like to be his. Hell, he'd definitely entertained thoughts of stripping her out of her tight, ass-hugging leggings and fucking her right up against a tree. Or bent over in the grass.

She'd probably look amazing spread out beneath him in the grass, too. Really, he wasn't picky. He'd take her in any position.

When his cock started pressing urgently against his zipper, he knew it was time to go. He'd set a relentless pace to get back to his house while urging his cock to calm down. Rover followed slowly behind them, practically dragging his paws on the way home. The sooner they got back, the sooner they could go their separate ways. He'd pack her some dinner he'd left warming in the oven, walk her back to her place, then run back to his home like a nervous teenager with his first crush.

A cold shower was also in his future to take care of his raging libido.

He should probably consider talking to his doctor about this. It could not be normal for a man his age to have so many erections in such a short span of time. The last time he'd been this horny was in his prime. Unfortunately, it was at least a decade ago.

Now, in his early forties, he didn't exactly get excited at the sight of just any beautiful woman anymore.

These days, he was more interested in what was between their ears than their cup size. He supposed this was a sign of maturity.

While his experience with being in a relationship was based on a much younger, much more careless person, he didn't have much luck in that department either. Living and working in a small town also limited his options. The rare occasion he'd have female company would only happen if he sought it out.

Maybe every couple of months, he'd have business out of town. He'd end up going down to the hotel bar for a drink to wind down. It wouldn't take long before a brazen woman approached him. Though the conversation was brief, he always made sure his intentions were clear. He was only ever interested in a one-night stand, and he made sure his partner was on board. They'd usually have another drink or two before heading up to her hotel room.

Once things were over, he'd cleaned up and left. No strings attached. No emotions. No kissing.

Those were the rules he'd set.

He wasn't a selfish lover. He made sure his female companion always came first before he found his release. Before Quynh, though, he'd never had the urge to taste anyone.

Which was a mistake, clearly. Now, he couldn't get

the memory of how she'd tasted out of his mind. Or the sweet noises she made when she came.

What would she sound like stuffed full of my cock? Would her breath hitch when I breach her entrance with the tip of my cock? Would she scream when she came with me buried deep inside of her? What would my name sound like on her lips when she broke apart?

Fuck.

Now there was no way to hide his massive erection straining against the zipper of his jeans. He quickly shrugged out of his coat and folded it, bringing the fabric across his lap as they rounded the corner to reveal his back porch.

The sight of his house in the distance filled Griffin with relief. It was the home stretch now. Griffin looked over his shoulder to find Quynh walking at a more sedate pace. Rover trotted next to her with his pink tongue hanging out of his mouth. The adorable traitor kept her company instead of sticking to his side. She was much better company, and Rover hated when their walk was over, oftentimes spending the next hour pouting in his dog bed.

He waited for the pair at the walkway, ignoring the way his heart seemed to clench at the sight of the happy pair. Quynh seemed so relaxed and content. He couldn't help but wonder what her life was like back in the city. Griffin knew she wasn't dating anyone seriously, but it didn't mean she was single. Though, after last night, he sure hoped there were no other males in the picture.

Griffin's fist clenched beneath his coat at the thought of another male in her life. He should not be this possessive about someone who was bound to leave him behind when she went back to her big city.

"Come on."

If his voice sounded louder than he wanted, he blamed it on the wind. He turned his back and went inside the house.

By the time the happy duo made their way inside, Quynh was wiping her shoes off on the mat. She moved to slip her sneakers off when he barked at her to keep them on. Her hands went up in front of her as if she had been caught doing something wrong.

"No need to take them off." He lifted his arm to show her the warm dinner he'd placed in a Tupperware container. "I made you some dinner."

Quynh's smile fell as she saw the container. Her eyes shuttered, cutting him off to her emotions. She nodded curtly as her lips rolled together. Slowly, as if to defy him, she slipped out of her sneakers and picked them up in her hands. He watched as she carried them down the hallway, walking past him with her head held high, her vanilla scent almost smacking him in the face as she moved away from him.

He felt a punch to the gut. He hadn't meant to hurt

her by rushing her out of there. It was for the best. They couldn't spend any more time alone and still be friends.

Do I want to be her friend?

Fuck if he knew what he wanted.

One thing he knew, though. The way her face looked when he'd basically told her to get out of his house made his stomach hurt. He didn't like the way her eyes had dimmed when she'd seen the dinner he'd prepared for her to go, even though he didn't want to send her mixed signals and have her stay for dinner.

Something snapped. Watching her walk away from him made him irrationally angry.

Tossing the offensive container on the counter, he marched down the hallway.

"Quynh," he growled at her back.

She picked up her pace, ignoring him, as she tried to put on her shoes with jerky movements.

He heard her curse under her breath as he rounded on her.

"Quynh, stop."

She didn't stop. If anything, she renewed her efforts to leave.

"Thank you for the walk. And dinner. It was very nice of you."

She had both shoes on and went to open the door, but before her hand could turn the knob, Griffin was on her.

He yanked gently at her arm, pulling her away from

the door, and backed her up against the wall. He kept his body from touching hers, knowing the contact would snap his barely leashed control. It would drive him crazy. He needed to be sane and not act like a complete caveman right now.

Her chest heaved with her heavy breathing.

"Look at me," he commanded in a low growl.

She refused to look at him, averting her gaze by looking over his shoulder.

"Quynh, look at me, please."

Griffin watched in horror as her bottom lip quivered.

Gently, he gripped her chin until her eyes met his. He cursed at the tears she was holding back.

"Fuck. Quynh, I'm sorry."

He rested his forehead on hers as he shook his head from side to side.

"It's fine." She sniffed.

It clearly was not fine. Griffin was being an insensitive ass.

"No, really, I appreciate it. I'll just get out of your hair."

She made to move away. He reacted instinctively, pinning her body against the wall with his. His arms braced on either side of her head to effectively box her in.

"You are not leaving here like this."

His control was hanging on by a thread.

She looked up at him. All traces of her tears were gone

as if he had imagined them. Instead, her eyes sparked with defiance he'd missed. Her jaw was set at a determined angle as she glared at him.

"Or what?"

She challenged him to action. His control snapped.

His hand gripped the back of her head, twisting her hair around his fist as he slammed his lips to hers. Her shocked gasp was like music to his ears. It left her wide open for his assault as his tongue delved into her dark heat and wrestled for control. Their tongues dueled for dominance, and the other hand moved to grip her around her waist, sliding down to grip her outer thigh in a bruising hold.

She tugged at his hair as if to pull him away but changed her mind at the last second. Instead, she used his hair to direct him on how she liked to be kissed.

Griffin was simmering, barely restrained from erupting. He was like a wildfire, scorching everything in his path. He never felt so out of control before.

Quynh was like a cool thunderstorm, bringing vital rain to temper his fires and bring life back to the scorched earth. Her lips were like a balm to his soul, her touch both calming his nerves and igniting the fire inside of him. The fire threatened to consume her if she wasn't careful.

He broke the kiss abruptly, yanking his lips away and letting their panting breaths fill the space between them. Griffin gripped her thigh tightly, which crept up to cradle his hip at some point. He wasn't even sure if it was his doing or hers.

"We shouldn't do this." His voice came out in a husky rasp.

She shook her head, agreeing with him.

"No, we shouldn't."

She withdrew from his touch, and the thought made him burn with rage. No, they shouldn't be doing this, but fuck if he didn't want to.

He halted her retreat by gripping her other thigh in his hand, hoisting her up so she was eye level with him. Her eyes widened in surprise as her arms wound themselves around his shoulders.

"Fuck it."

He was going to take what he wanted. And right now, all he wanted was the woman in his arms. Consequences be damned.

20

Quynh squealed in delight as he whirled them around and ran up the staircase with her wrapped around his body like a koala bear. He would never let her fall, but he reveled in the way she gripped him tightly in her arms. He enjoyed the way her thighs clenched around his hips. Pretty soon, he'd be able to feel it without the barrier of their clothes between them.

This time, instead of tossing her on the bed. He let her cling to his body as he pressed her against the bedroom door he'd slammed shut behind them, hands creeping under her top, aching to touch her skin just beneath his fingertips.

"You good?"

God, he hoped she was ready for this. *Please say yes.*

"Yes," she said, the words coming out on a soft exhale.

Not giving her a chance to change her mind, he pressed another demanding kiss to her lips. Like a flower unfurling its petals in the spring, Quynh seemed to blossom with his gentle caresses.

His cock was unbearably hard and pressing insistently against his pants. If they continued like this, he wouldn't last longer than a few minutes. But he needed to make this good for her.

He gently unwrapped her legs from his hips, placing her down slowly on the ground and breaking their kiss.

Griffin took a step back, admiring her freshly kissed lips and the flush to her skin. He did that to her. It made something primitive inside of him puff up with pride.

He reached an arm behind his head and yanked his shirt off, smirking when he realized she was watching him undress with rapt attention. He cocked a brow at her, his smirk widening into a grin when her blush deepened.

When she reached for the hem of her sweatshirt, slowly pulling it up and over her slender hips, his smile fell. She teased him with her bare abdomen. Each inch she revealed to him was a treat. He gulped when he glimpsed the bottom of her bright pink sports bra. She worked her arms out of the sleeves before pulling the sweatshirt over her head.

She squared her shoulder and met his gaze, shooting him a smirk. Like she was daring him to look. She stood with her back straight as he let his eyes drift down, taking in her slender neck, leading to delicate collarbones. The pink straps of her sports bra held up her small, pert breasts in a tight embrace.

The thought of getting the garment off her made his teeth ache with anticipation. He wanted to see what she looked like, completely bared to him.

His eyes drifted lower, over her soft abdomen, her hips hugged by those distractingly tight leggings.

His eyes whipped back up as she tucked her thumbs into the waistband of her leggings and shimmied them over her tight hips.

Inch by delicious inch, she revealed her matching pink panties before sliding one leg out of the leggings and tossing it to the side.

She stood before him like a goddess, confident in her ability to bring him to his knees. She need not ask for a sacrifice. He was more than willing for the chance to worship her at her altar. All she needed to do was ask, and he would be her willing champion or servant. The urge to kneel at her feet and worship her was strong, but he remained standing as she sauntered up to him.

He braced himself as she placed a warm hand on his naked chest, running her fingernails down his pecs and over his flat nipple. He shuddered at the sensation as she trailed her fingers lower, over his tight abdomen, which clenched reflexively at her touch and found their way into the coarse hair leading straight to his cock hidden beneath his pants, the incessant member begging for her attention all day. Or, really, since he first laid eyes on her days ago.

He held himself still while she explored his body. His abs rippled under her light touch, and goosebumps erupted across his arms. Griffin held his breath as she teased the waistband of his jeans with a finger. When she went to unbutton his jeans, he grabbed her hand to stop her.

He wouldn't last much longer if she touched him right now. No. Right now, he needed to regain some of his control and take care of his woman first.

She looked at him in shock.

"You first, sunshine."

Without another word, he bent at the waist, picked her up, and tossed her over his shoulder. He smiled at her delighted shriek as he tossed her onto his king-size bed. Her body bounced before he pounced on her.

He gripped her ankles and pulled them apart so he could fit his body between her legs. He crawled up her body until they were chest to chest, hip to hip. He braced his hands on either side of her head as they took each other in.

Slowly, he relaxed his body into hers, allowing his weight to press her deeper into the mattress. Her soft skin against his hard chest was a pleasure in itself, but still, there were too many garments between their bodies. He'd need to rectify the problem immediately.

He braced a forearm against the bed and used his other hand to trace the pink strap of her sports bra. He pulled on it, letting it flick against her skin, and she gasped at the sensation.

Was she into pain?

He'd have to explore it later.

He leaned down, rubbing his nose against hers gently, breathing in her sweet vanilla scent that drove him crazy. With his lungs full of her scent, he let out a soft breath over her lips, laying a gentle kiss on her soft lips, taking his time to explore the way her lips responded to his in a sensual embrace. This time, the kiss was not frantic and desperate. As if they had all the time in the world to get to know each other. To appreciate each other's bodies, both knowing where the next steps will lead them.

He broke the kiss, trailing kisses along her jawline. She turned her head to allow him access to her sensitive neck, her hands coming up to grip him around his biceps as he laved at the juncture where her neck and shoulders met. He teased her with gentle nips, her body coiled tightly at the anticipation of his bite.

With his other hand, he reached beneath the soft fabric of her sports bra and teased her nipple, fingers caressing and plucking at her peaked nipple, teasing them into sharper points. He moved to her other nipple, giving it the same attention before finally biting her flesh in his teeth.

He reveled in the way her body arched at the pressure of his teeth, biting hard enough to leave a mark but not to bruise. Her body quivered, breaths rapid as she clung to him. Her moan made his cock twitch.

Griffin had the urge to bury himself deep inside her, but at this rate, he'd blow his load before his cock ever touched her sweet pussy.

He released her neck, leaving open-mouthed kisses as if to kiss her pain away. The sports bra was up over her breasts, and he took a moment to appreciate the darkened areola topped with a pert nipple begging for his mouth. He leaned down and acted on his urge, pulling a nipple into his mouth. Using his tongue to tease the sensitive bud, his teeth nipped gently.

Her hands made their way into his hair, tugging urgently as she lost herself to the pleasure. He released her nipple with a soft pop, tugging her sports bra off and over her head to reveal her small breasts to him. He cupped them in his hands, massaging the soft flesh between his fingers.

"Mmm, I love how you fit in my hands."

Griffin bent his head and kissed each breast before releasing them to continue his exploration of her body. His lips followed where his hands led as he kissed and licked at the soft curves of her abdomen. Finally, when he was at the juncture of her legs, he teased the edges of her underwear with his fingers, giving her time to stop him if she changed her mind.

When she responded by arching her hips to greet his face, he chuckled.

"Is your needy pussy aching, sunshine?" He blew a breath against her damp center, her arousal soaking through her panties. "Look how wet you are for me already."

He tugged at the hem of her panties, sliding them off her hips. She bent her knees, and he slid them off. Before she could relax her knees, he grabbed hold of them and pressed them back against the bed, spreading her open for his ravenous gaze.

He'd tasted her pussy before, but this was the first time he'd seen it in all its glory. The dark skin of her pussy lips glistening with her arousal made his teeth ache with longing; her clit peeked out behind its hood, taunting him.

"You look so beautiful spread out for me, sunshine." He brought her knees over his shoulders as he leaned in. He groaned in pleasure at the first taste of her on his tongue. He would never tire of the way she tasted. If anything, she was quickly becoming an addiction. One he could never quit.

He'd have to tread carefully. Griffin knew he would never fully recover if he became too attached.

But, for right now, he reveled in the way she felt

beneath him. Quivering. Gasping. Moaning. Her hands gripped the bedsheet and his hair as he brought her to her orgasm, relishing in the way she shattered beneath him.

"So responsive." His murmurs were lost to her moans of pleasure.

As she was coming down from her orgasm, he worked a finger into her tight pussy, loving the way it gripped at his digit desperately. He worked another finger in, thrusting in and out and prolonging her orgasm.

Her channel was so slick with her arousal it made it easy to add a third finger. He brought her to another screaming orgasm. Hearing her scream his name was something he'd never tire of.

Sitting on his haunches, he worked his cock out of his pants. The tip of his cock was leaking with pre-cum. He probably wouldn't last very long at this rate. Griffin grabbed his stiff cock, stroking it once, twice, then releasing it with a curse.

Condoms. He didn't have any condoms. If he had any, they'd be expired by now. He never took women back to his place, so he didn't keep any stock.

"Fuck," he groaned, dropping his head back.

"What's wrong?" Her tentative touch on his arm brought his attention back to her.

She looked so magnificent, cheeks and chest flushed from her multiple climaxes. Her eyes were slightly glazed from coming down from her high.

"I don't have any condoms."

He moved to get off the bed. His cock bobbed at the movement. Quynh stopped him with a warm palm to his chest.

Griffin's brows furrowed in question.

"Umm...it's okay. I...uh...I haven't been with anyone in...a while." Her fingers curled in his chest hair. He didn't know it was possible, but she flushed even further by the admission.

Did she mean what I think she means? Has she been celibate for a while before me?

The thought sent a thrill through him, a surge of possessiveness he'd been unsuccessfully trying to bottle bursting free.

He pushed her down on the bed with a palm.

"Are you saying you want me bare?" he growled as he bore down on her.

Quynh gulped nervously but met his gaze unflinchingly.

"Yes."

What little control he had left snapped.

His lips smashed into hers in a bruising kiss, tongue demanding entrance as he fully claimed her.

There was no turning back after this.

He needed to be inside her like his next breath. Vital. Non-negotiable.

He braced a forearm by her head. His other hand

guided his cock to her slick entrance. Griffin teased her with the head of his cock, getting it wet from her arousal. She tried to lift her hips so he was left with no other choice but to breach her entrance. Except, he evaded her expertly. He almost chuckled when she let out a growl of frustration.

"You want my cock, sunshine?"

She nodded.

"Say it."

She tried again to coax his cock into her heat. By some miracle, Griffin maintained enough control over himself to evade her. Even though all he wanted to do was sink his cock so deep inside her, she'd never be able to walk without feeling him inside of her.

"Griffin!"

"Say it, sunshine."

"Please. I need it."

"Need what?"

She let out a cry of frustration, though judging by how wet she was, she was enjoying the teasing.

"I need your cock! Please!"

Her last word ended in a shriek as he pushed his cock inside her in one swift thrust.

Fuck, she was tight.

Griffin held himself still; being buried deep within her was sweet torture. He waited until her hips moved beneath his, letting him know she was as desperate to feel him move as much as he was.

His thrusts were slow at first. His tenuous control slipped away with each thrust, and their rhythm increased gradually.

In and out. In and out.

The obscene sounds of their coupling filled the room, amplifying their pleasure exponentially.

Quynh's hands dug into his back, leaving marks he'd proudly wear.

Her hips met his enthusiastically as they found a relentless pace that made them both groan and gasp.

Griffin changed the angle of his thrusts, hitting her G-spot. He growled at how the change made her throw her head back, and her thighs shake in response. He leaned away from her to make space between their sweat-soaked skin. Griffin placed a hand on her lower abdomen and applied gentle pressure.

"Oh, god."

"Say my name when you come, sunshine."

"Oh-oh."

Her words were incomprehensible as he brought her closer to her orgasm.

Using a thumb, he flicked at her clit a few times.

"Oh, fuck, Griffin!"

Her body clenched around his, her wet heat squeezing his cock in a pulsing rhythm, and his balls tightened in response. He sank his cock deep inside of her. Once. Twice. On the third, he lost all control.

His cock jerked as hot spurts of cum painted her insides with his release, her walls milking his cock for every drop of his cum.

The edges of his vision blackened. The release was so intense he swore he saw stars. Griffin collapsed, completely drained. He was conscious enough to catch most of his body weight so he didn't crush her beneath him. Barely.

They lay together, naked and sweaty.

Her gentle hands rubbed at his back as they both came down from their high.

His last coherent thought as they lay there drifted through his sex-addled brain.

He could get used to this.

21

Griffin's heavy weight on top of her was a welcome sensation, grounding her in reality while providing her with a sense of comfort she had never experienced before. Thankfully, her ever-present and swirling thoughts were quiet for what seemed like the first time all day.

She could get used to this.

This, of course, meant the sense of belonging. Even if it was short-lived, it was such a nice feeling. The orgasms were a perk, obviously.

But lying here, with Griffin's giant body pinning her down like a human weighted blanket, she felt safe. Cherished. Loved.

Loved?

It was way too soon for it, but she imagined this was it.

Their bodies moved together in a sensual rhythm, a timeless dance of desire and passion. It was as if their bodies were magnetically drawn together, each curve and angle complementing the other. His hardness to her softness. Like yin and yang, or two missing puzzle pieces needed to complete the picture.

Griffin's softening cock slipped out of her body. The telltale sensation of his cum trickling out of her was new. She never had sex without condoms before Griffin. The mere thought of his cum inside of her drove her to the brink of orgasm.

Do I have a breeding kink I wasn't aware of?

She'd have to find some new romance books with breeding kinks to explore the next time she went to the bookstore.

Griffin groaned as he lifted his head from the crook of her shoulder.

"You okay?"

His husky voice sent shivers through her body. There was no way she could go another round.

Griffin kissed her softly on her forehead, bringing her attention back to the present.

"I'm fine." Her hands continued their stroking motion against his firm back.

She nearly groaned in frustration when he lifted himself to look down at her.

"Just fine?" His eyebrow quirked in question.

"Better than fine," she amended with a smile.

"Oof, tough crowd."

She laughed as he pushed off of her, his cock slipping completely free. She hurriedly squeezed her thighs together as he heaved himself out of the bed.

Well, this was awkward.

How am I supposed to take care of the mess and not leave a trail behind?

Griffin disappeared into the ensuite bathroom. She heard the sink run as she contemplated her options. His cum continued to leak out of her.

Jesus, how much more of this stuff is inside of me?

Griffin returned with a damp washcloth in hand just as she contemplated doing an awkward waddle to grab her discarded underwear, unabashedly naked as the day he was born.

He sat down on the bed and gently pried her thighs open. Carefully, he used the damp washcloth and cleaned her. He kept his touch tender, yet she still flinched when the rough fabric grazed her oversensitized clit. She always took care of the cleanup alone. This was a first for her. She relaxed into the bed and let him take care of her.

When he was satisfied, Griffin got up and went back into the ensuite to ditch the washcloth. Slowly, she sat up. Her muscles were sore and tender in places she never knew possible. Sitting on the edge of the bed, sheets rustling with her movement made her wince. Griffin tossed something by her side. She looked down to find one of Griffin's T-shirts with the name of his shop across the back.

She glanced up just in time to see his delectable round ass before they disappeared into another pair of grey sweats.

God, does he own any other type of sweatpants, or did he just have grey ones?

It should be illegal for men to wear grey sweatpants. Why does he have to look so good in them?

She pulled on the worn shirt, its soft cotton gliding across her skin, trying not to overthink the gesture. When her vision cleared, Griffin was standing by the door. Shirtless.

She tried not to drool at the sight.

Down, girl!

"Let's eat." His knowing smirk made her blush.

He didn't wait for her to respond before he opened the bedroom door.

The sound of nails over the hardwood floor was the only warning she got before Rover came running in and launched himself at her.

She laughed as they fell onto the bed, his giant tongue assaulting her face with his happiness.

"Rover. Get down. She's mine."

Rover whined but followed his owner's command.

Quynh ignored the way her body tingled at how he'd claimed her as his.

He means nothing by it, right?

No. Of course not.

She was probably reading too much into it.

Griffin whistled, and Rover jumped off the bed to his side.

"We'll be downstairs. Come down for dinner when you're ready."

He didn't wait for her response as he headed down the hallway.

Quynh attempted to make herself presentable in the bathroom. Unfortunately, her hair was a giant, frizzy mess, her lips were swollen, and her skin was hopelessly mottled in multiple areas from Griffin's rough beard. She tried to stamp down the glee she experienced at the sight of his marks on her. Placing a hand over her neck, she recalled the way it felt when he'd sunk his teeth into her. She was dismayed when she couldn't see any marks. It was the first time anyone ever bit her during sex. Apparently, she liked it. Or, at least, she liked it when Griffin bit her.

She was learning so much about herself in the past week. She wondered if she ever truly knew who she was before now.

She splashed cold water on her face and attempted to control her unruly hair, using her fingers to detangle the mess. She made her way back into the bedroom. The wet stain on the bedsheet made her flush with embarrassment.

Quynh went searching for her underwear. Spotting them at the end of the bed, she stepped into them. No way was she going to attempt putting on her leggings again. She pulled off the dirty bedsheets and went hunting for clean ones. She found a spare set in the bedroom closet.

When she finished making the bed, she eyed her leggings again. She couldn't possibly go downstairs without pants. It would probably be a bad idea. Plus, it was chilly. Then something caught her eye.

There, at the foot of the armchair in the corner, were the pair of sweats Griffin wore earlier. She tiptoed across the carpet, biting her lip with indecision.

It was probably overstepping by wearing more of his clothes.

"Quynh? Dinner's ready!"

She jumped at Griffin's shout. It sounded like he was at the bottom of the stairwell. Grabbing the giant pair of pants, she hurriedly put them on, rolling the top a few times so they didn't slide off her. Then, she rushed out of the bedroom.

Quynh found Griffin and Rover in the kitchen. She tiptoed across the cold linoleum and sat at the table. Griffin already placed the utensils on the table. He didn't seem to need any help with dinner.

Griffin came over with two plates piled high. The delicious aroma of freshly baked chicken and pasta made her mouth water. She caught a whiff of it earlier when they first entered the house.

She murmured her thanks as he set a plate in front of her. She bit back on a moan when the flavors hit her taste buds. The only other sounds in the room came from their utensils scraping gently while Rover ate his dinner in the corner.

"This is delicious. You're a very good cook."

When Griffin didn't respond, she glanced up from her plate and gasped.

"Are you blushing?" She couldn't help giving him a hard time.

"No. Of course not."

"You are!"

"A man never blushes."

"Ha!"

He shot her an unamused look, which made her chuckle.

It was cute that he was embarrassed about his culinary skills.

Did he ever cook for anyone else?

She hoped not. The thought of him sharing this part of himself with another woman made her burn with unwarranted jealousy. Quynh had no reason to be possessive about Griffin. Besides sharing several intimate moments, they made no promises to each other.

Her time in Willowbrook was limited. The ever-present hourglass hanging over her head as the sands of time slipped by, marking their passage of time, knowing, inevitably, her time would run out here, and she'd have to face reality. Go back to the city and deal with the mess she left behind.

She still needed to find a new job. The prospect seemed incredibly daunting. She wasn't quite ready to tackle the obstacle. The thought of having to find a new job where she was not valued made her want to break out in a rash. She could really use at least another week before she needed to get her act together.

On top of her severance pay, her mother taught her the importance of saving her money, so she had a comfortable nest egg to last her a while, if necessary. She didn't have many bills other than car insurance. Her previous employer paid for her to relocate. As part of the relocation, they also paid for her apartment. The lease was good for the rest of the year.

Ugh. This was the first time she had even thought about her boss since she got to Willowbrook. Or, former boss. She hadn't seen the obituary notice yet, but funeral services were probably happening soon. She should at least go and pay her respects. Quynh made a mental note to contact one of her other coworkers for any updated information on funeral arrangements.

Not to mention, her car wasn't ready yet, but hopefully, the parts she just ordered will arrive soon.

"Quynh."

Griffin's voice broke her out of her spiraling thoughts.

"Hmm?"

"You okay?"

"What? Oh. Yes, of course."

"Don't lie to me."

Quynh put her fork down, folding her hands in her lap. She glanced at his face, which was set in determination as he waited for her to say something.

She fidgeted with the material of the borrowed grey sweatpants, pinching it between her fingers as she thought of what to say.

"I'm fine. Really."

"But..."

"But...I guess I was just thinking about how I should probably check up on things back home."

Griffin's expression hardened at her words, and his lips set in a thin line as his eyes assessed her. After a tense moment of silence, he gave her a curt nod.

"Once the parts to your car get here, it won't take me very long to get it fixed. You should be back on the road in no time."

Griffin got up and brought his plate to the sink, his movements jerky as he washed them.

"I can take care of the dishes since you made dinner…" The sound of the running water drowned her voice out.

"No need."

Quynh furrowed her brows in confusion.

Did I upset him?

She didn't mean for what she said to upset him. She stood up from the table, grabbing her dirty plate and utensils. Cautiously, she approached an irate Griffin.

She placed the dish on the counter with one hand, her other hand coming up and reaching tentatively for his stiff back. She kept her touch gentle, almost like she was reaching out to a wounded animal. She didn't want to startle or anger him.

The muscles on his back tensed impossibly further beneath her touch. He turned the faucet off, arms gripping the sink. Griffin hung his head between his shoulders.

"Did I upset you?" she asked in a low voice.

He shook his head in response but didn't look at her.

"It's nothing. It's getting late."

She dropped her hand back to her side, a sharp jab to her heart at his rebuke.

"Yeah, okay. I should probably get going." She backed away from him, making a hasty retreat from the kitchen.

"Thank you again for dinner." She tossed the words over her shoulder as she hurried to find her sneakers.

Where the hell are my sneakers?

They weren't at the front door. Then she remembered how she'd lost them on the way to the front. She turned around, only to find Griffin blocking her path. His looming figure felt larger than before. His muscles were taut with tension, his hands flexing at his sides as his dark gaze stared her down.

What was his problem?

"Um, I just need my shoes…" Her words trailed off as he took halting steps toward her.

Her senses were suddenly on high alert at the danger he presented. She didn't think he'd hurt her, but her body reacted to his unexpected aggression. Her skin tingled with awareness while a buzzing noise filled her ears. She became acutely aware of every heaving breath as she mirrored his movements. She took a step back, slowly backing away from him.

Griffin snapped.

He rushed at her before she could make another move. She gasped as a rough hand wrapped itself around her throat. He didn't squeeze her to apply pressure, but the threat was there. With a thumb, he lifted her chin.

Quynh ignored the way her body responded to him. Her pussy ached, begging to be filled again with his girth, her panties damp from his light but possessive touch.

"Don't go." She shivered as his deep voice came out in a low growl. "Stay."

His command almost brought her to her knees. He wrapped an arm around her waist and brought their bodies together. Her nipples were taut against the soft cotton of her borrowed shirt. The sensation was more erotic than it should have been.

"O-okay." She nodded at his request.

She sensed the moment he relaxed. His deep intake of breath filled his chest, rubbing against her aching nipples. His deep exhale across her lips made her want to catch his breath with her own lips. She stuck her tongue to lick her lips, wanting his mouth on hers again. As if he read her mind, he tilted his head towards her.

Griffin's kiss was surprisingly gentle, a contrast to his turbulent mood, as if he was making a promise to her with his body, the way he was incapable of words. A promise she understood. He'd never hurt her. Not unless she wanted it.

She kissed him back fervently, answering his promise with her own. She wouldn't hurt him either. A promise she wasn't sure she could keep. For now, it was enough.

It had to be enough.

22

The phone was ringing off the hook. Quynh could hardly keep up with the phone calls. She'd already talked to Henderson twice this morning. He'd called early this morning to find out how much more time until Griffin would work on his vehicle. The second time, he'd called to flirt with her. She'd let him go by pretending to be called away by Griffin. She never met him, and he seemed awfully flirty with a complete stranger.

The weekend was approaching fast. Griffin and the gang, as she started referring to them in her head, were hard at work since they arrived this morning. They worked quickly, yet diligently, to get people back on the road. Already, they sent home two vehicles, and it was barely noon.

Quynh welcomed the busy pace. It kept her distracted from her roaming thoughts. She couldn't keep the memories from last night from drifting in when she wasn't busy.

She ended up staying the night. Griffin gave her a new toothbrush and thanked her for making the bed. He didn't seem too upset about it, though she worried she had overstepped.

Before she even made it out of the bathroom, teeth freshly brushed, he'd tackled her into the bed. His eager antics made her laugh.

She wasn't laughing for long when he made her see stars again with just his skillful fingers before they both collapsed into a restful sleep. Griffin's alarm woke them up early this morning, rousing them from a deep slumber.

She'd woken up to find Griffin's entire body wrapped around hers, almost as if he was afraid she'd disappear in the middle of the night. There hadn't been enough time for them to fool around before starting the workday. Especially since she needed to hurriedly get back to the apartment to get dressed, escorted by a particularly grumpy Griffin.

He'd mumbled under his breath about how unfair it was to have to ignore his very impressive morning wood. She heard him grumble about how he didn't get the chance to make her come again on his tongue before having to rush out of the house.

His grumblings only made her smile. She tried to soften the blow with soft kisses and hugs. He was hardly appeased, but he went into the garage bay while she ran upstairs to get ready.

By the time she'd come downstairs, Julio and Sean were already hard at work. She'd opened the side door to shout a good morning, smiling at their answering response.

She ordered lunch to be delivered today from the local sandwich shop. It was too busy for her to step out to grab lunch for the guys. She knew if she didn't order lunch, the whole gang would work through the day without a meal. Everyone deserved a lunch break, and at the pace they were all working today, they needed the fuel.

When lunch arrived, she'd made the announcement through the side door. She'd left the lunch on the counter. The guys came in shortly after washing the dirt and grime off their hands. The smell of motor oil and musk assaulted her senses as she kept her head down while the guys chattered.

By the way the hairs on the back of her nape stood at attention, she knew Griffin was standing close behind her. She pretended to be unaffected by him while he reached over her and grabbed a sub. While she wasn't ashamed of what they were doing as two consenting adults, she didn't want her personal affairs to be gossiped about, either.

Julio grabbed the turkey grinder while Sean opted for the meatball. She ordered a salad for herself while Griffin tore open the wrapping for the Italian sub. They spread out around the reception area around her while they ate.

It was so nice to be a part of the team. Julio and Sean never made her uncomfortable. Though she knew by the knowing smirks and winks they'd toss at her that they were aware of the less-than-professional arrangement between her and their boss. If it bothered them, they said nothing to her.

Something she was very thankful for. She would probably die of embarrassment if it were ever brought up. Even if her deal with Griffin was temporary. And, though, technically, Griffin was her boss, it was unlike her to be involved in any type of scandal. Certainly, having an affair with your temporary boss, who also put you up in lodging while fixing your car at an unknown cost, was scandalous.

Sadly, it was probably the most rebellious thing she ever did in her entire life. As a teenager, she never had the urge to rebel, knowing how fragile her mother's mental health was after having to move in with her aunt. She didn't want to add to her burden. Instead, she followed all of her mother's strict rules.

While she was too young to fully grasp it at the time, memories of her mother's smile still haunted Quynh. The upheaval of leaving her father seemed to drain her mother of all joy and happiness.

Her mother used to smile all the time before they

moved. As a child, she took for granted how much her mother showed her love and joy. It was almost like the sunshine came from her heart. Mostly, Quynh recalled having a happy childhood. They were poor, but they were happy. Her mother worked at the local nail salon, often bringing Quynh with her to work while she did her schoolwork in the back.

She'd seen her father once in a while. He didn't live with them in their small one-bedroom apartment above the laundromat. Her mother told her he was a businessman who was away frequently for business trips. She never elaborated on how the two met, but the infatuation was obvious.

Her mother's world was shattered the day she realized Quynh's father had another family. He never intended to marry her.

It was on a Sunday. Her mother took her to the park. It was a rare occasion since her mother was often working. But that day, she got out of work early. The weather was unseasonably warm for the winter.

When they arrived at the park, Quynh was so giddy about running around. She made her way towards the playground when she spotted a familiar figure in the distance. She squealed in delight and took off. Her mother yelled at her to slow down behind her, which she ignored. In her naïve mind, she thought her father was there to see her.

She'd run up to him, screaming, "Daddy, Daddy," when he'd whirled around and spotted her. Instead of the delight she was used to seeing, there was a look of horror on his face. She didn't understand what it meant at the time. After a moment, she realized there was a strange woman by his side.

The woman glared at her with so much venom it made her stop short, pigtails swinging. Her mother, who didn't expect her to take off so quickly, ran after her. Her hands came around her shoulders, kneeling down to ask her what was wrong.

The moment her mother realized why she took off was permanently etched into her memories. Quynh pointed to her father. He pasted on a polite expression by the time her mother arrived. Her mother looked toward where she had pointed with confusion.

"Arthur?" Her mother dropped her hands from Quynh's shoulders. "What are you doing here?"

Her mother's thick accent was even thicker with her confusion.

"Who are these people, Arthur?" the mean woman by his side snarled, her lips curled in distaste.

"Papa? Come play!"

A small figure appeared suddenly, her blonde hair plaited in French braids, gleaming in the bright sunshine. Her small cheeks were rosy from the chilly air or running around.

The world tilted on its axis the moment the little girl gripped her father's hand.

Why was she calling him her papa?

"Arthur? Who are they?"

Her father looked at her with sad eyes. She didn't understand it then. It took years working with her therapist before she could make sense of that day. His eyes held regret as he uttered the heartbreaking words that destroyed both her and her mother's entire world, effectively breaking the strongest woman Quynh ever knew and reducing her to the shell of the woman she became until her death.

"They're nobody. Come on, Ruth. Let's get out of here." Without a backward glance, she watched her father pick up the little girl, Ruth, she assumed, into his arms. With his other hand, he grabbed the mean-faced woman's hand and tugged her along. They both watched as the mean-faced woman tossed them a look of disgust over her shoulder before they disappeared beyond the parking lot.

It was the first and last time she saw her mother cry.

"Thanks for lunch, Quynh." Sean's cheerful voice startled her back to the present. She shook away her depressing memories and glanced up from her salad. Griffin was studying her intently.

She blushed as she continued eating her salad, avoiding Griffin's eyes for the rest of the meal. Julio cleaned up and offered to take her trash. She'd bit back a smile at Griffin's scowl but handed her trash over to Julio's waiting hands.

"You're the best, little lady." Julio flashed her a wink and walked to the back with the trash bag.

She was alone with Griffin for the first time since this morning. Her heart pounded in her chest like a drum. The room suddenly was too hot.

She wondered if she would ever get used to being around him without feeling like a teenager with a crush on the captain of the football team. It was so cliché she could almost laugh at herself.

Instead of being a football player, though, Griffin was the hot mechanic with a way in the kitchen. She'd never really been into older men, but the salt and pepper hair Griffin sported was a major turn-on. Honestly, everything about Griffin was a turn-on.

His moodiness. His dark aura. Almost like he was a thundercloud ready to unleash a torrent of rain on her. His grumpy demeanor didn't bother her. He wasn't mean. He was just...prickly. She noticed he seemed a little less prickly around her. The sex probably helped, too.

Despite his cantankerous nature, on the rare occasions when she could make him smile, it was like she had won the lottery. The look of joy on his face was one that took her breath away.

"Henderson called again. Twice."

"Hmph."

"I told him he wasn't allowed to call more than once a day anymore."

"Good."

The tension was so thick she could cut it with the plastic cutlery.

"I'm going to organize the office. Excuse me."

She got up and made her way to the back, realizing too late that he was hot on her heels.

The office door snicking shut behind her made her whirl on her heels.

"Griffin."

He prowled toward her like a predator. She backed away slowly.

"Griffin, what are you doing?" Her voice sounded breathless to her own ears.

"What do you think I'm doing? I'm taking a break."

"Don't you have to finish up the job for today?"

"It can wait a few minutes."

"Only a few minutes?" She couldn't resist teasing him.

At his growl, she gulped as her hips encountered the hard edge of the desk.

He loomed before her, only a foot of space between their bodies.

"Quynh."

"Y-yes?"

"I only need a few minutes to make you scream my name."

"O-oh. Is that so?"

"Mmhmm." He lowered his head and closed the distance between them. His nose grazed the side of hers as he took in a deep breath.

"You drive me crazy." His rumbling voice was low, stirring an ache in her center. She was already on edge since he'd set foot inside the office. Now, she felt like she was going to combust, her pussy already dripping with her arousal.

"Turn around."

"Wh-what?"

"Turn around and lift your skirt."

She gulped. When she didn't immediately move to obey, he smacked her ass with a firm hand.

"Ow!" she yelped.

"You heard me, sunshine."

"So bossy," she grumbled beneath her breath, though her knees were shaky. She used the edge of the desk to turn around, trying to disguise the way he affected her.

"Lift your skirt, sunshine."

With shaking fingers, she slowly lifted her skirt. She bit her lip when she heard his sharp inhale.

"No panties. Dirty girl."

She held onto the edge of the desk, looking over her shoulder as Griffin unzipped himself from his coveralls, revealing his undershirt. He unzipped further to reveal his jeans, leaving the coveralls hanging from his hips. He unbuttoned his jeans and slid the zipper down slowly over the swell of his erection. His hard cock bounced as it escaped the tight confines of his jeans.

She nearly swallowed her tongue. She never got a good look at his cock last night, but knowing the giant dick had been inside her made her thighs shake. He felt large, and this morning, she was tender and sore. She chalked it up to her lack of experience. Not to mention, it had been a while since she was intimate with anyone other than Rip, her battery-operated boyfriend named after her favorite fictional antihero.

But, now, looking at Griffin's thick, veiny cock, fear skittered down her spine.

"Don't worry, sunshine, you can take it." His words should have reassured her.

"Now, be a good girl and bend over the desk for me."

She licked her lips and bent at the waist, presenting her naked ass to him.

She expected him to fuck her like that, so when his hot tongue probed at her pussy she nearly jumped at the contact before melting into his erotic kiss.

Griffin was skillful with his tongue. He laved at her center and flicked at her clit, alternating between shoving his tongue into her entrance and torturing her clit. Within minutes, she was on the edge of an orgasm.

Just when she was about to go over the edge, Griffin stopped. She growled in frustration at his answering chuckle.

"I want you to come on my cock." His lips left wet kisses on her butt cheeks. Her pussy throbbing with neglect made her want to reach down with her fingers and take care of business.

Before she could, Griffin stood up. She gasped as the head of his cock probed at her entrance. Instead of penetrating her, he slipped his cock through her pussy lips.

"That's it. You're getting my cock nice and wet."

Her fingers fisted on the table at the erotic sensation of his hot cock rubbing in her juices. Finally, after torturing her for a few more moments, he notched himself at her entrance. This time, he took his time as he worked himself inside of her with shallow thrusts, letting her get used to him. He knew she was still tender. All too soon, she felt the telltale pressure building in her belly.

"Oh, fuck, Griffin, please, I need to come."

Whatever restraint Griffin had until then fractured. He fucked her. Hard. So hard she held on to his desk for dear life. Griffin grabbed her right leg, placing her knee on the table.

"Oh, fuck." Quynh hung her head at the deeper angle of his thrusts, his cock hitting a sensitive part, making her spasm around him.

Griffin reached a hand around and played with her clit

between his fingers, rubbing and pinching the sensitive bud. It was too much.

"I'm going to co-come!"

Griffin's hand came up to cover her mouth as she screamed her release, her walls squeezing and milking his cock for all its worth. He kept his relentless assault on her clit, wringing every ounce of pleasure he could from her, prolonging her orgasm until she was certain she would die. *La petite mort.* The little death.

How apropos.

Her thoughts were hazy. She was still coming down from her orgasm when Griffin cursed and came with a low groan. His stiff cock jerked with his release as he spilled himself inside her.

His arms squeezed her to him, head resting at the crook of her neck as their breathing slowed down.

For the second time in less than twenty-four hours, she felt his cum leaking out from around his softening cock. She shifted as the thought turned her on.

What does it look like when he comes inside of me?

"Ah, sunshine, you'd better stop wiggling if we want to get back to work. Otherwise, we'll never leave this office."

He leaned over her, picking up the box of tissues on the desk and pulling a few out. When his cock slipped completely out of her, his tissue-covered hand was there to catch his mess.

She should be embarrassed, but if anything, she was more turned on by his willingness to clean up after himself. When he pulled the sopping tissues away, he balled them up and tossed them into the trash bin.

She pulled down her skirt and turned around to plop on the edge of the desk. Her legs were still shaky. She wouldn't chance trying to walk yet.

Her nose scrunched up in distaste. The office smelled like sex. She needed to light some candles or something to clear the air.

She watched as Griffin tucked his semi-hard cock back into his jeans, his tongue licking at his bottom lip, eyes hooded as he watched her watching him.

"Quit looking at me like that, sunshine."

"Or what?"

"Or I'll stuff that pretty mouth of yours with my cock."

Quynh squeezed her thighs together to relieve the ache that returned in full force at his filthy words.

"I don't think Henderson would appreciate any further delays to his Camaro. He will be here in an hour to retrieve it." She cleared her throat and straightened her skirt, pretending to be a professional after being freshly fucked.

His answering smirk made her toes curl in her flats. God, he was sinful.

"Okay, boss. Let's get back to work." He winked at her, giving her a once-over before opening the door and walking out into the hallway. Thankfully, he shut the door quietly behind him to allow her some more time to get herself together.

She really needed to find a candle or air freshener, though. And the office really needed some organization. She could answer the phones from back here. They weren't expecting any clients for at least an hour. The bell would announce any newcomers.

She rounded the desk and sat down in the giant office chair, adjusting it to her preference, and she started on her new tasks.

Maybe it was the combination of the amazing sex and doing something productive, but happiness bubbled inside of her. She hadn't felt this way in a long time.

Maybe, just maybe, things were looking up for her.

Maybe she was no longer down on her luck.

23

Quynh was in heaven.

Or, at least, this was what she imagined heaven would be like.

For the first time in her life, she was truly happy. Like a soul-deep, goofy smile at random times throughout the day, happy.

Was this what being in love felt like?

She didn't have anything to compare it to, but she imagined this was what the romance books she loved to read were trying to capture.

Quynh was no pessimist; rather, she was a realist. But the past week was one of the best weeks of her thirty-two years of life. She wished this feeling would last forever.

The past week, she spent more time with Griffin outside of work. After he'd fucked her thoroughly in his office, they wrapped up the workday. He'd followed her upstairs and waited while she fed Pickles. She hurriedly packed some of her clothes and essentials, the unspoken agreement she would spend the night with him.

One night turned into a week.

Each evening started out the same. They'd go for a walk around the lake while dinner cooked in the oven. When dinner was ready, they'd sit across from each other, sharing little tidbits about their lives with each other. Before dinner was done, though, they took turns as to who would make the first move to leap across the table.

The entire evening, sitting across from each other, was like foreplay. Of course, playing footsie under the table only ratcheted their desire. He'd nearly snapped her toe when she started rubbing her foot on his hard cock under the table.

Griffin was insatiable. She did not know where his energy or vigor came from, but she was not complaining. Most nights, he'd make her come first. Alternating between his mouth and fingers, or, if she was really lucky, both.

Quynh appreciated the foreplay to prep her for his girth. She did not want to risk being split in half by his giant appendage without proper prep. She was starting to think he had a breeding kink, too. He never missed an opportunity to come inside of her. She wanted to attempt to give him a blowjob, but she needed to work on some jaw exercises. Or learn how to unhinge her jaw in order to handle his sausage link.

Every night, they fell asleep wrapped in each other's arms to the soundtrack of a quiet countryside. Exhausted but content.

Quynh was getting used to how calming living away from the city was. It certainly helped that she had her own giant teddy bear to keep her company at night, though she missed Pickles's presence something fierce. She made it a habit to take more frequent breaks to check in on her feline friend. Pickles pretended like he didn't miss her, but when she was putting on her shoes to leave again, he'd make a frantic dash to curl his fluffy body around her ankles.

She needed to make more of an effort to stay at the apartment so Pickles wouldn't be so lonely.

In the past week, Griffin drove her to her father's place a few times. Each time she showed up, Cindy was always delighted to see her. She wasn't sure what the nature of Cindy's relationship with her father was, but she was nice enough.

Most of the time, she'd find her father already waiting for her in his sitting room. She ignored the way he seemed to become more and more frail as each day passed.

Their conversations were usually pleasant. Quynh talked for the most part since talking took a lot out of him. He always listened attentively to every word she said as if she led such an interesting life when really it was probably the most boring thing to recite.

Still, he missed nearly every important event in her life. Quynh ignored the way his eyes glistened as he listened to her tell him about the time she nearly tripped when she went to shake hands with the dean during her undergraduate ceremony. Or the time her heel broke off during her graduate ceremony, so she walked across the stage without shoes. He'd nod along to her stories, offering warm smiles when appropriate.

Today was no different. Quynh was enjoying a cup of coffee Cindy brought her, knowing how she liked to have a little afternoon pick-me-up. She finished telling the story of how she came to adopt Pickles.

She vowed to never leave him behind, though guilt pierced her at how often she had stayed at Griffin's place the past week. She'd have to spend more time in her temporary apartment.

"Quynh."

Her father's raspy voice brought her back to the present. She looked at him curiously. He rarely talked when they were together since it took so much out of him. She noticed he looked particularly lively today. There was more color to his cheeks, and he seemed to be sitting up straighter.

"Your mother…"

Her eyebrows raised as she waited patiently for him to say what he needed to say.

"I…I loved her…very much."

Quynh's lips parted.

"I'm s-so sorry. I tried t-to find you. After..."

She knew what he meant by after. Her mother packed their bags and left in the middle of the night after the incident at the park.

After a moment, he huffed out a breath of frustration. This was the most words he'd spoken to her since she started visiting him.

"I love you, Quynh."

The words were clear. Not punctuated with gasping breaths.

Quynh didn't know what to do. A part of her had been waiting to hear those words for so long, but her chest tightened as tears pooled in her eyes. A high-pitched noise filled her ears as she thought of all the pain and suffering she and her mother went through in the years following the incident.

The right thing to do was to probably forgive him. She knew he wanted her forgiveness before he met his maker.

Am I ready to forgive him for everything?

"Oh, um, I should get going." She plopped the coffee mug on the table a little harder than intended. Quynh winced as some coffee spilled over the edge. "Shit."

She used the napkins to clean up the mess she had made before bowing her head and making a hasty retreat.

"I'll...uh...I'll see you soon."

Typically, Griffin would drop her off and come get her

after about an hour. Today's visit was shorter, so she didn't expect Griffin to show up for at least another few minutes.

She hid in the sitting room. That's where Cindy found her pacing the floors.

"Are you okay, dear?"

Quynh jumped at the sound of Cindy's voice. She hadn't heard her approach.

"I'm fine." Quynh shook out her hands.

What's happening to me?

"Is it alright if I sit with you for a moment?" Cindy didn't wait for an answer before she sat down gracefully on the loveseat.

Quynh stopped her pacing and sat down across from Cindy. It was an awkward silence as they both took each other in.

"I don't mean to overstep, but...you see, I've been with Arthur for most of his life." Quynh stopped breathing as she watched Cindy. She must be having some internal struggle as her lips twisted in a thoughtful pout.

"You see...you and I...we've met before...before this," Cindy gestured vaguely at Quynh. "You were probably too young to remember me. That's okay, dear, but I used to take care of you when you were a baby."

Quynh's stomach bottomed out.

"Your mother and father met when he was in town doing business. Love at first sight, I imagine. They were both young, but times were different back then. Your mother being...well...you know...of a different ethnic background...it just wasn't allowed."

Quynh knew what Cindy meant. Interracial marriages were illegal until 1967. Her mother and aunt were both Vietnamese refugees who came to America looking for work. The sisters had to leave their parents behind, though they always sent money back home to their family. Quynh never got to meet her grandparents. They died when she was young.

From what she recalled from her mother's stories, the sisters were together for the first year but eventually separated to pursue different job opportunities. Her mother went east, while her aunt went west. They remained apart for nearly a decade before Quynh and her mother showed up on her aunt's front step.

"Your parents tried to keep it a secret, but your mother became pregnant. She had to work long hours, so she would leave you with me when you were a babe. Eventually, she could take you to work with her." Cindy continued. "Your grandparents were furious when they found out, naturally. They tried to keep it a secret. They gave your father an ultimatum. Either he joined the family business, or they'd make your mother disappear. Now, I don't pretend to know what that meant, but it scared your father an awful lot. He joined the family business, and his father made it a mission to keep him away from your mother as much as possible. That meant he was frequently sent away on business trips."

Quynh listened with her heart in her throat. This was all so much to take in. She grew up most of her life thinking her father never wanted her in his life. To find out maybe he didn't have a choice was...devastating. It threatened to fracture everything she believed to be true about her world.

"That summer...before you and your mother...disappeared...your grandfather had forced your father into an arranged marriage. A business merger, really. Sara was a widow with a little girl, Ruth. The marriage was important for the family business."

Quynh's memories brought her back to the fateful day in the park. How confused she had been when she saw the little blonde girl calling her father, 'daddy.'

"He tried to find you and your mother for years. It was like you had vanished into thin air."

Something wet splashed against the back of her hands. She realized she was crying. Quynh reached up to wipe away the tears. Cindy leaned over and handed her a handful of tissues.

"For what it's worth, I'm so happy to see you again."

Quynh's lips thinned in an attempt at a smile. She couldn't think of a proper response.

What am I even supposed to say to such a bombshell?

Griffin's approaching truck rumbled in the distance.

She almost jumped out of her seat. She was so grateful to hear the familiar rumble as it made its way to the front of the house.

She sniffed and wiped her tears away, thanked Cindy, and took off to meet Griffin in the driveway.

His truck barely pulled to a stop before she ripped the door open and hopped in. Griffin looked at her. His face tightened at what he saw, but he didn't say a word. She was grateful for the reprieve, however brief it may be. He'll probably grill her for answers later.

But right now, she needed a break from the emotional roller coaster.

Quynh felt lost.

Was everything I thought I knew a lie?

24

The drive back to Griffin's was silent.

Her thoughts spiraled, and a thousand questions flashed through her mind. One question kept coming back.

She wondered what would have happened if her mother had waited just one day before deciding to move across the country.

Would my life be completely different?

She likely would have grown up knowing both her parents loved her. Undoubtedly, life would be different. She didn't think they would have acted like a happy family, but she would have been closer to her father.

If the "incident" never happened, Quynh wouldn't have watched her mother deteriorate from her heartbreak over the last decades of their lives together.

However, she wouldn't have gotten to spend time with her aunt if not for her mother's impulsive move.

And, though it was hard, she didn't regret a single moment she had with her aunt.

Griffin pulled to a stop in his driveway. Neither of them made a move to get out. One arm rested against the back of the bench while his fingertips toyed with the edges of her hair.

She noticed how his raw energy seemed to soothe her frayed nerves. His masculine scent wrapped around her as she took a deep breath. Her scalp tingled from the gentle pulling sensation of his fingers toying with her hair.

For the first time since this morning, they were finally alone.

Griffin's hand gripped the back of her neck as he pulled her close.

"You okay, sunshine?"

She gripped his forearm and rested her forehead against his, breathing him in.

She nodded.

Grounded. It was how she felt at this moment.

The world stopped spinning, just for a second. She could breathe again.

She opened her eyes, not realizing she had closed them, and looked into the mesmerizing green of Griffin's eyes. They seemed to change colors depending on his mood. Right now, they seemed darker. His pupils were wide, nearly drowning out the green.

How could anything be wrong with this mountain of a man holding me?

She pressed a kiss to his lips, relishing in his surprise at her making the first move. He returned the gesture in kind.

Quynh unbuckled her seatbelt without breaking their kiss and climbed into his lap. She wore a sundress today because of the unseasonably warm weather.

Griffin's hands gripped her hips as she settled her weight in his lap. The hard bulge beneath his jeans rubbed against her damp panties. Quynh nearly groaned in frustration, belatedly thinking she should have skipped the underwear again. It hadn't seemed appropriate to visit her father sans underwear, but now she wished she'd left it behind.

It would make things a lot easier for them if she didn't have underwear on right now.

Her hands gripped the back of his head desperately. She needed to get closer to him.

She broke the kiss and tugged at the button of his jeans. Griffin halted her movement with a large palm over her hands.

"You sure, sunshine?"

Am I sure? Yes. Am I okay? No.

She was so far from okay. But, right now, she wanted just one moment to herself. A single moment where her world wasn't falling apart around her. She deserved just one moment.

"I need you." She never meant anything more. She needed him like her next breath. Quynh couldn't imagine being alone right now. Griffin's quiet strength kept her from falling apart completely.

"Take what you need, sunshine." Griffin sat back on the bench while her eyes roamed over his magnificent physique.

Will I ever get tired of looking at him?

It didn't matter. She knew exactly what would make her forget the last hour.

She was sitting on it.

Her hands were no longer shaking. This time, she unbuttoned his jeans without struggling. She was careful to work the zipper over his impressive bulge. Quynh bit down on her lip as the tip of his cock poked above the waistband of his briefs. His tip was already slick with his arousal.

She hadn't even touched him yet, and he was already so hard for her. Bolstered by his eager response, Quynh tugged his boxers down. Her lips parted as his cock bobbed between them. Griffin's hands on her hips tightened briefly.

Slowly, she reached a hand to grip him experimentally. She bit her lip at Griffin's groan. It sounded like he was in pain, but one glance at his tightened expression confirmed his desire. She couldn't wrap her hand around the thick length as she moved her hand from the tip to the base.

Griffin's hips bucked involuntarily at her movement.

"Fuck. That feels good, sunshine."

She couldn't remember the last time she gave a hand job. It never appealed to her before. But watching the look of satisfaction cross Griffin's face made her want to try it. Another time, perhaps. Right now, she needed to feel his thick cock inside of her desperately. The thin line between pain and pleasure at how he stretched her wide open was addictive. She needed to lose herself to him.

She bent her head and spit on his cock. Quynh rubbed her spit around the head of his cock.

"Fuck, that was hot." Griffin's low growl made her pussy clench in response. She was so wet, her arousal was dripping onto her thighs.

Sitting back on his thighs, she tugged off her panties. He held her steady as she tossed the offending garment over her shoulder. Hands on his shoulder, she hovered over the tip of his cock, sliding her hips back and forth, making them both groan at the torturous contact.

"Quynh." Griffin's groan made her shiver. His threat was clear. If she didn't put them both out of their misery soon, he'd take over. Normally, she wouldn't mind if he took the reins, but she needed to be in control this time.

She reached a hand down to grip the base of his cock,

holding him steady at her entrance as she bore down on him.

Griffin's hiss fortified her as she impaled herself on his hard length. At this angle, he was deeper than he was before. She groaned at the fullness of having him fully buried to the hilt inside of her.

She gave herself a few seconds to accommodate the delicious stretch, rocking her hips experimentally as she found the angle that made her toes curl. With Griffin's grip on her hips, they set a sizzling pace, both desperate to reach the finish line.

Her skin was on fire. Sweat dripped around her hairline as she leaned further back, hips grinding into his as he brought his hips up to meet her eager thrusts. One hand braced on his thigh while the other squeezed her breast and pinched her nipple.

The windows fogged as they fucked.

It was sloppy. It was chaotic. It was everything she needed as she barreled into an orgasm with a hoarse scream. Griffin followed closely behind, pulling her down as he emptied himself inside of her. His arms circled her waist as he brought his head to her chest, his cock twitching as she squeezed him.

Their heavy breathing filled the cabin of the truck. When her ears stopped ringing, she opened her eyes cautiously. The setting sun over the lake was a beautiful backdrop to the otherwise frantic moment. She winced as she sat up, and he slipped out of her. Griffin grabbed napkins from the center console and held them to her as his cum dribbled out of her.

She'd longed to stop being embarrassed about how he took control of aftercare. After the first few times when he'd noticed she squirmed at the attention, he reassured her it was his mess and, therefore, his responsibility to take care of it. He'd finished the statement with a sweet kiss before telling her he took pleasure in taking care of her.

"Come on, let's get inside before the neighbors see us." Griffin picked her up by her hips and helped her get back into her seat. Her legs were still weak from the orgasm, and he got extra cranky if she tried to open the door herself. When he opened her door, instead of letting her hop out of the truck, he reached in and picked her up, arms wrapping around her back and waist as he carried her into his house like a bride.

Quynh wrapped her arms around his neck, resting her tired head against his shoulder. He set her down on the couch, bending down to take her shoes off for her before repositioning her so she was lying on the couch. He covered her with a fluffy blanket and turned on the television for her.

Rover came running in to greet them. His slobbering kisses instantly lifted her spirits. A pang of guilt pierced her as she thought about Pickles, who was home alone all day.

"I checked in on that cat of yours before I left to pick you up. He's still as cranky as ever." She smiled gratefully. Between Pickles and Griffin, she wasn't sure who was crankier.

Both of them shared their pricklier personalities to hide their squishy, tender hearts. She suspected Griffin was a gooey teddy bear beneath all the posturing.

Quynh tilted her chin up, looking up at him beneath her lashes. She was sure he could tell how the thoughtful gesture made her feel, but she thanked him regardless.

Griffin's soft kiss warmed her heart and made her toes curl. She could get used to this. Quynh was never anyone's first priority before, and being taken care of was nice.

It's too bad she needed to leave soon.

25

The weekend approached before they knew it. Quynh avoided seeing her father over the last few days, but eventually, the guilt ate at her. She knew their time together was limited, and regardless of their messy history, she did not want to miss another opportunity to spend time with someone she loved while they were still around.

Because even though her father broke her mother's heart long ago, Quynh was still the little girl who remembered her father's smiles and hugs. Losing him was difficult for her, and while they probably could never go back to what they had, they could try to build a new relationship. Make new memories.

Quynh had an epiphany when she finally opened up to Griffin about what she learned. They were lying in bed after having just finished cleaning up when the floodgates opened. Griffin stayed mostly silent as she dumped her family drama on him. Finally, when she was quiet, he offered some welcomed advice.

"Maybe you don't need to forgive him now, but would you regret not giving him a chance when he's gone?"

It hurt to admit, but she wanted to get to know her father. She just wished her mother were still alive. Her mother, who died thinking the love of her life had forsaken her for another woman. The reality was much more complicated.

She wondered if it would have helped her mother to know the truth. Quynh would like to think so. The strain on a person's emotional and physical well-being following a heartbreak was well known to end in illnesses and early death. It didn't really matter anymore.

She couldn't change the past any more than she could change the color of the sky. What's done is done, and she would make the best of the present.

Which included a sick father, a grumpy mechanic, a crotchety cat, a sister she hardly knew, and a car which was nearly fixed. She'd worry about finding a new job another day.

She'd called Cindy yesterday to arrange for today's visit. Quynh worked up the courage to unearth the precious bundle she hid in her suitcase. It was time to heal. No more hiding from the past.

It was a nice day, and she thought maybe they could

spend it outside. Cindy seemed so elated when she called and said she would help arrange everything.

By the time Griffin rolled up to the mansion, Cindy was already on the porch to greet them. This time, instead of dropping her off, Griffin put the truck in park and got out. Quynh glanced at him curiously as he rounded the hood of the truck to open her door.

He helped her hop down, and suddenly, it became clear why he ditched his usual T-shirt, flannels, and jeans ensemble for the weekend. Instead, he cleaned up his beard and dressed in dark jeans with a button-down shirt. He looked good enough to eat, though he wouldn't let her take a bite. Instead, he shoved her out the door before they could get distracted and risk running late.

She sat on her hands during the short drive to the mansion so she wouldn't touch him. After all, it probably was not a good idea to distract the driver. Even if said driver was looking like a yummy snack.

Quynh had yet to taste him today. Later. She'll make it a priority for next time. Griffin usually took the lead with their bedroom excursions. She appreciated the control, or rather, being able to relinquish control to someone else. It was freeing to have someone else take the reins. When she gave up control, she didn't have to be constantly on guard. Always trying to think ten steps ahead or worry about how much of a mess her life was.

She wondered what it would be like to watch Griffin lose control for once.

Would he let me take the lead once in a while?

The thought of a man like Griffin trusting her enough to take control was exhilarating. By the time they pulled up to the mansion, Quynh was squirming in her seat.

Thank god.

Another minute alone with Griffin and her wandering thoughts would have ended with them on the side of the road as she acted on her impulse. She didn't think Griffin would mind, really.

Griffin's hands reached around her waist and brought her body close to him. He held her against his hard body as he slowly let her feet touch the ground. Quynh held on to his biceps, a small smile curving her lips. He wasn't one for public displays of affection, but these small gestures were more meaningful to her than any PDA was.

She stretched onto her tiptoes, lips puckering in a quiet demand for a kiss. Griffin met her halfway, hands tightening around her. This kiss was different. It was gentle. A quiet appreciation between two people. It soothed her frayed nerves and bolstered her confidence. They broke apart when Cindy cleared her throat.

"Hello, dears. He's waiting for you in the garden."

Griffin took a step back, and Quynh moved to follow him until she remembered the small journal she brought with her. She reached inside the truck to grab her precious cargo and turned to follow Cindy. Griffin's hand took hers in his large paw. She glanced up at him, eyes gleaming with her appreciation.

Cindy led the way around the home. The lawn was well-manicured, with perfectly trimmed hedges and rose bushes along the path. The smooth stones led them to the back of the mansion with an expanse of green grass before leading into a dense tree line. Off in the distance, Quynh could make out a pool area.

When they rounded the bend, the trio stepped onto the stone patio with a covered pergola. Her father sat in a wheelchair at the table in the shade. He wore a nice shirt and slacks. Gone was his usual robe. He looked healthier for the first time in days. Almost as if a burden was lifted since their last visit.

"Hi." Quynh bowed her head in greeting, hands gripping the journal tightly in front of her. She fidgeted on her feet for a moment.

"Sir, it's nice to meet you. Griffin Kennedy." Quynh watched as Griffin shook her father's hand in a firm grip. A warm sensation flooded her chest, making it hard for her to breathe.

Her father offered a tight smile and gestured for the pair to have a seat. As they settled onto the cushioned seats, Cindy came out with a tray piled high with finger sandwiches and snacks. Quynh thanked Cindy before she left.

Her hands were damp as she nervously tugged at the journal in her hands.

"I...um...I wanted to read you something today. It's... It's my mother's journal." At the mention of her mother, her father's demeanor changed. His eyes seemed brighter, more attentive. His breathing was shallow, the quiet hum of the oxygen tank a reminder of his precarious condition.

"It took me a while to get it translated properly...I thought you'd like to know about her life after..." Her voice trailed off. It didn't need to be said.

Her father rolled his lips between his teeth, giving her a curt nod to continue.

Quynh glanced at Griffin nervously, his reassuring nod giving her the confidence she was lacking. She squared her shoulders, cleared her throat, and fumbled to open the journal. It took her years after her mother passed to even open the journal, and it took months before she could translate it to the best of her ability. She learned her native language when she was younger, but it was a different thing entirely to translate it into another language.

Tucked inside the journal were her translated notes. She probably should have had it properly translated, but the thought of having a complete stranger comb through her mother's private thoughts made her sick. So, she took on the painstaking task herself.

Side by side, she read her translated version, glancing

up once in a while to see the look of adoration on her father's face. Quynh's mother wrote about having to leave her elderly parents behind to pursue the American dream. The promise of a better life for her family kept her from giving up when she reached hardship after hardship. It was difficult to read about how much her mother and aunt went through to get to America.

Quynh couldn't even imagine leaving the only home she ever knew for a different country, having to learn a completely different language, and navigating an entirely different world. She wasn't sure she would have made it as far as her mother and aunt did. At least they had each other. Until they didn't.

Her mother wrote about how the sisters separated in pursuit of different opportunities.

After what seemed like an hour, she finally came to the part where her parents met.

Her mother had just moved to town and was staying with a local sponsoring family. They helped her get a job working at the local nail salon. She was just leaving work when she bumped into her father as she was leaving the shop. She apologized profusely, though her English was broken. Instead of being angered, her mother mentioned how kind he had been to her.

It was not the first time they bumped into each other. At first, they seemed like happy coincidences, but it became clear after a few run-ins that he was waiting for her to leave to approach her. Eventually, their run-ins became more intentional. They would meet once a week at the park. She would listen to him talk, barely understanding a word he said, but "he had kind eyes and a warm heart."

For the first time in her adult life, her mother felt like a woman. Not just a woman, but a desirable one. Though she knew it was inappropriate, they ended up having an affair. They planned to get married, but she became pregnant first. Her father put them up in their own apartment in town so they had privacy. Unfortunately, he was forced into the family business and traveled a lot.

Quynh stopped as the pages thinned. She reached the end of the journal. Tucking the pages back into the journal carefully, she placed it on the table. Her hands were shaking from reliving her mother's life. She wasn't prepared to see the tears gathering in her father's eyes. She hadn't realized how emotional the last hour would be for him.

"I'm sorry..." Her hand reached out to grasp her father's aged one.

"Thank you." His voice cracked on the words. Quynh watched helplessly as tears streamed down her father's face. He pinched his lips together with a curt nod. "Thank you."

Quynh wasn't sure what he was thanking her for.

Griffin reached over and clasped her hands in his, lending her his strength at this moment.

"We should probably get going," Quynh said hesitantly as she slowly stood up. She hesitantly approached her father, unsure of what to do. Her father reached out a hand, which she grasped, grateful for the olive branch. Holding his aged hand in both of hers as they smiled tentatively at each other. Then, he gave Cindy a nod, who tried to pretend like she hadn't been eavesdropping on the edge of the lawn. A gesture she knew meant he was ready to retire to his bedroom.

"Goodbye, dears." Cindy rushed to wheel her father back into the home.

She watched the pair as they moved toward the house. Her father glanced over his shoulder and offered a small wave of goodbye.

Griffin's warmth against her back made her tense muscles relax. When he wrapped his strong arms around her waist, pulling her against his hard chest, she let out a breath of relief. He rested his chin on her head. They stood together for a moment as she processed the last hour.

Griffin turned her around gently, hands framing her face. His calloused fingers wiped away tears she hadn't known were there. He kissed her on her forehead and pulled her in for a tight embrace.

She clung to him. Her rock. Her quiet comfort.

Not for the first time, her stomach fluttered with

awareness. This time, though, instead of pushing the sensation away, she embraced it.

She wondered if this was what her mother felt for her father. If what she was feeling was even a fraction of how her mother felt, she understood why losing it would break a person.

Quynh prayed she never had to know what her mother endured firsthand.

She wasn't sure she was strong enough to survive it.

26

Bright rays of sunshine peeked through the blinds. For a moment, Quynh forgot where she was. Last night, Griffin brought her back to his house. She was completely emotionally drained from her visit with her father. She'd wanted to collapse in his bed and curl up under his blankets for at least a few days. Though he didn't push her to talk, he'd silently prepared a hot bath.

He insisted she get in the hot bath while he cooked dinner for them. He'd given her an adorable frown when she'd tried to refuse.

"You're not going to waste all that hot water, are you?"

It took more effort than it should have to get undressed, but it was worth it when she sank into the slightly too-hot water. She'd let the lavender scents from the bath bomb Griffin tossed into the bath soothe her senses as her muscles relaxed.

By the time Griffin came back to retrieve her for dinner, the bath water was barely lukewarm, and she fell asleep. He shook her awake gently, having a giant fluffy towel ready to help her get out of the bath. Wrapped up in the towel, she'd felt like a princess as he helped her get dressed in another one of his shirts and sweats. Once she was fully dressed, he'd cradled her in his arms and carried her to the dinner table.

Quynh never felt so cared for before. And she was not complaining. It was a welcomed feeling after the emotional roller coaster of the past week. She never realized how lonely she was until she met Griffin. How empty her life was.

Dinner was delicious, as always. She marveled at how talented Griffin was. Not only was he a respected and successful businessman, but he was also an amazing cook.

How did I get so lucky?

She could get used to this. She could get used to him. For a brief moment, she imagined what her life would be like if she stayed in Willowbrook.

Can I stay here?

Pushing the thoughts away, she finished the dinner he had made of beef Bolognese. She was too tired to worry about anything else but the present.

Life seemed so much simpler this way, not worrying about the future but focusing on the present.

Later, after they'd cleaned up dinner, the sex was unhurried. Tender. Building each other's climaxes up slowly with gentle caresses and sweet kisses. Each touch of the hand was an exploration of not just their bodies but their souls. They came together, eyes clinging to each other as their climaxes peaked nearly simultaneously.

Quynh passed out before Griffin finished cleaning her up.

It was how she found herself this morning. Except something was different. There was a familiar furball curled up next to her head.

"Pickles?" She lifted her head to look around Griffin's bedroom.

Where was Griffin?

She rarely woke up alone.

Rolling over, she looked around the empty bedroom for any sign of him. It was quiet throughout the rest of the house. She reached over to grab her cell phone charging on the nightstand table.

One new message from Griffin.

> At the shop early this morning. Breakfast in the microwave. Your feral furball looks hungry. Hope he doesn't eat your face.

Well, that explained how Pickles showed up at Griffin's house. He must have gone over to the apartment and brought him back for her.

Her throat grew thick with emotion. She clasped a hand around her throat and tried to take calming breaths.

She was reading too much into Griffin's intentions. He was very clear he was not and would not be interested in a relationship. Griffin was just a misunderstood grump who really was just a teddy bear on the inside.

Quynh tried to ignore the giddy feeling in her chest. The kind that made her want to kick her feet with happiness and grin like a lovesick teenager.

Her phone pinged with a new message. This time, it was from Ruth.

A single sentence.

What she saw effectively wiped the smile off her face, a cold dread rolling in and making her stomach drop.

27

Four little words that can make anyone's heart drop.

RUTH

We need to talk.

Words nobody should be allowed to say unless it was an emergency.

Oh, god, is my father okay?

QUYNH

Everything okay?"

Her shaking fingers typed out the response. Quynh chewed on her lip as she stared at the three bouncing dots showing Ruth was typing a response.

RUTH

Can you meet me in an hour at the cafe?

Quynh gulped as she read the message. This couldn't possibly be good news.

QUYNH

See you soon.

Quynh jumped out of bed. The movement disrupted Pickles from his perch. She shot him an apologetic expression as she made a mental note to pick up some of his favorite treats on her way back. She hurriedly got dressed in the clothes she'd brought over last night. Rushing down the stairs, she forgot completely about the breakfast waiting for her.

She crossed the street and walked into the open garage bay doors. Griffin was working on Shelly when she walked in. He didn't notice her at first, face frowning as he worked under the hood, muscles flexing with the movement.

Griffin rarely worked on Sundays, but because he was so behind recently, it became a new routine.

Noticing her in the doorway, his face lit up as her heart pounded. His usual frown softened into a slight smile. Her stomach churned with nervous excitement as she noticed how he acted differently around her.

"Morning, sunshine." He took a step toward her, taking in her appearance. "Everything okay?"

"Oh, yeah, everything's fine. I'm going to meet Ruth at the cafe." She bit her lip anxiously, unsure why she needed to tell him her plans when she probably could have just texted him instead.

A part of her wanted to see him before the meeting. Waking up alone for the first time in weeks was disconcerting. She got used to seeing him first thing in the morning. And...she missed him.

"Need me to go with you?" Griffin wiped his hands on a rag as he stepped up to her.

She shook her head and met him halfway. He tossed the rag on the tool bench and reached for her. Quynh melted into his arms, grateful for his embrace.

For a moment, she breathed him in. He smelled of motor oil and grease, but underneath it, he smelled uniquely Griffin. A blend of sandalwood, spice, and musk. A scent she was quickly becoming addicted to. It centered her and calmed her. If only she could bottle his essence and bring it with her everywhere.

"No, I'll be okay." *I think.*

"Call me if you need anything." He gripped her chin in a firm grasp, tilting her head back so he could look into her eyes. She wasn't sure what he saw, but whatever it was, it made his mouth tighten. Quynh thought he'd object to her going by herself. Instead, he surprised her by placing a gentle kiss on her lips and patting her butt as if to say, "Get outta here."

Her lips tilted up in a grin.

Lightness filled her chest, a change from the heavy

weight Ruth's text left. It seemed like all she needed was a dose of Griffin to lift her spirits.

The walk to the cafe was uneventful. She waved to the pedestrians as she made her way to Main Street. The town was buzzing with activity as people went about their business. Sundays were a busy day for the otherwise sleepy town.

The bell chimed as she made her way into the cafe. She didn't see Ruth inside but waved to her favorite barista, Jodie. By the time she made it to the counter, Jodie had already rang her order up. She never thought she'd be one of those people who would be remembered by their order. Back in the city, she brewed her own coffee at home. There was never any time for her to stop at a coffee shop before work. It was a luxury she didn't have time for.

She would miss this part of her day. There were a lot of things she would miss about Willowbrook. A certain green-eyed, grumpy mechanic flashed through her mind.

Quynh grabbed her coffee and sat at a table in the back. Normally, she would enjoy people watching at the window, but since she didn't know why Ruth wanted to meet with her, it was probably best if there were no witnesses if it was bad news.

Her gut churned with anxiety. The prospect of meeting with Ruth made her so nervous, even if she was technically family. Even if they met under unfortunate circumstances.

The bell chimed again as another guest arrived. Glancing up from her coffee cup, she saw Ruth at the entrance. The glare Ruth shot her way made her want to shrink in her seat. Instead, she took in a calming breath and wrapped her hands around the hot coffee cup. It was too hot to drink, and she was not a fan of burning her tongue.

Ruth marched toward her, each step bringing her closer to Quynh. By the time Ruth plopped down in the seat across from her, Quynh's palms started sweating.

"Ruth. Good morning."

"Hmmph."

The silence between them stretched.

"Listen, Quynh. I don't want to dance around the issue here, but I need to be upfront with you."

Quynh waited with bated breath for Ruth's next words. She gestured for Ruth to continue.

"I know you came all this way hoping to cash in on my dad's inheritance, but that's not going to happen."

Rearing back in shock, Quynh gaped at Ruth's harsh words, confused at the hostility radiating off the woman sitting across from her.

"I'm not here for..."

"Cut the shit. Everyone in town knows why you're here."

Her heart dropped. The heat from her coffee no longer kept her warm. Instead, she was chilled to her bones. Tentatively, she looked around the small cafe, noticing for the first time Jodie and the other customers averted her gaze, pretending they couldn't hear every single word of the embarrassing exchange.

"Ruth...I-I don't know what to say." She fought the urge to sink further in her chair. If only the floor could open up and swallow her whole.

"Say you're leaving town." Ruth sat back, arms crossed across her chest. The glare she shot Quynh cut through her like a sharp knife. Any hope she had of getting to know her stepsister was gone like the wind.

"But..."

Her only remaining family didn't even want her. Heat crept through her, the shame threatening to consume her.

Ruth rolled her eyes at her, which only made her feel ten times smaller.

"Look. Dad doesn't have much time left. I've already talked to his lawyer and made sure that everything's taken care of. If you're looking for a fat check, you'll be sadly disappointed, so you don't need to stick around anymore." Ruth paused, hands adjusting the thin scarf loosely wrapped around her neck. "I only found out about you a few years ago, you know."

Quynh's brows pinched together in confusion.

"Dear old dad tried to find you for years. Hired

multiple private investigators too, but it was like you vanished into thin air." Ruth brought her fingers together and threw her hands up dramatically. "Poof. Gone."

Hearing someone cared enough to look for her should have filled her heart with joy, but what she felt was the complete opposite.

"He was obsessed with finding you." Ruth curled her lip up in distaste. "Couldn't be bothered to care for the daughter he actually had." She sat back with a huff of annoyance, blonde hair swaying with the movement.

At a complete loss for words, Quynh tucked her cold hands between her thighs.

"I'm sorry you feel that way..."

"Yeah, whatever. I mean, I get it. Mom was a complete bitch." She let out a dry laugh. "I didn't even know I had a sister until a few years ago, so I'm sorry if it's hard to welcome a new family member with open arms." Ruth turned her head, looking off in the distance, chewing on her bottom lip in a familiar gesture.

"Sure..."

"He only found you because you started searching for him, you know. If you hadn't put your information in the ancestral thing, he never would have found you." Ruth leveled Quynh with a withering glare. What was left of her hope for a happy reunion shriveled under her gaze.

"I'm sorry." The words were whispered under her

breath. There really wasn't much for her to say at this point.

Ruth glanced at her cell phone on the table. "Yeah, well, I have to get going." She got up to leave while Quynh sat glued to her seat. "Oh, and let's keep this between us girls, yeah?" Her hand moved between them. "Dad doesn't need to know that his girls aren't besties. Probably would kill him." Ruth rolled her eyes and turned away.

Quynh's lips parted, aghast at the implications. She watched helplessly as Ruth turned her back and left the cafe without a backward glance.

Fighting back tears, Quynh slumped in her seat. Her cheeks heated as she overheard people whispering about the encounter. Their harsh criticisms sliced her like a thousand paper cuts. For the first time since she arrived in Willowbrook, her heart felt heavy. Like heavy chains wrapped around the bleeding organ tied to a cement block weighing her down. It threatened to drag her under her waves of despair.

Sniffling, Quynh covertly wiped away the tears that escaped despite her best efforts, breath shallow as she fought for control over her emotions. She couldn't break down. Not now, and certainly not in a room full of strangers.

Strangers she was so hopeful of calling friends one day.

You're a fool, Quynh.

That was the thing about hope. It was a dangerous emotion. One she wished she never had, but the illusion of a happy life here in Willowbrook was so irresistible. One where she lived in a town where she could plant her roots. A family to call her own. A man to call hers. But it was all an illusion.

Now, all she had left were the broken fragments of her dreams.

Escaping from the cafe was harder than she thought possible. Trying to ignore all the curious glances and keeping her head held high was a testament to her strength. It was embarrassing enough to have witnesses to her family drama. She didn't need to add letting complete strangers see her cry in public to the list.

The walk to the bookstore helped Quynh's mood. When she opened the doors, the scent of books lifted her spirits. Just a tiny bit. Enough for her to forget about the last twenty minutes. As she browsed the latest romance books on the shelves, she almost jumped with joy at the new fantasy book she requested, yanking the thick book off the shelf and hugging it tightly to her chest.

There was nothing a good book couldn't solve.

Usually, she limited herself to one book at a time, knowing her pile of unread books was hopelessly longer than her lifespan, but today, she needed a pick-me-up. An instant mood booster. There was no way she was going back to Griffin an emotional wreck. He'd notice the change in her mood immediately, and she wasn't quite ready to divulge any of her family drama quite yet.

She wanted to stay in the happy bubble just for a while longer.

The universe owed her that much.

So, she went up and down every aisle of the romance section, picking up books she had been eyeing for weeks until she held a stack so large she couldn't see over it.

The bookstore owner, Lana, was more than happy to see how many books she picked out when she rang her order up. She barely resisted the urge to plug her fingers in her ears as she handed over her credit card. Her happy mood didn't need to be ruined by how much she spent.

It was a problem for future Quynh.

Present Quynh was as happy as she could possibly be in this moment, and it was all she needed.

28

The sound of a rock song blared through the speakers as Griffin finished installing the new alternator in Quynh's car. He'd also taken the liberty of updating a few other parts that desperately needed replacing. Normally, this job would have taken him no longer than a few hours at best and maybe a day or so at worst, as long as parts arrived on time. At first, when the manufacturer emailed him to notify him of a delay in shipping the parts he'd needed to fix Quynh's car, he was frustrated. He was already hopelessly behind with current orders and didn't need to pile on something else. At the rate the auto shop was going, they'd never be able to catch up before the season was over.

It ended up being a blessing in disguise.

The shipping delay meant Quynh had even more of a reason to stick around town. Obviously, the sex was a plus, but having her around the shop was a welcomed presence. He grew to enjoy being around her. The short time they spent apart made him feel like a caged animal, restless and irritable until he was reunited with Quynh again.

Griffin was not used to wanting to be around another person for any amount of time. Much less a woman. He successfully avoided any romantic entanglements for years. Being a bachelor suited his lifestyle perfectly fine.

But when Quynh blew into town like a devastating tornado in her beat-up VW Beetle sporting her tear-stained cheeks, expressive eyes, and kiss-me lips, he knew he was a goner.

So, he may have dragged his feet a little while fixing her car. If Julio and Sean suspected what game he was playing, they never said a word. Though the knowing glances and smirks clued him in they knew what he was doing. Those two clowns enjoyed having her around just as much as he did.

Quynh didn't need to know he could have had her back on the road a week ago. Griffin enjoyed the extra time he got to spend with her on the drives to her father's mansion.

But after the most recent visit with her father, Griffin was attacked by his conscience. He couldn't keep her if she didn't want to stay. She shared her past with him little by little. Knowing how close-lipped she was about her past made his head, chest, and dick swell with pride at being "the one" she trusted.

Yet, here he was, violating her trust. No, he couldn't keep up the ruse any longer. He had to make up for lost time. Griffin woke up early this morning to fix his mistake. Leaving her alone in his bed was torture, but he had amends to make. When he got to the shop, he'd heard the telltale sounds of scratching coming from upstairs. Griffin let himself into the apartment she'd been staying at and collected the grumpy asshole in his carrier. He had scratch marks all over his arms to show for it, too.

He'd carted the snarling motherfucker across the street. It was a ridiculous notion, having to sneak into his own bedroom, but he didn't want to wake her. Quynh was feeling guilty about leaving the poor critter alone every night. So, he let the rabid animal loose, knowing Quynh could fend for herself against the fiery furball. Griffin would likely lose an eye if he stuck around for another second.

His good deed accomplished for the month, he'd trotted across the street to get to work, Rover right by his side for the adventure.

When Quynh found him hours later, he could tell something was bothering her by the strain on her face. She also chewed on her lip when she was anxious or over-whelmed. Whatever was bothering her, he hoped she was fine.

Having her car back should help.

It took most of the morning and well into the afternoon before he had Quynh's car running like a dream. He also took the clown car to Ricky's, who also operated the car wash in town. Since Ricky owed him a favor for the prank he pulled with the tow job, Ricky personally detailed the car himself. The bastard only laughed at the sight of Griffin arriving in the clown car.

He'd known Ricky from grade school. He'd always been the class clown, which he clearly never outgrew, constantly playing pranks on everyone. Although Ricky grew up to be a successful businessman, he never outgrew his goofier side. Like when he went out of town and conveniently forgot to notify Griffin he'd left Griffin's contact information for emergency calls that came through.

Normally, Willowbrook had little in the way of vehicle emergencies, but it must have been his lucky day. Who knew how many times Ricky pulled the same prank before a certain dark-haired beauty became his damsel in distress. Griffin didn't believe in luck, but he couldn't deny he was happy it had been him who answered the call instead of Ricky.

Ricky was an attractive guy. Objectively speaking, of

course. He was a smooth talker and often had a gaggle of ladies hanging off his every word. Griffin had no doubt that if Ricky was the one to answer Quynh's distress call, she probably would have met the charming bastard himself.

He wondered if Ricky had not pulled his prank, if he and Quynh would have ever crossed paths.

Griffin didn't believe in fate, but there's something to be said about everything happening for a reason. He strongly believed Quynh was brought into his life to shake things up, bringing his life into perspective, even if he had been content with how his life was progressing.

And the too-tight squeezing sensation in his chest whenever thoughts of Quynh crossed his mind. It made him warm and fuzzy inside. He should probably be evaluated by a doctor. There was no way it was normal that another person could stir up so many strange emotions.

But when he thought about how her eyes lit up every time she saw him, it almost brought a smile to his face. Most of the time, he tried to suppress it, but when he was caught off guard, he'd find himself smiling like a lunatic. He probably looked insane standing in the woods behind his house with a smile on his face. Thank goodness he didn't have any witnesses, though he saw the house next door to his was just sold.

Pretty soon, he'd have new neighbors, and his privacy would be over.

He sensed her presence before he saw her. It was like his life was dull and colorless until she came into the scene, bringing with her all the colors of the rainbow and the heat of the sunshine. And, sure enough, when he turned away from cleaning a spot on the hood of her clown car, there she was.

She wore another sundress today. This one was a light pink paired with a jean jacket and sunglasses. She had a brown bag in her hand from the bookstore, no doubt. The woman was addicted to buying books. He'd have to build her a bookshelf to store all the books she bought.

Griffin shook his head at his wayward thoughts. A bookshelf was probably necessary if she stuck around, but since she still had an apartment in the big city, it wasn't looking very promising. Not to mention the lack of jobs in town of her pedigree. The local health clinic wasn't hiring, and the nearest hospital was close to an hour away from town.

Unless she had any interest in sticking around and helping a grumpy mechanic run his auto-body shop, his chances of convincing her to stay were slim to none.

Griffin pretended to be busy with the car, tightening up bolts that were already tight, and wiping away nonexistent stains while he glared at Julio and Sean for taking her attention. He watched as she threw her head back and laughed at whatever Sean said, making the muscles in her neck look both delicate and delicious. It shouldn't make him jealous she was giving any other male attention, but he couldn't control the irrational urge riding him to stomp over to Sean and punch him in the face.

Thankfully, Griffin was aware of how impulsive those urges were, and instead, he unlocked the passenger side door and sat in it while rubbing at the immaculate leather. Ricky did a phenomenal job, bringing the dull Beetle back to life with his waxes and whatnots. The interior smelled clean. Griffin lamented the loss of her sweet vanilla scent when a small hand touched his shoulder.

He knew who it was before he turned his head to acknowledge her beaming face.

"Took you long enough," he groused while wiping his hands on the rag. Quynh's smile only widened into a grin at his grumpiness. Most people would run away scared of him, but not her. Not his Quynh. If anything, she grew bolder the grumpier he was with her.

Griffin had one leg in the car and the other on the road since he was not built for clown cars. Somehow, Quynh plopped herself on his lap without hurting herself or banging her head against the side of the car.

"Hi." She smiled up at him as she wrapped her arms around his neck, fingers threading themselves into his thick hair.

He grunted in reply before tossing the rag and placing his hands on her small hips.

"You're back." *Finally.*

"I am." She bit her lower lip as her eyes gleamed playfully at him. It was as if she knew what he was saying without having to say it. That he missed her when she was gone, and now she was back, he felt like he could breathe again.

She leaned in to kiss him, and he met her halfway, letting her know how much he missed her. When she was a gasping puddle beneath his hands, he pulled away and smirked at her flushed face.

"Well," she said breathlessly, "it seems like you missed me a little."

"Just a little." He could admit that much.

"Uh-huh." She leaned back against the glove compartment.

His eyes drank in the sight of her splayed in front of him, her dark hair curling around her face in soft waves as the setting sun streamed in through the window, casting a halo around her gleaming body. Her tan skin seemed to glow under his attention. Griffin watched as her dusky lips parted and her breath quickened. His hand on her knee tightened as he fought to restrain himself from pouncing on her.

He was too big to properly service her in this car. His truck would have more space, but then there was the annoying fact of having to deal with the two idiots who were now whistling and making catcalls from the garage bay doors. Guess the cat was out of the bag.

"Oops." Quynh's fingers massaged his scalp as she smiled up at him. "I think they figured it out."

"Yeah," he grunted, not as bothered with the guys knowing about them as he probably should be. It was unprofessional at best and a disaster waiting to happen at worst. But, right now, at this moment, as his eyes roamed over her body, he couldn't bring himself to care at all.

A problem for another day.

"Did you fix my car?" Quynh's soft voice brought him back to the present. Instead of answering, he lifted her and placed her gently on the ground. He was less graceful climbing out of the car. Placing his hands on her shoulder, he guided her around to the driver's seat, opening the door for her, and he gestured for her to get inside.

Her delighted smile sent his heart rate into overdrive. The keys were still in the ignition, and he watched proudly as she turned the car on. Instead of the clunking noise it was making a few weeks ago, the car purred to life.

"Oh, my god! You fixed Shelly!" Her excited voice pierced his heart. He should be happy for her, but Griffin couldn't help the dark cloud that threatened to take over his mood. Or the sense of dread as he stared down at her smiling face.

He realized with horror that he had just given her the means to leave him.

29

Quynh jolted awake, her heart hammering against her ribs like a trapped bird. A chilling sense of foreboding washed over her as the vestiges of her nightmares faded away. The details of her night terrors escaped her, though the uneasiness the visions provoked still gripped her.

Try as she might, she couldn't shake the dreadful feeling clinging to her like a menacing phantom. She tried to stay busy in the office, but the pit in her stomach persisted. It didn't help she had trouble falling asleep despite Griffin tiring her out with his insatiable appetite. Her mind whirled for hours while she grappled with Ruth's hostility until she fell into a fitful slumber.

After Griffin fixed her car yesterday, they celebrated with him down on his knees while he spread her out across the dinner table. Her toes curled in her flats at thoughts of how voracious Griffin's appetite had been. Only when Griffin was satisfied that he brought her to climax properly did he reward her with another home-cooked meal.

If she wasn't careful, she'd get used to being spoiled. On top of probably gaining much-needed weight with how much he loved to cook for her. Her days of eating ramen seemed so far away now.

When taking Rover for a walk around the lake, they ran into their new neighbors, Ben and Emily, who were surveying the property to prepare for the move. They seemed like a lovely couple, and it was nice to see another Asian woman in town. They revealed they were moving for their growing family. Pretty soon, their quiet neighborhood will be filled with the sounds of a small child. The thought made her smile, and thinking about how Griffin's mood darkened at the prospect of noisy mornings made her chuckle to herself in the otherwise quiet office.

The day passed by in a blur. She pushed thoughts of her encounter with Ruth into a box and sealed it up tightly. There was no time to examine how she felt about her sister right now.

Before she knew it, it was already lunchtime. The bell chimed, announcing the entrance of a customer. The guys only used the side door, which didn't have a bell, but it was pretty obvious when it was opened because of the noise filtering into the office before it was shut.

Quynh emerged from the office with a practiced smile

as she greeted the newcomer. She placed the files she was sorting through on the front desk as she sat down in her chair.

"How can I help you?"

A stunning younger woman stood in the lobby, hands clenching bags with what smelled like food. Quynh furrowed her brow in confusion. She hadn't heard the guys mention ordering lunch. Usually, Quynh took care of making sure the guys all took their lunch breaks. Sometimes, they'd order food from the local deli or pizzeria.

"I brought lunch for the boys. They usually eat around this time. I'll just bring it back to them."

The woman made to move around the desk when Quynh stood up to stop her. She didn't know who the woman was, but she couldn't just prance back there.

"Do they know you're coming?"

"Who the hell are you?"

Taken aback by her rude tone, Quynh inspected the blonde bombshell in front of her. She was taller than Quynh by a couple of inches, even without the stiletto heels adorning her feet, hips wrapped in a tight miniskirt with a low-cut form-fitting top which revealed more than it covered.

"Why don't you have a seat, and I'll grab Griffin."

Quynh gestured to the open seats in the lobby and watched as she stomped off, heels clacking loudly against the tiles. It was a marvel to her how anyone could walk in heels that high without falling. Didn't seem comfortable. She'd probably break her damn ankles if she tried on a pair, much less try to walk in them.

Once the sour-faced blonde plopped in a chair, Quynh made sure the computers were password-locked before entering the garage bay.

Griffin was bent over the hood of a Mustang when he spotted her. His contemplative eyes seemed to brighten when they landed on her before the corners pinched together in a frown.

"What is it, Quynh?"

She tried not to flinch at his harsh tone. He'd been grumpy all morning.

"Um...there's a woman here asking to see you."

She wasn't sure it was possible for his frown to deepen, but somehow, he pulled it off.

A hundred questions ran through her mind, but she ignored them. Instead, she backed away when Griffin approached. She could have sworn he growled before stopping before her. He grabbed a rag and wiped his dirty hands on it, wiping them free of the grease coating his fingers. She bit her tongue so she wouldn't drool and focused on the pain. The sight of his forearm muscles flexing as he completed a mundane task was causing her libido to go wild.

Get yourself together, Quynh! Stop drooling over the man!

She was probably making a fool of herself by staring

at him. When she looked at his face, a knowing smirk replaced his frown.

Oops.

So what if he caught me checking him out? He shouldn't be so damn handsome.

She pulled her shoulders back and stood taller, as tall as her 4'11" frame could get, before walking back into the main lobby. Griffin was hot on her heels. Shivers racked up and down her spine at his body heat.

Quynh took her place behind the computer and pretended to go back to work. She watched out of the corner of her eye as he walked past the desk to the main lobby.

The squeal of delight almost shattered her eardrums.

"Griffin, baby! I missed you!"

Quynh shrank in her seat in embarrassment.

Baby? Oh my god, was that his girlfriend?

He told her he wasn't seeing anyone.

Did he lie to me?

She watched in horror as the woman launched herself into Griffin's arms. Her stomach churned at the thought of another woman in his arms.

I'm going to be sick.

Clutching her stomach, she murmured a quiet 'excuse me' as she made a hasty retreat into the hallway. This was all too much. First Ruth, now this woman.

Why can't I catch a break, for once?

Her ragged breathing sounded loud in her ears as she raced to the back. She needed to get out of there before she passed out from hyperventilating. The walls were closing in on her. Once she was in the stairwell, she ran up the flight of stairs, quickly locking the door behind her.

I am such an idiot.

She slammed her head against the door a few times and groaned, her heart still pounding in her chest.

She was about to walk away from the door when she heard stomping steps echoing from the hallway. Only one guess who it might be. Quickly, she fumbled to deadbolt the door and backed away just as a hard fist pounded at the door.

"Quynh! Open up!"

She jumped at his angry tone. She wasn't scared of him hurting her. She just didn't want to talk to him right now. It was humiliating enough being the other woman. She didn't need to listen to any excuses or lies from his filthy mouth. Not when she needed to sort through her own thoughts first.

She owed it to herself to at least figure out what she wanted. It wasn't like they were dating or exclusive. While she asked him if he was seeing other women, it never crossed her mind he would lie to her face.

It stung more than the betrayal. She didn't think he'd been physical with any other women in the short time they'd been together.

What do I even know?

Griffin pounded at the door again.

"Goddammit, Quynh. Let me in. It's not what you're thinking."

"Go away!"

Her voice was thick with tears, catching her by surprise.

"Sunshine, please."

There was a soft thud at the door.

What was he doing out there?

"I don't want to talk to you right now." Her voice came out strong, unwavering in her conviction. This was a boundary she wasn't ready to relent. She needed to be clear-headed and not let his eyes or body sway her from seeing the truth.

Despite being a mostly rational person, she was not immune to Griffin's charms.

"This isn't over, Quynh."

She heard him swearing under his breath, having her ear pressed against the door when he'd stopped pounding on it.

When his footsteps retreated, and she heard the door close downstairs, she let out a breath.

"Yes, it is."

Finally alone, she let the tears fall. Griffin could deal with taking care of his business without her for one afternoon while she hid and licked her wounds. She'd barely processed what her encounter with Ruth meant for her, and then this happened. It was all too much. She needed to be alone.

Wincing, she was attacked by her conscience. She was planning to drive the newly revived Shelly to her father's place later this afternoon for a visit, but there was no way she was fit for company. The time she spent with her father was mostly her talking. It was almost like a therapy session she hadn't meant to sign up for. Sorting through her mother's memories and wading through the emotional implications of her father's guilt was...a lot. Sometimes, it left her emotionally raw, and she just wasn't up to it today.

Tomorrow, though, she'd suck it up and be a big girl. She would pick herself up by her bootstraps and soldier on. Just like she had always done her entire life.

She didn't need a man to make her happy. Even if Griffin was the first man in a long time to truly see her. Or the first man to take care of her. She hadn't known how lonely she was until he started showering her with his attention. He was the desperate thunderstorm during a drought, providing the life-giving hydration to a wilted flower like her.

That's what she was. A wilted flower that lacked the water or sunshine necessary to flourish.

She needed to deal with reality. It had been weeks since she thought about her apartment and what waited for her there. She needed time and space, and going home was exactly what she needed to do.

Except, when she thought about home, it wasn't her empty apartment that came to mind but the gruff mechanic who stomped all over her heart.

Regardless of the possible misunderstanding, she needed to take care of business. Quynh had avoided her responsibilities long enough. Though it hurt, she needed to leave town.

The sooner, the better.

30

Griffin never thought he was capable of committing murder until he walked into the mess Delilah left for him. If he could get away with it, he'd strangle her until she was blue in the face. When she'd shown up with her peace offering of his favorite meal, he knew she was up to no good. Combined with launching herself at him and calling him baby? She signed her death certificate.

After forcibly removing Delilah's arms from around his neck, he cursed when he realized Quynh had taken off to the apartment upstairs. He wasn't fast enough to catch her before she slid the deadbolt home. The sound of it sliding into place was like a nail to his coffin.

He had some serious explaining to do, even if it was just a misunderstanding. Delilah was nothing to him except for a disgruntled, scorned ex-secretary whom he should have fired months before she pulled her last stunt, but he hadn't wanted to deal with the administrative work. He'd hoped she'd get the hint if he continued to ignore her advances, but obviously, she'd taken it as encouragement when he didn't follow through and let her go.

What a mistake.

A mistake that might cost him so much more.

He'd wait her out and give Quynh some time to cool down. It would also help if he didn't commit murder. Jail time would put a damper on his case. It would be hard to talk to her when he was behind bars.

So, even though it pained him to walk away, Griffin forced himself to move away from the locked door. He'd banged his forehead on the door when he realized it was futile, short of kicking the door down, but then he'd have to fix it. Worse, he didn't want to scare her with his antics.

He was an adult. A grown man with impulse control. Even if inside, he wanted to rage like the caveman he was. He wanted to kick down the door, toss Quynh over his shoulder, march her across the street, and lock her up in his bedroom. He might give her a good spanking to let her know how frustrated he was with the situation. Then he'd kiss it all better.

When he stomped back down the stairs, Delilah was wringing her hands in the lobby. He had no idea what she was waiting for. If running off after another woman wasn't a clue, Griffin wasn't sure how much more obvious he could be.

"Delilah. What the fuck are you doing here?" The words were low and laced with a threat. If Delilah were smart, she'd run back through those doors she waltzed through before it was too late for her.

"I missed you," Delilah practically whimpered, tears shining brightly in her big blue eyes. They did nothing for him, though. No, if anything, it angered him to think the woman he cared about was upstairs thinking the worst of him because of the person standing in front of him right now.

"You need to leave." Hands on his hips, Griffin's withering stare would make any grown man shake in his boots.

"I brought you and the boy's lunch!" Her shriek was grating to his ears. As if she thought the sight of food would soften his resolve towards her.

"Thanks, but no thanks." Griffin resisted the urge to forcibly remove her from the premises. Delilah did enough damage. If she stayed a second longer, who knew what other trouble she could get into?

"It's from your favorite pizza place..." Delilah's lower lip quivered. Griffin sighed and brought a hand to rub at his face. His frustration was evident in the tense muscles of his shoulders.

"Delilah, I am going to say this for the last time." Griffin ran a hand through his hair before leveling her with a glare. "You are not welcome on the property anymore. If you return, I will call the cops and have you removed."

He stared unmoving as tears started falling.

"But...I love you." She sniffed through her tears.

Griffin scoffed.

Love? What did this twenty-something know about love?

Outside of work and shared lunches, they had nothing in common. He was almost two decades older than her, for god's sake!

"You're a young woman who has her whole life ahead of her. I am not who you think I am." Griffin tried to soften the blow. "But you need to leave, or I will call the cops for trespassing."

Griffin handed Delilah a box of tissues and tried not to wince when she blew her nose. She tossed the used tissues into the trash can before offering him a watery smile. After another awkward moment, she finally left with her shoulders hunched and tail between her legs. He waited to see her car leave the parking lot before he went back to the garage bay. He rang the bell to let the guys know he had an announcement, and when Julio and Sean stopped their tasks, he told them about the pizzas waiting in the lobby.

Though the food smelled delicious, Griffin lost his appetite. His stomach was in knots over the woman upstairs. He hoped she'd let him explain what she overheard.

He was finishing up the final touches to Henderson's car when he got a message from Ricky asking him for a favor.

Griffin did not want to leave without talking to Quynh, but in this case, he didn't have much of a choice.

He just hoped she would be more willing to talk to him when he got back.

And it wasn't too late to set things straight.

31

Quynh went through every range of emotion possible. First, she was in disbelief at what she overheard. She didn't want to think the worst was possible, but there was no denying what that woman called Griffin.

Second, there was anger at his audacity. If Griffin was seeing other women, he could have been upfront with her from the get-go instead of implying he was a single bachelor.

How dare he lead me on like that!

Third, after anger was irrational rage. She wasn't sure if it was an actual step in the grieving process, but what she knew was how the thought of his betrayal incensed her. It was as if there was a raging inferno living inside of her at the thought of Griffin lying to her. Coupled with Ruth's abrasive encounter, she was ready to erupt.

Am I perfect? No. But I do not deserve to be lied to or

cheated on. Did he cheat on me? Am I the other woman in this scenario?

She had so many questions, but she was far too emotional to have a rational conversation at this moment.

She needed time and space. Quynh needed to be alone to sort out her own thoughts and feelings. During her rage, she spotted her suitcase poking out from the closet and packed her meager belongings into it. It didn't take her long, and she realized she couldn't leave town without a very important person. Pickles. Who was still at Griffin's place.

Quynh cursed her luck. Of course, she would need to get the grumpy cat before she could make a getaway. This only made things more uncomfortable if she ran into Griffin before she was ready.

Her phone dinged on the bed just then. She approached it slowly. Not wanting to see who messaged her, but also dying to know. Griffin's name lit up her phone with an unread message.

She ignored it. She needed to stay strong. She collapsed on the bed and buried her head under the pillow. Quynh resisted the urge to scream, not knowing how thin the walls were.

She wasn't sure how long she stayed lying there, letting her thoughts spiral, when she heard the garage bay doors shutting. Quynh rushed to the window and peeked through the slits of the blinds as she watched

Griffin's muscled back as he walked across the street. Rover ran happily along his side, but instead of going inside the house, she watched as he got into the truck and drove off toward town.

Quynh frowned. This deviated from his normal routine, but she wasn't about to look a gift horse in the mouth. Jumping into action, Quynh grabbed her suitcase and ran down the stairs. Her car keys were already in hand by the time she made it to the parking lot. She popped the trunk and threw the suitcase in it before shutting it with a loud bang.

Hurriedly, she ran across the street, across Griffin's yard, and opened the front door. She found Pickles's carrier in the hallway closet and went in search of the creature. He hated the carrier, but there wasn't much she could do at the moment. Normally, she'd sweeten up the deal with loads of catnip and treats, but time was of the essence. Who knew when Griffin would be back, and she had a long drive ahead of her.

She found Pickles snoozing on the bed. It wasn't long before she wrestled him into the carrier, and she was out the door with a growling Pickles. She let out a breath of relief when Griffin's truck was nowhere in sight.

At the end of the driveway, she turned around to look at the colonial that felt more like home than her apartment after just a few weeks. A small smile touched her lips as she turned away and made her way back to Shelly.

Gently, she placed Pickles in the back and adjusted her mirrors before turning the ignition. She took in a deep breath, squared her shoulders, and put the car in drive.

There was no turning back now.

She needed to leave, and it was now or never.

Quynh knew she was being a coward, leaving before talking to Griffin, but she needed to do this.

She just hoped she wouldn't live to regret this.

32

Griffin cursed as he sped down Main Street. Ricky's favor ended up taking him a couple of hours longer than he expected. A couple of hours too long to leave Quynh alone. He hoped the time apart allowed her to cool down, but all it did for him was ratchet his anxiety to unbearably high levels. It had been ages since he'd experienced this restlessness.

The last time the anxiety rode him this hard, he was still abusing narcotics and alcohol, using substances to dull his senses when life became too overwhelming. An unhealthy coping mechanism passed down by his deadbeat father. His mother left them when he was barely a toddler.

Whenever his father was reminded of his mother, it would often send his father into a rage. A flurry of fists against his small body until his father decided his belt would do a better job. His cries for help went unanswered until he learned not to make a sound. There was nobody around to help him. Nobody cared enough about him to bother.

The cycle of abuse continued for years. Unfortunately, the brutal beatings he endured left a permanent mark on his already dark soul. One he spent years trying to purge with drugs and alcohol, but nothing ever seemed to work.

His father died following a brawl that broke out when he was at the bar downtown, his favorite hangout spot every weekend. Griffin was usually left to fend for himself when he went on his binges. He enjoyed the short reprieve, even if he'd known the beatings tended to be worse when his father came crawling back to him. Except that night, his father pissed off the wrong person. A witness reported he instigated the fight by insulting someone's wife. His father was shoved so hard his head cracked on the sidewalk. He never got back up again.

Griffin was just about fourteen years old when the police came to their rundown home to notify him. He should have been upset, but all he remembered was a great sense of relief at knowing his father could never hurt him again.

Though Griffin tried to stay straight when he entered the foster system, he didn't stray too far away from his father's footsteps. He spent the next few years of his wasted youth finding the bottom of the bottle and fucking any willing woman he could. Eventually, alcohol turned into pills.

Nothing he did ever drowned out his father's screams or blocked the memories of his meaty fists flying toward his face. The drugs and alcohol helped, but even those were a brief reprieve until his next high.

Though it was a difficult habit to break, Griffin had a rude awakening when he killed his best friend. While Griffin walked away from the wreck, there was no denying that life had stopped for both of them. It had been an accident, but it never negated the incessant guilt he'd been living with ever since that night. Sometimes, it was as if the guilt ate away at his sanity like acid, corroding his will to live.

Brian had been a year older than him. They practically grew up together and shared deadbeat dads and nonexistent mothers. Brian was always the life of the party, often working with the dealers to get them the next hit. Marijuana, cocaine, pills, alcohol...it didn't really matter much to them.

They were at Brian's dealer's place, drinking, smoking, and enjoying any willing pussy. Normally, Griffin would drive them home, but that night, he hit the bottle a little too hard and had done too many lines. Brian volunteered to drive the pair across town.

The drive was normally fifteen minutes, but Brian jumped on the highway, traveling in the wrong direction.

Griffin had been unconscious in the passenger seat. As their car struck a semi-truck, the impact slammed him against his seatbelt, jolting him awake as pain seared his chest. The car flipped end over end before plunging into a ditch. His ears rang as the screeching noises of metal being crushed echoed around him.

When the car finally rolled to a stop, they ended up upside down. The roof of the car crushed beneath his head. The disorienting angle of his body hanging upside down, held in place in his seat only by his seatbelt, snapped him out of his drunken stupor. He'd yelled for Brian, who hadn't uttered a single noise. Frantically, he'd tried to unbuckle himself but was kept pinned in place by the mangled metal surrounding him.

The rattling sounds of twisted metal, shattered glass, screeching tires, and the sounds of his near-death experience still haunted him. The flashing lights, the metallic shriek of the jaws of life tearing through metal, and the pungent smell of gasoline replayed in his mind like a personal horror movie. A nightmare he couldn't escape.

Thankfully, by some divine intervention, he remembered to buckle up.

Brian died on impact. A blessing in hindsight he didn't suffer for long. The gruesome image of his mangled face will forever haunt his nightmares.

Being so incapacitated, he hadn't been able to help his friend when he needed him most. It was something he would have to live with for the rest of his life. The blood alcohol levels were so high in their systems that it would have warranted jail time, but somehow, he walked away with merely a few cuts and bruises.

His car was completely wrecked. After the hospital released him, he walked to the bus station. With the spare change in his pocket, he'd taken the bus back into town and gotten off near the auto shop where they kept his vehicle to claim it. Old Man Murphy owned the only auto shop in town. He'd taken one look at Griffin and walked off.

Griffin wasn't sure what to make of the grumpy old man, but he wasn't one to judge. He'd spotted his mangled car at the end of the lot. Even from a distance, he could tell it was divine intervention he was able to walk away from such a wreck. The thought sobered him. A turning point in his miserable life.

It was probably an hour or so later when Murphy found him sitting against his destroyed car. He'd been unimpressed with Griffin, but he must have seen something in him. Something he found worth redemption. The next thing he knew, Murphy offered him a job. It would be off the books, and he would be paid under the table, but Murphy needed an extra set of hands around the shop. His only condition was that he not use drugs or alcohol while working for him.

One act of tragedy and one of kindness permanently changed the course of Griffin's life.

Murphy set him up with the unfinished apartment above the shop with the condition he could live there as long as he fixed up the place. A task Griffin took on happily. Up until that point, he'd been couch surfing. It was nice to call a place his own.

At first, Murphy only allowed him to help with the small tasks around the shop, like cleaning or organizing the tools or mopping the floors. Sometimes, he answered the phone, but for some strange reason, Murphy didn't let Griffin do that often.

Keeping his hands busy kept his mind calm. His old habits tried to reel him back in, but he avoided everyone from his previous life, effectively isolating himself from his past. Though his future was still bleak, he had a purpose for the first time in a while.

Eventually, Murphy encouraged Griffin to get his high school diploma. He would go to night school after he was done at the shop, but eventually, he earned his diploma. Once the diploma was in hand, Murphy taught him how to fix engines. It was a skill that came naturally to him. With two pairs of hands working at the shop, they could take in more work.

Murphy died in his sleep nearly a decade ago. Murphy was widowed and didn't have kids to call his own. In a twist of fate, he left the auto shop in Griffin's name with the demand he rename it Griffin's Auto Body.

Thoughts of the old man who changed his life made him nostalgic. If not for Murphy, he could only guess where his life would have led him. Probably down the same path as his worthless father. Dead in the ground.

His tires squealed when he pulled to a stop in his driveway. The keys were still in the ignition when he'd jumped out of the truck. He ran across the street, not even bothering to check for oncoming traffic. Luck was on his side that he didn't get hit by a speeding car as he raced into the shop. He barely took notice of how the office was neatly organized as he barreled down the hallway. His footsteps echoed in the stairwell as he took the steps two at a time.

"Quynh!" His voice sounded desperate, even to his own ears. He pounded on the door a few times, giving her the illusion of choice before he kicked the door down. He paced the hallway, but when he still heard nothing on the other side, he tried the door handle.

It was unlocked.

His heart dropped. Suddenly, he wasn't sure what to expect.

The door creaked open ominously. He could sense she was gone before he even stepped one foot inside the doorway. The energy in the apartment was dull. She took her sunshine with her when she left.

Now, all he was left with were the memories of her smiling face.

Griffin resisted the urge to punch a hole in the wall. He'd only have to fix it later, and he had other things to worry about.

Even knowing she was gone, he still checked the bedroom. Finding it empty, an ache started in his chest, spreading deeper into his core.

She couldn't have at least waited for me? After everything we've been through, don't I deserve a chance to explain?

"Fuck!" His barely controlled rage was a volcano waiting to erupt. He needed to get out of here.

Belatedly, he wondered if she took the damn cat with her. Though a seedling of hope was buried beneath layers of frustration, it was quickly squashed when he found his house empty of the feline creature.

She would need to return, eventually, didn't she?

After all, she still had her father and stepsister. Griffin knew how important those budding relationships were for her. He didn't think she would abandon them. Maybe he didn't deserve a second chance, but he knew Quynh well enough that she wouldn't let the opportunity of having a relationship with the last remaining members of her family go to waste.

What did it make me? Someone expendable in her life?

He couldn't help but think as he jumped in the shower and washed away the dirt clinging to his skin.

Quynh was just a woman. He'd lived his whole life before her and was fine. He could do it again.

The lies he told himself tasted bitter even to himself.

His heart would never recover from her departure.

Griffin's biggest regret was not telling her how much she meant to him when he still had her in his arms.

Now, it was too late.

She was gone.

33

The drive away from Willowbrook was harder than she thought possible. The further she drove, the more painful it was. Almost as if she was leaving her heart behind while her body traveled away from its home. Her heart and her mind warred with each other, cleaving her apart until she could barely make sense of what was left.

When she crossed over state lines, though, the gut-wrenching sensation of having her heart ripped in half was visceral. A bloody mess left oozing in her chest. She never realized how painful leaving Griffin would be. Instead of turning the car around, she soldiered on. Focused on her navigation app as it directed her back to her old life. She kept the radio off. She didn't need to hear anyone else's heartbreak. Hers was enough to last her ten lifetimes.

About a few hours away from the city, she pulled over and pretended to fuel up at the gas station while the tears started up again. They finally stopped falling when she was about an hour outside of city limits.

You're being ridiculous.

She was acting as if she were in love and was leaving him far behind.

Love.

What a scary concept.

Was this love?

A deep sense of dread at the idea of no longer seeing Griffin's grumpy face or how her life now seemed colorless at the prospect of being on her own. Again.

She missed Griffin more than she should for someone she really only knew for a few weeks.

Was it even possible to love someone in such a short time?

The sex was amazing. Their connection seemed to transcend anything she ever thought was possible. Griffin knew her body better than she did.

The way he seemed to know what she needed, even when she didn't have a clue. Or how he cooked for her and made sure she always had a full plate of warm food to eat. And the adorable way he'd frown when she didn't clean her plate, as if he was worried she was too skinny.

She couldn't forget the way he'd begrudgingly showered Pickles with affection when he thought Quynh wasn't looking. Griffin often complained about the cat, but the way he cared for Pickles was in opposition to his grousing. Beneath his gruff exterior was a heart so big it would swallow her whole if she wasn't careful.

The thought terrified her.

Can I trust another person with my heart?

Everyone in her life had left her. Her past relationships proved it. Even her aunt and mother left her behind. And her father was close to leaving her behind, too.

Ruth was a different story. Things seemed irredeemable with her, but with time, she hoped there would be a relationship between them. Even if it were a fragile thread holding them together at the moment. She was probably a fool for hoping to be able to nurture a relationship with the prickly woman.

And what about my career?

She had still done nothing to salvage it. The prospect of returning to a job that was so soul-sucking did not make her happy. The thought of wasting all those years of school, training, and mountains of student debt overwhelmed her. It seemed foolish to throw all of it away just because it didn't make her happy.

When did life become so messy?

Am I better off where I'm headed? Back to the city where I was alone, but life was predictable?

Quynh knew the answer, but she wasn't ready to acknowledge it.

The sting of Griffin's betrayal was too fresh. The harsh

words Ruth threw at her were just salt to the wound. It was all too much for one person to handle.

She'd turned all of her notifications off so she wouldn't be distracted while making the eight-hour drive. Quynh needed to be alone. She needed to figure out what she wanted.

It was now or never.

34

Quynh had been gone for two weeks. He'd tried to call her after he realized she had left town, but didn't leave a message when her voicemail picked up. Hearing the sound of her voice sent a fresh stab of pain through his chest. His stomach has been in knots ever since she left town. He'd typed up a hundred messages but never sent them.

Words were inadequate.

Life continued on in the shop as if she were never there, but her absence was like a missing limb. Julio and Sean asked him where Quynh was, but they didn't press for answers when all he managed to do was growl at them in response. He didn't have it in him to go into the office and see how she took care of his business. Everything she touched was better for it. He knew the office was spotless and well-organized. He possessed half a mind to go in there and make a mess so he wouldn't be reminded of her in there anymore. Griffin didn't even bother answering the phones at the risk of biting off the heads of anyone on the other line.

Even his bed felt empty without her and that mangy cat of hers warming it. His sheets still smelled like her sweet vanilla scent. Griffin stopped sleeping in his bed for fear her scent would disappear completely. He couldn't handle knowing all traces of her were gone.

It was pathetic how he was moping over a woman. Someone he barely even knew, no less. But he was man enough to admit when he missed her. He missed waking up next to her. Her face being the first thing he saw when he woke up was something he took for granted. If he ever got a second chance, he'd never take any moment spent with her for granted ever again.

Griffin was banging around under the hood of a Ford Escalade when he lost his grip on the wrench. Letting out a growl of frustration, he backed up and kicked the tire. If not for his steel-toed boots, he'd break his foot for sure.

"Whoa, there, buddy. You okay?" The sound of Sean's worried voice made him whip his head around with a snarl.

"I'm fine," he spat out between clenched teeth.

"You seem fine..." Sean replied, though he was obviously being sarcastic.

The urge to tell Sean to fuck off was strong, but Griffin resisted. Barely.

"Listen, uh, I know it's been slow around here, so if you need to take off for a couple days or anything, you know Julio and I can handle the shop while you're away, don'tcha?"

"What do you mean?"

"Oh, nothing. I was just saying if you wanted to go chase after that city girl of yours, she left her address on her invoice."

Her address on the invoice?

As if a lightbulb went off, he realized Sean was right. When she ordered the parts he'd needed to fix her beater, she'd left her contact information behind.

Why didn't I think of that?

"It's alright, buddy. You've been a little preoccupied." Sean chuckled at Griffin's expression.

Griffin moved to punch Sean in the shoulder, but he was too slow. Must be his old age slowing him down.

"Well, go on. Get outta here, already!" Sean's shout made Griffin jump into gear.

If he left in the next twenty minutes, he could probably make it there in time to find a hotel to crash for the night before trying to look for her apartment.

"Thanks, Sean," Griffin shouted over his shoulder before running across the street to shower and change. He couldn't show up smelling like grease and motor oil. He'd have to figure out what he wanted to say when he got there. There were plenty of miles between him and his prize.

When he got out of the shower, he threw on a pair of jeans and a long-sleeved tee. He grabbed his phone off the nightstand and opened up her message thread.

GRIFFIN

I miss you.

He probably should have said something more, but it was the most important thing he wanted to tell her at the moment. Whistling to Rover, he grabbed his car keys, and the two of them jumped into his truck.

"You ready to go get our girl back?" he asked Rover, who barked in response and licked his face. "Gross." Griffin shoved Rover's face away.

He pulled up to the auto shop and ran into the office. It didn't take him long to locate the invoice. Snapping a picture of her information, he put the address into his navigation app and ran back out the door.

He could hear Julio and Sean whistling and laughing at him as he ran like his ass was on fire.

Griffin was a man on a mission.

He had a woman to bring back home.

35

 wo weeks.

It's been two whole weeks since she made her dramatic exit from Willowbrook. Away from Ruth. From Griffin. Instead of giving Griffin a chance to explain, she fled town like a coward.

In hindsight, she knew a small part of her left because of Ruth, but a bigger part of her knew it was because she was scared of having her heart broken. Of being vulnerable. Again. But with Griffin, it was different. She wouldn't have survived the heartbreak if he had been lying to her the whole time they were together. Even if they had only been together for a few weeks.

She was the happiest she had ever been in all of her adult life. Which was saying a lot, considering her age. She worked hard for her college degree and a successful career. Well, she considered herself to be pretty successful before she was fired. And her boss possibly committing insurance fraud.

Her heart ached as more time passed.

And they said distance would make things easier.

She scoffed. If anything, she felt worse as the days passed.

Most nights, she'd cry herself to sleep thinking about what she walked away from.

Did he even miss me?

She'd only seen one missed call from him, and he didn't leave a voicemail. Quynh resisted the urge to text him. She needed to figure out her life first.

What do I even have to offer a man like Griffin right now except for the broken pieces of myself?

Instead of being abandoned, she left Willowbrook behind in a delusional attempt at controlling her situation. All she ended up doing was making a bigger mess of her life.

During the daytime, she kept herself busy with fixing her resume and looking for jobs around the city. There were dozens of positions she was more than qualified for, but nothing seemed appealing. The idea of going back to long hours in the clinic, followed by long hours working from home every night, didn't seem appealing to her.

She realized losing her job was a blessing in disguise. It pulled her out of a haze of her own making. The burnout she experienced was so pervasive, she assumed it was a normal part of her life. Except when she worked for

Griffin at his shop. Only then did she realize what it was like to actually enjoy what she was doing. Not to mention, her creative juices started flowing again.

Quynh recalled a time when she wanted to be a writer. She spent some time writing short novels and fan fiction, but when her aunt became ill, she realized a career as an author was not what would help pay her bills. Having close proximity to her aunt's declining health and then her mother's subsequent demise opened Quynh's eyes to the role of nurses. At first, she went to nursing school and worked in the field for a couple of years before deciding to further her education to get her master's degree. She'd landed a job as a nurse practitioner before she even graduated at a prestigious practice affiliated with the local major health corporation.

She'd tucked her head down and soldiered on despite her unhappiness. Through her years of hard work, she squirreled away a healthy nest egg. It was a bonus her employer paid to move her and for her housing. Her lease would be up at the end of the year. She'd have to figure out her next steps soon. She couldn't push it off any longer.

Sitting in her living room with her laptop open to the job listings, Quynh resisted the urge to scream. All she wanted to do was lie in bed with a tub of ice cream and mope. But doing so meant she'd have to think about

Griffin and how much she missed him. She missed everything about him.

How can I miss someone I barely know so much? How much time is appropriate to get to know a person?

Her mother and father's courtship was brief before she ended up pregnant, and look how well that turned out.

Did the passage of time dictate how well you knew someone? Or, is it true 'when you know, you know'?

It wasn't like either of them was in their early twenties anymore. At this stage in her life, Quynh knew what she wanted out of a relationship. And, right now, that person was Griffin.

Thoughts of what their future might have looked like if she were brave enough to stay taunted her. She imagined what it would be like to be a permanent resident of Willowbrook. To be within walking distance of everything she needed. She imagined herself still working at Griffin's auto shop while writing during the downtime. Maybe she'd be able to finish the book she'd been thinking about writing for the past few weeks. Her parents' tragic love story inspired her to rewrite their history.

What if they ended in a happily ever after instead of how it really turned out?

Her mother's translated journals added some necessary background historical and cultural elements to their story.

She'd been so excited at the thought of writing a book. It was a small and humble dream, but it was hers. Reality was a much harder pill to swallow. Eventually, she'd run out of funds to fuel her passion. She didn't want to consider being broke, homeless, and living off of ramen again.

Her stomach gurgled at the thought of food. She'd forgotten to eat breakfast, and now it was nearing lunchtime. The fridge was empty of any fresh food, and all she had were some stale chips and Pop-Tarts. The thought of eating made her queasy. She missed Griffin's home-cooked meals.

She missed Griffin.

Her thoughts always circled back to Griffin.

Pickles let out a grumble as she flopped back on the couch. She let out a big sigh as she stared up at her popcorn ceiling.

What a fucking mess.

Just as she was contemplating whether she should just woman up and call Griffin, there was a loud buzzing at her door. Frowning, she swung her legs off the couch and got up. The buzzer sounded again. She rarely had visitors unless it was for food delivery, but she hadn't ordered anything to be delivered today.

Pressing the talk button, she leaned in to speak into the speaker box.

"Hello?"

"Quynh. It's me," a deep, gravelly voice sounded through her apartment.

She knew exactly who 'me' was. Griffin. He was here.

He was here! Wait, why was he here?

36

"Quynh. Let me up."

She tried to suppress the shiver going through her at the sound of his low voice. With a deep breath to steady her nerves, she pressed the button quickly before she could change her mind. She heard the faint click as the lock disengaged.

Oh, God. He was really here. What do I do?

Quynh bit her short nails and paced the small walkway. She lived on the third floor, so it would take Griffin some time to find her apartment. She was thankful for the extra time, using it to take deep breaths and shake the tremor from her hands, hoping to calm her racing heart.

Suddenly, she realized how disheveled she appeared. Her hair was a hopeless mess of tangles on top of her head. She was in the most unattractive outfit she owned —an oversized sweatshirt riddled with holes that drowned her petite frame. A relic from her nursing school days. Her stained sweatpants hung loosely around her hips. Unfortunately, it was much too late to make herself presentable. She was not expecting visitors. At least she remembered to brush her teeth this morning.

All too soon, there was a loud knock on the door, making her jump. The sound seemed to echo in her otherwise quiet apartment.

It was now or never. Time to face the music. The impending encounter sent a jolt of adrenaline through her, making her heart hammer against her ribs with a frantic rhythm.

Another loud knock at the door made her jump, and her muscles tensed. She padded toward the door on socked feet. Her shaky hands, trembling with a mixture of fear and anticipation, were inches from the deadbolt when another, more forceful knock rattled the door frame, making her jump back.

"Alright, alright!" *So impatient.* She let out a puff of air in annoyance as she unlocked the door and yanked it open.

Nothing could have prepared her for what came next. Standing in front of her was her grumpy mechanic. He looked worse for wear, with his tousled hair and unkempt beard. She never saw him look so tired before and briefly wondered what put the bags under his eyes. Come to think of it, he seemed to have lost a bit of weight.

Still, she thought he looked like an absolute snack.

And she was starving. Quynh took a moment to feast her eyes on the sight gracing her doorstep.

"Quynh. You're drooling."

Her head whipped back in indignation.

She was not drooling.

"I was not drooling!" Her face heated when she realized he was joking. God, it was so good to see his grumpy face light up as a small smile stretched across his face. A smile she caused. It did dangerous things to her heart and made her want to jump into his arms and profess her undying love and devotion to him.

"Are you going to let me in?" His eyebrow quirked up at the question. Though she didn't kid herself into thinking she had a choice in the matter. She knew if she didn't let him in, he'd likely kick the door down.

Griffin must have driven the whole night to get here, judging by his wrinkled appearance.

Instead of answering his rhetorical question, she slowly stepped aside and pressed her body into the wall. Quynh held her breath as he walked past so she wouldn't get a whiff of his intoxicating scent. It was dangerous to have a predator in her safe space. She'd have to keep her guard up, or else she'd fall prey to his tricks.

She shut the door hesitantly before turning around to face her new visitor. Leaning against the closed door, she watched as Griffin looked around her small apartment. The living room was separated by a counter, which led into the small kitchen. Her tiny bathroom was nestled between her bedroom and the living room. It wasn't much, but it was hers.

She tried not to gasp in outrage when Pickles emerged from her bedroom and sauntered right up to Griffin. He wound his fluffy body around Griffin's legs, demanding attention. She barely got the same greeting from the furry traitor.

Quynh watched as Griffin bent down on one knee to give Pickles a chin scratch in greeting. Pickles's purrs of pleasure could be heard from across the room as Griffin continued to shower him with affection. Quynh's knees became weak from watching the two males in her life reunite. She probably would have ended up on the floor in a puddle if not for the door holding her up.

After a couple of moments, Griffin cleared his throat and looked up at her from his kneeling position.

"Wha-what are you doing here?" she asked.

"Isn't it obvious?"

With eyebrows furrowed in confusion, she shook her head slowly.

"I came here for you." His gruff voice made her core clench with need, but his words made her heart stop.

"For me?"

"You left without letting me explain." Griffin's words were like a knife slicing through her chest.

She knew this was coming; of course, she did, but the

reality of the situation made her nervous. Quynh resisted the urge to run out the door and not look back. Instead, she took in a deep breath and squared her shoulders.

Griffin stood up from his crouched position and took a step toward her. His steps were slow and measured as he advanced, as if he was aware of how much she wanted to retreat. She watched him warily, resisting the urge to press further into the door. He approached her like she was a wounded animal, giving her time to adjust to his presence, letting her know she was safe with him. She would always be safe with him.

Finally, after what seemed like hours but was only seconds in reality, they stood toe to toe. Her breath hitched in her throat at having him within reach after so long. She clenched her fists and glued them to her side to stop them from reaching toward him. The urge to run her hands up his hard chest to reassure her this wasn't a dream was nearly impossible to resist. Instead, she focused on her breathing as her eyes trailed up to meet his eyes.

His green eyes collided with hers. She was caught in his trap. Helpless. Transfixed by the intensity of his gaze on her. The storm that had raged around her for weeks finally calmed to a quiet dullness, as if they were now in the eye of the storm.

She suddenly forgot why they were separated for so long, or why she was upset with him. Captivated by his gaze, she experienced the disorienting feeling of falling. He saw too much. It made her vulnerable.

The air crackled with tension between them. The air grew thick with anticipation as they studied each other. The hairs on the back of her neck stood on end as he slowly raised a hand. She closed her eyes in anticipation of his touch, but nothing could prepare her for how her skin erupted in goosebumps when his hand cupped her cheek. She leaned into his touch and almost whimpered in relief.

Finally, she could take a deep breath for the first time in weeks. His touch paradoxically soothed her and sent her pulse soaring.

Griffin's thumb brushed over something wet against her cheek. She wasn't aware she'd started crying until he wiped away her tears. His other hand came up to grip the back of her neck in a gentle hold. She opened her eyes and looked up at him beneath her wet lashes.

"Please don't cry, sunshine. You're breaking my heart." The rumbling of his voice resonated deep within her chest. "Shh. It's okay." He bent his head until his forehead touched hers. The tickle of his breath across her lips was a teasing caress. Quynh watched as he licked his lips as if he was itching to kiss her but held himself back. "I'm sorry."

What was he apologizing for?

Griffin must have seen the confusion on her face as he

cleared his throat and lifted his head, giving her some much-needed space from the temptation of his pouty lips.

"Nothing happened between Delilah and me. Nothing." He took in a fortifying breath as his grip tightened at the base of her neck, as if he was willing her to believe his words through his possessive touch.

Her eyes roamed over his face, taking in his pinched expression, lines bracketing his eyes as if he were in pain. His jaw was clenched so tightly she could see the muscle ticking as he fought for control.

She believed him.

She ignored the voice in her head whispering she was an idiot for believing him. Instead, she listened to what her heart was telling her for once. The same bleeding heart that wept for the man whose strong arms cradled her so gently, as if she were made of fine China and he wouldn't dare to break her.

She knew in the deepest parts of her heart he would never intentionally hurt her. She'd always known that about Griffin, but she let her insecurities about being vulnerable drive her decisions, letting her fears of being abandoned take her away from this man who likely drove all night to get to her.

With shaky hands, she reached up and gripped his forearms. Her throat was tight with emotions, and words escaped her, so she nodded as a fresh round of tears spilled over her lashes. Her lower lip quivered as she tried to get a handle on her raging emotions. Her breaths were shaky as she leaned her head back against the door; the contact grounded her in the moment.

"Sunshine, say something." His Adam's apple bobbed as he swallowed. "Please."

"I'm sorry, too." She sniffed, licking her dry lips as his face scrunched with confusion. "For leaving without talking to you first."

His face morphed into anger at the reminder she left him without a word.

"Never do that again. You hear me?" His grip on her tightened as he brought their bodies closer together. Her peaked nipples grazed his chest. She gasped at the sensation.

I should have worn a bra.

"Say it, sunshine." He shook her gently. "Say you'll never leave me again." A hand traveled down her side and gripped her waist as he melded their bodies together. He took a step forward so she couldn't escape with the door behind her and his solid form in front of her. She couldn't move an inch without rubbing herself all over him.

Her body was on fire. For the first time in weeks, she felt alive. Every nerve ending was electrified, making her body hum with energy and anticipation. Her core ached to be filled as her arousal dampened her panties. She nearly whimpered as the sensations overwhelmed her.

How did I go so long without feeling like this? Without Griffin?

She was a walking zombie until she met Griffin.

Her ears buzzed as she tried to form a coherent sentence. She nodded, though his tight grip restricted her movement.

"I need to hear you say it, sunshine." Griffin's low growl sent a pool of moisture to her pussy. She gulped.

"I'll never leave you again." Her words were raspy, but the vow in the words echoed between them.

Griffin's eyes bounced over her face. She watched as his expression changed from cold determination to wicked glee.

His lips came crashing down in a possessive kiss. His tongue forced her lips open as he claimed her thoroughly with each stroke of his wicked tongue. Their teeth clashed as he continued to dominate her. She loved every second of it as she relinquished complete control to him, answering his demands with promises of her own, both asking for forgiveness with their dueling tongues. Their kiss conveyed more than words ever could.

Before she knew it, he let go of her abruptly, leaving her bereft at the loss of his touch. Her lips tingled from the onslaught. Quynh reached up a hand to touch her sensitive lips. Griffin backed up a couple of steps. She watched as his hands went to his belt. He started undoing his belt buckle. The clanging of the metal was loud in the otherwise quiet apartment.

She thought she knew what fear was like before. It was nothing compared to this. Quynh wasn't scared Griffin would hurt her. No. She knew he had decided on what her punishment was for leaving him. Whatever it was, she wouldn't walk away from it the same person.

The sound of his zipper dragging down made her quiver in anticipation. She fought the urge to cross her arms across her chest as she watched his careful movements. She marveled at the way his dark, tanned hands looked against the blue denim of his jeans as he revealed a dark patch of hair. The outline of his cock pressed against his pant leg. It looked painfully erect, and her mouth watered when it bounced free of its denim restraint. The tip of his cock was already wet with pre-cum. No boxers, she noted.

Quynh licked her dry lips as he pushed the jeans down to reveal his balls hanging beneath his curved cock. Griffin gripped the base of his cock and stroked himself a few times while he watched her. She knew he was watching her by the heat of his stare on her face, though nothing could pull her eyes away from watching Griffin as he milked his cock.

She wanted a taste.

Quynh realized she had never tasted him before, and now all she wanted to do was feel him sliding against her tongue. She wanted to taste the bead of pre-cum and see if she could coax more out of him. She wondered how long it would take for him to explode down her throat.

Clenching her thigh at the unbearable ache which had intensified since seeing him, she looked up to meet his eyes. With one hand still wrapped around his cock, he pointed to her and then to the ground.

"Get on your knees, sunshine." His command was low, but it left no room for argument. "You're going to learn what happens when you misbehave."

It looks like she'd get her wish after all.

Slowly, Quynh lowered herself to her knees. She sat back on her heels and looked up at Griffin. He seemed so large and imposing standing above her. She knew without a doubt he would never hurt her. Not unless it was something she wanted. And right now, she wanted his brand of punishment.

In her kneeling position, she was even achier with her heels pressed into her groin. Quynh resisted the urge to rub herself against her own feet as she waited for Griffin to make a move.

His eyes were hooded with lust as he gave himself leisurely strokes. Griffin seemed pleased with what he saw as he took a couple of steps to breach the distance between them.

"Now, open your mouth, sunshine," he said as he rubbed the tip of his cock across her lips, rubbing the pre-cum over her face like he was painting. "You're going to let me fuck that sweet throat of yours until I come, and you're going to swallow every last drop of it, you hear me?"

Quynh gave a jerky nod and opened her mouth as moisture soaked through her panties at his order. Her hands gripped her thighs when he pushed the tip of his cock into her parted lips, the taste of his pre-cum making her quiver with arousal. She fought the urge to moan as he continued to feed his cock into her willing mouth.

"Good girl." His hand gripped her hair as he angled her head the way he wanted. "Ah, fuck, you look so good with my cock in your mouth. I hope you're ready because this will not be sweet. Tap my thigh three times if you want me to stop."

His warning was barely out of his mouth before he started thrusting his hips. Griffin's thick cock slid in and out of her mouth. She tried to suction her lips around his length, but he grabbed her head with both hands and increased the pace of his thrusts.

When he hit the back of her throat, it brought tears to her eyes. He worked his way into her throat and held her head at the base of his cock, limiting her ability to breathe for what seemed like hours before pulling out and allowing her to take in a much-needed breath.

Quynh's saliva was everywhere. Tears streamed down

her face every time he hit the back of her throat and with-held her breath. It was messy. Sloppy. Wet.

She was so turned on she could come on the spot. All she needed was a gentle touch against her clit, and she'd erupt.

"Don't you dare touch that pussy. It's mine," he growled as he yanked her head back, bending over her to snarl in her face. Quynh hadn't realized her hand had inched its way toward her aching center. "Do you hear me?"

She nodded frantically. The tight grip on her hair was almost too painful, but she liked the bite of pain, judging by the fresh wave of arousal that gushed out of her center.

"Good girl. Now suck my cock."

She opened her mouth obediently as he shoved his cock deep inside her throat, making her gag on his cock.

"Fuck, that's it. Choke on my cock, sunshine." His pace quickened as his balls tightened. "I'm close."

It was the only warning she got before he shoved her head down his length until her nose touched the coarse hair at the base of his cock. Her hands came up reflexively to grip his thighs, helpless in his strong grip. His cock jerked and spasmed as hot spurts of cum spilled down her throat. In her position, she could barely breathe, much less swallow, as her saliva mixed in with his semen. Her throat spasmed reflexively as she gagged around his cock.

Finally, he pulled out, and she gulped in lungfuls of

air, trying to catch her breath. Griffin gripped her gently under the chin and tipped her head back so he could look at her face. He made a sound of approval as he used a thumb to wipe the corner of her mouth. He shoved the thumb into her mouth, and her lips closed around the digit reflexively. Griffin groaned as she sucked and pulled out his thumb with a pop.

"God, you look so good like this. I've been wanting to see you on your knees, choking on my cock, ever since I laid eyes on you. You're better than what I envisioned." Griffin bent down and kissed her hard on the lips, uncaring that the taste of him still lingered on her tongue.

Pulling back, Griffin tucked his semi-hard cock back into his jeans but left it undone before he bent down to pick her up under her arms. He hoisted her up and carried her bridal style into the adjacent bedroom.

He tossed her onto her unmade bed and pounced on top of her.

"Let's take care of this needy pussy, yeah?" She yelped as he yanked her pants and underwear off of her in one swift movement and dove in like a man starved.

She tossed her head back and groaned as his lips and tongue moved over her. Griffin's tongue teased at her opening, applying enough pressure to drive her crazy. Quynh was embarrassed; she was so close to the edge already, and he'd barely begun. Her thighs clenched around his head as she felt the telltale signs of her building climax. The pressure intensified as he switched gears and teased her clit with his wicked tongue. He flicked at the oversensitive bud as he worked two fingers into her slick opening. Instead of thrusting his fingers, he curled them as he laved her clit with attention. Her toes curled as her orgasm crested, making her thighs shake as she came on his tongue with a scream.

The pleasure rolled through her in waves as Griffin kept up his ministrations, wringing every ounce of her pleasure like a pro. She collapsed against the bed in a boneless heap and fought to catch her breath, the edges of her vision returning as reality came crashing down.

She closed her eyes as Griffin climbed out of bed. Quynh listened as he made his way into the bathroom. The sound of the water running seemed louder in the quiet space. She held still when he approached the bed and ran a damp towel between her legs.

She loved how he always took care of her needs before his own. And the way his touch was always so gentle. So reverent, as if he worshiped her body.

Tears clung to her lashes as she suppressed a sob. She wasn't sure why she was crying, other than the fact she walked away from this. From Griffin. He didn't deserve what she did. *She* didn't deserve a man like Griffin in her life.

Quynh sniffed as he finished cleaning her up. The bed dipped as he climbed in next to her.

"Hey. Look at me." His voice was soft. Gentle.

She could have easily turned away from him and pretended like she was fine. Instead, she took a deep inhale to steady her nerves and turned to face Griffin. The time for running away was over. Quynh needed to own her mistakes and make amends. She sent up a silent prayer to whoever might be listening that she didn't completely mess everything up.

Meeting Griffin's warm gaze, she wiped away her tears. "I'm sorry." Her voice was hoarse, and it broke on the last word. She only hoped he heard the sincerity in her voice. "I'm so, so sorry."

"Sorry?" His face scrunched with confusion. "You're sorry? For what?"

Quynh studied his baffled expression. He didn't seem angry at her, which gave her the strength she needed to continue.

"For leaving you. Before talking to you. About..." Her voice trailed off.

"No." She shrank away from him at the harsh tone. Griffin ran a hand through his hair, a sign she knew betrayed his agitation. Griffin cleared his throat. He brought his hand to cup her cheek. He turned her face to look at him as he stared down at her. "I meant...no, I'm the one who should be sorry. Not you."

Now it was her turn to be confused. Griffin blew out a breath and collapsed on his back with a groan.

"This is not going the way I imagined it would." He let out a self-deprecating chuckle as she sat up to look at him.

"What do you mean?"

"I came out here to apologize to you."

"For what?"

"For…well, being an idiot, for starters." He laughed before turning his head to look at her. "For letting you walk away thinking I had another woman in my life."

"Oh."

"There has been no other woman in my life since I met you." He paused, and she watched in fascination as his cheeks became flushed.

Oh my god, is he blushing?

"There is only one woman in my life," he finally said. "You are the only one I want in my life, Quynh."

If she were standing, she would have swooned. Luckily, she was lying in bed. Realizing she was half-naked, she reached down to pull the blankets to cover her. She fussed with the material, needing the distraction to buy her some time to form a proper answer.

Her stomach fluttered as she tried to form a coherent sentence.

She couldn't think of an adequate response to his statement.

Griffin's hand covered hers, still fidgeting with the blanket, halting her movements. The warmth of his hands soaked into her cold ones. It centered her and calmed her racing thoughts. Her fingers curled around his instinctively, solidifying their connection.

Her racing heart slowed even as heat crept through her body. It's unnerving how a simple touch could affect her so profoundly. Almost as if she was numb, her body encased in ice, until Griffin released her from the icy prison, warming not just her body but her heart and bringing her back to life.

She licked her lips. She met his eyes with determination.

"I'm scared," she admitted in a whispered voice, worried speaking them into existence would shatter the happy bubble they constructed around themselves.

"I know." His hand squeezed hers. "I am, too."

He didn't waste time giving her any platitudes. Instead, he pulled her body closer to his and tucked her head under his chin. His arm slid around her waist to cup her hip as their legs tangled together.

She lay on his chest with her ear pressed against his heart, the sound of its soothing rhythm lulling her back into a happy state. She felt safe. Secure. Loved.

Love?

Was this what being in love felt like?

Her experience with love was nonexistent. In the weeks since she left Griffin, she imagined this was the feeling she had been searching for. The fear of losing

Griffin forever made her sick to her stomach, while the thought of never seeing him again made her cry herself to sleep every night since leaving him behind. Or how her chest felt hollowed out like she was missing a vital organ. She was barely alive, yet her body continued to exist without the missing piece.

Quynh never wanted to feel that way again.

Now he was here, the hollow space was no longer empty.

37

At some point, they must have fallen asleep because the next thing she knew, she was being woken up by a desperate mewling. Jerking awake, she tried to sit up, only to be pulled back by powerful arms.

"What the..." The memories came back to her in pieces as she recalled how Griffin showed up on her doorstep. Her cheeks flushed as she relived the moments after that led her to be imprisoned by his steely embrace.

Pickles' wailing escalated to a fevered pitch when he realized she was awake. A glance at her bedside clock showed she was barely late with Pickles' dinner by a few minutes.

Rolling her eyes at the dramatic furball, who was acting as if he were starving to death, Quynh tried to wiggle out of Griffin's tight embrace. He grumbled in his sleep and squeezed her tighter to his chest. She was essentially a human teddy bear for the large, grumpy bear in her bed. He squeezed her so tightly it was almost hard for her to take a deep breath. She shoved at his chest, and he relaxed his hold slightly. Griffin glared through narrow slits at her.

"Let me go, you brute. I need to feed the animal before he eats my face." She sighed dramatically. The last thing she wanted was to deal with an extra irritable Pickles. He could be a real dick when he wanted to be.

Griffin merely closed his eyes without acknowledging her. Quynh let out a huffed breath as a smile stretched across her face when he refused to let her go. Just when she thought she'd have to figure out another way out, Griffin reluctantly loosened his hold, his fingers lingering on her arm a moment longer. She leaned over his sleepy form, planted a kiss on his pillowy lips, and whispered, "I'll be right back."

He grunted before letting his hand finally fall to the bed. Quynh made a hasty escape before he could change his mind, swiping up her discarded sweatpants from the bedroom floor and hopping into them as Pickles paced frantically in front of her. His meows became louder at the prospect of getting fed.

On bare feet, she padded into the kitchen for the wet food she kept in the cabinet. The sound of the can opening stirred another round of frantic meowing and pacing from Pickles. She'd barely placed the wet food into his food dish before he buried his whiskered face in it.

Quynh chuckled at the sounds he made while he devoured his dinner. You'd think she was starving the poor guy, not that he got fed wet food twice a day. And he had a steady stream of dry food throughout the day.

"What are you doing?" The sound of Griffin's gruff, sleep-raspy voice made her jump. Startled, she whirled around with her hand on her chest. She hadn't heard him approach.

"Feeding the dying rabid animal," she said. Her words came out more breathless than she intended. "I was late with his dinner. Pickles hates it when I'm late."

Once, she was stuck at work with a patient, which meant his dinner was delayed. She came home to her apartment completely trashed. He ripped through her couch pillows, which were more expensive than any pillows ever needed to be. Pickles pushed the glass cup she had left out on the counter over. The gleaming of the shattered glass and water taunted her when she finally came home.

After cleaning up the broken glass, she found another surprise in her bathroom. Pickles had completely unfurled her new roll of toilet paper. Lying in a heap of toilet paper was Pickles. Licking his paws. He gave her a mean side-eye and continued to clean himself. Pickles acted like he hadn't destroyed her apartment, and when she only gaped in outrage, he'd merely gotten up and sashayed past her. She knew exactly where Pickles was going. Right into the kitchen, where he sat pointedly staring at his empty food dish.

Since then, Quynh tried her hardest not to run late with a client. In the grand scheme of things, it was probably the least damage Pickles was capable of. His giant Maine Coon frame probably could break her window if he tried.

With Pickles happily chowing down on his food, Quynh straightened up and wiped down the countertop. She could sense the heat of Griffin's eyes on her as she moved around the kitchen. She shivered helplessly, trying to ignore the dull throbbing between her legs at the sound of his voice.

It was late evening, judging by the time on the oven. She ate nothing today, and her stomach growled in protest.

Quynh heard Griffin's muffled curse as he made his way into the kitchen. She turned around to see him open her fridge to look inside, though she winced when he slammed it shut a second later. Fighting the urge to slink back into the bedroom and hide from his wrath, she shifted her weight on her feet as she waited for Griffin to say something. She knew what he saw. Or didn't see. It was empty, and had been for some time.

"You don't have any food in here." Griffin's voice was a low, gravelly rumble sending shivers down her spine. She grimaced, knowing she was on shaky ground. Griffin stood with his back to her. The tightness in his muscles and the stiffness of his spine betrayed his simmering rage. His body was a coiled spring.

"When was the last time you ate anything?" The low growl resonated in Griffin's voice. Despite its quiet tone, she sensed the warning of an impending storm.

When she didn't answer him right away, he whirled around to face her. Quynh took a reflexive step back as he slowly approached her. His taut muscles, corded and tight, belied his barely controlled agitation. She gulped even as her panties became soaked with her arousal.

"Um...I can't remember." She gasped.

"You can't remember the last time you ate?" he echoed in disbelief.

"N-no...?" It shouldn't have been a question. She really couldn't remember what she ate.

Griffin stopped just short of her, hands planted firmly on his hips. His eyes burned with fury as he glared at her. His face was a mask of repressed rage. She knew he hated it when she forgot to eat. She had no excuses that would placate him. Quynh looked up at him from beneath her lashes as she worried at her lower lip between her teeth. His gaze softened, though she still sensed his ire. He stepped closer and wrapped his arms around her.

"You need to stop forgetting to eat," he whispered quietly against her hair. He pulled back to look down at her. "Or else." His face hardened with the looming threat.

His words hung heavy in the air. The unspoken menace in his words was clear enough. The thought of his punishment sent a shiver down her spine, a strange blend of dread and exhilaration she couldn't explain. It was an inappropriate reaction. When it came to her eating habits, she knew it wasn't worth provoking his anger. He was right.

"We can order delivery?" she offered, her voice coming out in a squeak, trying to placate her angry boyfriend.

Boyfriend? Is he my boyfriend?

"Fine. Only because we don't have time to go to the store to get ingredients to make a proper meal," he agreed begrudgingly.

"Okay," Quynh sighed, relieved to have avoided his anger this time, though she knew next time she wouldn't be so lucky.

He grabbed her hand and led her back into the bedroom. Quynh found her phone at the bottom of her bed. She snatched it up and looked up her favorite local Asian fusion restaurant, which offered a variety of Asian cuisine. It was expensive, but she was starving.

She put in her regular order and handed her phone to Griffin. While he figured out what he wanted to eat, she went to the bathroom to freshen up. Her hair was a tangled mess. She tried running a hairbrush through, but there was no use reviving the limp strands. She piled her hair high on top of her head and secured it in a messy bun.

Turning on the faucet, she washed her face, breathing in the calming aromas from her favorite foaming Korean facial cleanser as she washed traces of sleep away. She dried her face on a towel. Quynh debated for a quick second but decided it didn't hurt to brush her teeth again, even though she knew they'd be eating food soon.

Who doesn't want fresh breath?

Plus, it would be a miracle if they could keep their hands off each other before dinner arrived. The likelihood of that happening was slim to none. A pulse of excitement shot through her at the thought.

When she walked back out into the main living area, Griffin sat on her tiny couch. Pickles was curled up on his lap and purring contentedly as Griffin absentmindedly stroked the cat across its back. Pickles must have finished his meal and was now trying to steal her man's attention.

She huffed out an annoyed breath at being jealous of a cat getting Griffin's attention.

"Where's Rover?" Quynh asked as she settled into the seat next to Griffin.

"He's at Sean's house. I dropped him off on my way here." Griffin didn't take his eyes off the television, where he was scrolling through the options. She only subscribed to Netflix since she rarely spent time at home, nor did she enjoy watching television. She preferred to read, and her massive stack of books, which she needed to read, sat on the opposite side of the couch.

She glanced nervously at the titles. She wondered if he would be mad if he knew what she liked to read. She knew some men were insecure when women read romance, like it affected or challenged their own masculinity when, in reality, romance novels were her happy place. The smut was a bonus she enjoyed. It was a refreshing and safe way to explore her sexuality with no pressure. She found with Griffin, it was easier to let him take control. She absolutely loved it when he dominated her in the bedroom.

Would he let me take control?

She had a feeling he would. Griffin didn't seem to be the type of person to be emasculated by her desire to be in control. He'd never made a comment about her reading when she was staying at his apartment. Or when she was at his house.

Griffin picked out a show and set it on. He finally turned his full attention to her. Her body tingled with awareness at his hooded eyes. She knew what that look often led to, and her core pulsed with anticipation.

At her age, she never would have imagined she would still be interested in sex, but Griffin made her feel like a horny teenager for the first time in her life. She never felt this way about anyone else before.

Is it Griffin that made me feel this way?

"When will the food get here?" he asked nonchalantly.

"Um…" She pulled out her phone and opened the app to show her order status. "The app says about forty-five minutes." Quynh yelped as he picked her up and placed her in his lap. The movement dislodged Pickles from Griffin's lap, who meowed angrily before stomping away.

Something hard pressed against her bottom. Her phone clattered to the floor as her hands came up to clutch his shoulders. Quynh fought the impulse to squirm against the hard ridge pressing against her bottom. His cock was hard, taunting her with how close it was to her already-soaked center.

Suddenly, she was breathless at the memory of how his cock felt. The way his hard length stretched her, filling her empty core and making her see stars with every thrust. It had been weeks since he'd been inside her. The throbbing ache between her thighs pulsed in a relentless rhythm, making her desperate to have him inside of her again. To be close to him again.

Gulping, she took in a shaky breath. Her hand came up to the back of his neck and played with the soft strands of his dark hair. It had gotten longer during their separation.

"This is new." Her other hand gently rubbed against the bristles of his beard he'd let grow out.

"Hmmph." She smiled at Griffin's grunted response.

"I like it."

"Don't get used to it." Even as he burrowed his face into her hand, his soft bristles tickled her palm, reminding her of Pickles.

"Why not?"

"It's a pain in the ass," he said as if it was obvious.

"Oh. Well, it makes you look like a real grumpy bear."

The air in the room changed. She sensed his mood shift but ignored the threat.

"What did you call me?" His low voice deepened.

"I said," she continued, "you look like a real grumpy bear with that scowl on your face." I chuckled at his expression.

"That's it."

She squealed in shock as he flipped her over and began tickling her. Her peals of laughter echoed throughout the apartment.

"Oh my god, stop!" She begged between laughing breaths. "Please!"

After another moment of agonizingly sweet torture, Griffin finally relented, a sigh escaping his lips. He stared down at her as the sounds of the television filtered back into her awareness. She forgot it was even on, so engrossed she was with Griffin.

A warm smile bloomed on her face as she looked up at him. A weight lifted from her chest. Happiness bloomed inside her like a flower in spring. Her heart melted as she saw her own emotions reflected in his gentle gaze.

The intensity of her emotions overwhelmed her. She desperately wanted to confess her feelings. The words burned on the tip of her tongue, but she swallowed them down as a knot tightened in her throat. She wasn't sure if the time was right. The weight of her confession pressed down on her.

She loved him—so much it hurt. She could almost taste the regret, bittersweet on her tongue, as she thought of what she almost lost.

"Can I ask you something?" she said instead of what she really wanted to say.

"Yeah?" Griffin tilted his head as he studied her.

"What...I mean...Why are you here?" She avoided his gaze and picked at the imaginary lint on his shirt.

"I missed you." His voice rang with conviction. Their eyes met, and a strange, dizzying sensation washed over her like she was falling from a great height. Only this time, fear did not grip her. She let herself soak it in while lying securely in his arms. It was terrifying just as much as it was exhilarating.

Griffin leaned down until they were nose to nose, their breaths mingling. His hips nestled between her thighs as she cradled him. He didn't apply any pressure as their bodies met. A palpable tension crackled in the air between them.

"I came here for you." His words hovered above her lips.

"How did you know where to go?"

"Sean reminded me I had your address from the invoice when you first came in."

"Oh. That's smart." Quynh licked her lips and swallowed. "Are you still mad at me?"

He paused, thinking over his answer.

"Yes."

Her face fell, and she attempted to look away. His hand gripped her chin and turned her head so they were face to face. Griffin rested his forehead against hers, taking in a deep breath.

"I am mad that you left without talking to me. I wish you had let me explain. I've been worried about you for weeks." His admission made her stomach flutter.

He was worried about me?

"Why were you worried about me?"

"I always worry about you." He gestured with his head toward the kitchen. "You don't even have food in your kitchen. I didn't even know if you made it to your destination. You didn't call or text—"

"You didn't either..."

"I know. I should have, but I'm not good at this...relationship thing."

"Relationship?" Her heart skipped a beat.

"Yeah..." His cheeks flushed adorably.

"Are we…in a relationship? A knot of anxiety tightened in her stomach. She needed to be absolutely certain.

"You bet your ass we are. Did you think you could escape me a second time? I'm not letting you go that easily," he growled, his grip tightening.

"So does that mean you're…my…boyfriend?" Her voice was shy. Unsure. She reached up to tuck her hair behind her ear.

"I'm too old to be anyone's boyfriend," he said. At her disappointed expression, he continued. "But I'm definitely your man. And you're my woman."

"Your woman?"

I like the sound of that.

"My woman."

"Okay."

"Okay? That's all you have to say?" His voice cracked with astonishment.

"Well…yeah, what else do you want me to say to a grumpy bear that's smothering me beneath his weight?"

"Oh, so now you're calling me fat?" Griffin reared back, his eyes wide with a mocked, affronted look, a snort escaping his nostrils.

"I would never." She laughed and pushed at his chest in jest.

Griffin leaned down to kiss her. What started out sweet quickly became heated as he deepened the kiss.

When their tongues touched, it sent a tingle straight to her clit, making her moan.

"I love the sounds you make," he said between kisses as he carved a trail down the side of her jaw and neck.

She waited with bated breath as he approached the sensitive underside of her neck. He grazed the area with his lips teasingly and continued his path down her shoulder. She groaned in frustration even as she grew wet with his teasing ministrations.

Griffin chuckled against her collarbone. He tugged at the hem of her top, pulling it over her head in one swift movement. His large hands cupped her breasts, kneading them as he stared down, his dilated pupils a sign of his growing lust. As was the outline of his erection in the band of his sweatpants.

Where did those pants come from?

She wondered why they looked familiar. Before she could figure it out, Griffin yanked her pants and underwear off her, leaving her completely naked on the couch.

She resisted the urge to cover herself with her hands. Instead, she watched Griffin's face closely as his heated gaze roamed over her. A shiver of anticipation rippled through her, making her skin pebble. Her hands clenched the couch cushions beneath her reflexively.

The tip of Griffin's tongue peeked out as he licked his upper lip like a hungry predator about to take a bite out of its meal. She should be scared of the way he was looking at her. Instead, she felt powerful.

She did this to him. Made him hunger for a taste. A rush of excitement at the prospect of affecting someone as strong as Griffin. She brought him to his knees with just her body.

Despite her prone position, she knew she was in control. Bolstered by her newfound confidence, Quynh bent her knee next to his hip. She opened her thigh, exposing her wet center to him.

Quynh watched as his nostrils flared with the movement, his attention on her every move as she exposed herself to him.

"Oh, sunshine, you shouldn't have done that." His threat was issued in a low tenor.

Before she responded, Griffin pounced. He leaned down and laved at her pussy like a man starved for water, as if he was drowning. He needed to taste her.

He licked and sucked. He kissed and flicked. It all sent her toes curling as a hand gripped his hair. The other hand went behind her head and gripped the side of the couch.

A gasp escaped her lips as her body arched, sensitive to his every touch. The pleasure rolled through her in powerful waves. She came to a screaming climax all too quickly.

Her clit was overly sensitive from their earlier activities. But really, she had been in a hyper state of awareness since she woke up wrapped in his arms not even an hour ago.

Before she could catch her breath, Griffin sat back and pushed the waistband of his sweatpants down over the crease of his ass. His cock popped out, hard and erect, standing at attention. Griffin gripped his cock in one hand while the other came down to squeeze his balls that hung heavily between his legs.

He smoothed a thick palm over his hard cock, smearing the pre-cum across the tip before leaning over her body, still reeling from her orgasm. He slid his cock slowly against her, giving her teasing strokes against her wet folds, getting his cock wet with her arousal.

"Mmm, look how wet you are for me. You're soaking my cock." He lined the tip of his cock against her center, giving her a moment to brace herself.

Griffin didn't give her any other warnings before he sank himself deep inside of her. He buried himself to the hilt, giving her only a breath to adjust to his size. Groaning, he set a relentless pace.

It was fast. It was hard. It was everything she needed at this moment.

Moving together at a furious pace, their bodies spoke what their words could not. The electrifying friction between their sweat-slicked skin crackled with unspoken hurts from the past couple of weeks, the tension between them melting away as they came together in a primitive dance.

Quynh tried to hóld on. She struggled to hold out until he was on the edge with her, but another orgasm crashed into her. As she regained awareness of her body, she heard Griffin's deep grunt, which signaled his impending climax. She gripped his hips with her ankles, locking him deep inside of her as he came with a low groan. The feeling of his cock jerking and pulsing inside her sent her over the precipice again.

Three orgasms in one day must have been a record.

When her vision cleared, she realized Griffin was collapsed on top of her. His heavy weight was a welcome as he caught his breath. Their sweat-slicked skin clung together. She ran lazy circles on his back as they both came back down to earth.

After a quiet moment, Griffin lifted his head to look down at her.

"Are you okay?" he asked, though she knew his words meant more than what just happened between them.

"Yes, I'm okay." She smiled up at him.

They were going to be okay.

No matter what happens next, they'll figure it out.

She was going to take things one day at a time and stop worrying so much about the future.

38

Dinner arrived shortly after they both cleaned up, as they worked up quite the appetite. Quynh leaned against Griffin's side as they ate, enjoying the warmth of his strong body next to her as the new crime thriller played on Netflix. The show got a lot of hype, but neither really paid attention to what was happening. It was nice. Domestic.

Not for the first time, she wondered what their future would look like.

Would we live together in Willowbrook, or would he consider moving here?

It was probably presumptuous to assume they had a future together.

What did it mean that he drove all the way here?

They still had not talked about what had happened. Or the next steps, which weighed heavily on her mind.

"Hey." At the sound of Griffin's voice, Quynh turned her attention to him. "Tell me what you're thinking."

She finished chewing her lo mein before putting the chopsticks down. She bought herself some time hunting for a napkin to wipe her mouth as she thought of what she wanted to say. There was so much she wanted to know. The questions were bubbling up inside her, waiting to burst free. After an internal battle that took entirely way too long, she finally turned to face him. Griffin mirrored her movements, so they sat face-to-face.

"Why did you follow me out here?" she asked cautiously.

"Isn't it obvious?" His tone was incredulous, eyes wide with disbelief.

"No, not really." Her brow furrowed in confusion.

Griffin gently placed his to-go container down on the coffee table. "I came here because of you." The words came out slowly, as if he wasn't sure how else to say them. Like the answer was obvious when she still didn't know why.

"But...why?"

Griffin paused. She watched his pensive expression as he mulled over the words to say to her. "Because I need you in my life, and I miss you."

Her heart melted at his confession. "I miss you, too. But what do you see of our future?" She needed to know.

"Quynh," Griffin reached over and gripped her hands, "the only future I see is you. Wherever you are is where I want to be. It's where I need to be."

She was at a loss for words. Her eyes watered as she took in his heartfelt words.

"Do you really mean that?" Her voice was thick with unshed tears.

"I do." His tone brooked no arguments.

"You do?" She bit down on her lower lip.

"Absolutely. We will figure everything out. Together."

Before she knew what was happening, Griffin scooped her up and placed her on his lap.

"I need to tell you something. I've told no one this before." His voice trailed off. Quynh looked at his pinched expression. Her heart raced as she prepared herself for the worst.

"Okay. What is it?"

"I—well, there's really no other way to say this, but... I'm an addict. Recovered. Drugs and alcohol." His voice was rushed as if he needed to get them out before he lost his nerve.

She stared at Griffin in shock.

"My father was an alcoholic. He gambled too, but his drug of choice was alcohol. My mother left when I was young. I don't know much about her." Griffin paused as he looked off into the distance. Quynh rubbed her hands across his shoulders, not sure what to do with herself but wanting to soothe him. This was obviously causing him distress to relive old memories.

"I started drinking when I was really young. Did some

stupid shit, too. Drugs and girls were part of my life for a while until..." Griffin gulped. "Until I killed my best friend."

Quynh's heart dropped. She tried not to react or judge, instead waiting patiently to hear the rest of the story. A part of her was proud he trusted her with this part of himself.

"He was driving us home from a party. We had no business being in the car. I fell asleep, and the next thing I knew, I woke up to the car being flipped upside down. He...he died on impact." His voice choked on the last word. "I'll never forget the way he looked. They needed to use the jaws of life to get us out, but it was too late for him."

She rested her head on his shoulder, giving him time to process his traumatic memories. She placed a kiss on his neck, reassuring him she was still there with him.

"It wasn't your fault, you know," she murmured softly against his side.

"I know that now, but I'm telling you this because my fucked up past...It's a big part of who I am. I quit drinking and drugs. It wasn't easy, but I did it. Old Man Murphy took me under his wing and helped me get out from under the shadow of my father. Murphy left me the auto shop when he died a few years ago. And that apartment that you've been staying in? That's where I lived for a while before I built the house across the street."

Griffin took in a deep breath, his hand coming up to cup the back of her neck as he pulled her in so he could see her. She stared into his expressive eyes, watching the emotions flickering through them. Fear. Anger. Loss. She knew it took a lot for him to tell her about his past.

She leaned forward and kissed him, his lips automatically welcoming hers. She pulled away before he could deepen the kiss, not wanting to distract from the gravity of his words.

"Thank you for telling me."

"Yeah. I know I'm fucked up, and I'm hard to be around. I don't deserve you, but I need you."

She smiled at his gruff words.

"I don't deserve you," she finally said and refrained from laughing at his huff of disbelief. "It's true. You're strong, and you're brave. It takes hard work to straighten yourself out. You took a tragedy and remade yourself. Look at how successful and respected you are. Everyone in Willowbrook has nothing but great things to say about you."

He narrowed his eyes in disbelief.

"I need to tell you something." Now it was her turn to share. "I'm not very good at being in relationships. I've always had this fear of being abandoned...and I have a bad habit of leaving before I'm left, if you know what I mean."

"I know." He tilted his head at her in a comical gesture.

"I'm sorry that I reverted to my old habits. I was.... scared."

"Scared? Of what?"

"Of you. Of us."

"Why?"

"Because...I've never felt this way before...about anyone. You make me feel so many things, and I wasn't ready for you to leave me behind. So I left first, but it was a mistake." She swallowed and blew out an anxious breath. "Please know that it was a mistake to leave you."

He said nothing for a while, studying her expression, the way she was chewing on his lip. Griffin reached up a hand and pulled her bottom lip away, teeth tearing through her flesh.

"I would have never left you."

She nodded, but before she could respond, he hushed her.

"I would have never left you," he repeated. "Because I love you."

39

"I love you." His words hung heavily between them. He'd known for a while what this feeling was. The moment he laid eyes on her, he knew he was in trouble. There was no turning back from her. Destiny came screeching into town disguised as this dark-haired beauty.

He tried to convince himself it was simply an attraction. A fleeting interest. Though it was undeniable when he was around her, there was a physical pull that made him acutely aware of her presence. Of her scent and her every movement. The way her laughter seemed to dance in the air between them, or how her radiant smile lit up her entire face.

Anyone could see she was breathtaking. Her tawny skin, smooth and begging to be touched, seemed to glow with an inner light, as if she somehow captured the luminance of the sun and kept it trapped beneath her skin. Her love for sundresses, with their vibrant colors and the way they flowed around her, was maddening. But it was the piercing gaze of her dark brown eyes that ensnared him instantly. He was a goner.

How does a man like me end up with a woman like her?

Where he was quiet and reserved, she was vibrant and outspoken. She was everything he wasn't. Though their personalities clashed like fire and ice, their connection was undeniable. The connection between them was so strong, you could almost feel it like a physical being. Their souls were bound together with a thick, rough rope, the fibers intertwining and making them inseparable.

It was sheer luck, a twist of fate, that brought her into his life. He was silently thanking his lucky stars Ricky hadn't answered her desperate call for help. The thought of Ricky touching her sent a surge of furious, red-hot anger through him. He doubted Quynh would have wanted someone like Ricky, but he hadn't liked the odds.

Go figure: the one time Ricky played a prank on him, it helped him land the woman of his dreams. His confession left Quynh speechless, her eyes wide. A look of disbelief painted across her face, as if it were the most absurd thing anyone ever said to her.

He wondered if any other man had ever said those words to her. Irrational jealousy threatened to consume him at the thought. Griffin wanted to be her first. And her last.

He'd make certain she'd never want for anything. He

pledged to provide for her completely. First things first. He needed to figure out what she wanted.

"You don't need to say anything, sunshine. Just know that I love you," he reassured her. It wasn't the ideal time or place to confess the true nature of his feelings for her, but it was now or never.

She rested her head against his forehead, her hands tangling with the long strands of hair at the nape of his neck, making him shiver with pleasure.

"Can I tell you something?" she whispered, voice tentative, as if unsure if she should say what was on her mind.

"Anything."

"I know it's crazy, but...I love you, too."

A warmth spread through Griffin's chest, making it three times larger with her confession. He let out a breath of relief.

"Thank god," he said with a smile as he cupped her face and gently freed her lower lip from her teeth. "You're mine." He crushed his lips against hers in a passionate kiss before she could refute his statement.

They still needed to figure out the next steps, but for now, this was enough.

Griffin lay awake in bed later that night. Quynh was curled around him, her head on his chest, while he held her close. They didn't really talk about what came next after their heartfelt confessions. The future still loomed ahead of them. Though he was confident they'd make it work, he was leery of letting fate decide their future.

He knew one thing for sure. He was not leaving here empty-handed. No matter how long it took, he was prepared to sacrifice everything to win her over. He'd never been in a long-distance relationship before, but it would be worth it to have Quynh in his life.

He could manage the shop on weekends and fly in to be with her every weekend if she wanted him to.

Whatever the resolution, he would do whatever was necessary to make sure they had a future together. There was no way he would let Quynh walk away from him again.

Quynh moaned in her sleep and wiggled closer to him. Griffin's arm tightened around her as he gripped her. He never wanted to let her go. Not now. Not ever.

Love is such a wild feeling. Knowing his heart was no longer beating in his chest, but was lying next to him disguised as this sleeping beauty, made him fearful. Out of control. A sensation which terrified him more than the possibility of relapse.

With them being miles apart, the possibilities were

endless and fraught with danger. There was so much uncertainty stretching between them. He was too far away to protect her.

The thought of anything happening to her terrified him more than anything he thought possible. His restless mind whirled with possibilities.

40

"So, what do you think?" Quynh asked over her shoulder, smothering a smile at his disgruntled expression.

"It's...something," he finally admitted, his voice flat as he tilted his head to look at the sculpture from a different angle.

It was Sunday afternoon. They spent the day sightseeing. Quynh took him to her favorite diner around the corner, where she watched in awe as he ordered everything off the menu and ate everything that arrived. The plates were piled high everywhere. When she only gaped at him in astonishment, he scowled at her and ordered her to eat her breakfast, which sat cooling on her plate.

She merely smiled at him and took small bites from her veggie omelet. When she took bites from the pancakes he ordered, he'd playfully swatted her fork away from his food. Though she saw the look of pleasure as he watched her eat raptly.

She knew he was worried she didn't eat enough food. It's not like she was concerned about her weight, more like she often forgot to eat with how busy she was with her life. Most days, she would be running around at the clinic and barely had time to eat. It became second nature to miss meals.

You'd think she'd be skinnier than she was, but the roundness of her abdomen contradicted her lack of eating. It was a frustrating conundrum. She didn't forget to eat when she was with Griffin, who often went out of his way to feed her.

After their brunch, she'd taken him on a walking tour of her block. There wasn't much to see besides busy restaurants and chain stores. Then they hailed a cab to take them across the city so she could show him the historical sights, which included the park with its many artistic and unique sculptures. That's where they were when he finally straightened up with raised eyebrows.

She laughed at his expression before tugging on his arm and dragging him to the next sculpture.

They continued on through the park, occasionally stopping to people-watch and rest on the metal benches. They kissed beneath the cherry blossom trees, which were no longer blooming for the season. It didn't make the moments less romantic, though.

Griffin's disgruntled expressions at being dragged

around the city made her laugh. Despite his grumbling, she knew he was happy by the twinkle in his green eyes.

She couldn't remember the last time she had so much fun with another person. Despite his gruff exterior, Griffin was a softie inside. He was down for almost anything she suggested.

Later, she dragged him inside a lingerie store and pulled out some items to try on. She was inside the dressing room trying on a light purple teddy when something was tossed over the door and plopped to the ground.

"What's this?" she asked, bending down to retrieve the new garment. Her eyebrows shot through her hairline as she observed the barely there outfit of lace and ribbon barely held together with straps going every which way. The material was soft and thicker in areas like the nipple and the crotch. She did not know how she was going to even get into the garment without ripping it to shreds.

She modeled the teddy for Griffin, who'd grunted his approval before walking back into the dressing room. She pulled off the teddy over her head and tackled the ribbon and lace. After a few moments, she assembled all the parts appropriately and admired herself in the full-length mirrors in the dressing room. She turned and twirled as she admired how her ass looked from all angles.

She looked good.

She started opening the door to the private dressing

area. Griffin was sitting slouched against the couch and perked up with attention when he saw her peek through the door.

Bolstered with confidence, she pulled the door open wide and stepped out, trying to feign confidence as she strutted slowly toward him on her bare feet. She watched as his face tightened while his pupils dilated. His big hands clenched into fists on top of his thighs as if he was fighting the urge to not jump up and grab her.

It was probably illegal to have sex in the dressing room, but she knew the outfit was a keeper by the way he stared at her and watched her every movement.

She loved this feeling. She felt powerful. Beautiful.

Griffin had a way of making her confident in anything she wore. Even when she was in her grungiest outfit, he still looked at her as if she were the sexiest woman he'd ever laid eyes on. It was unnerving.

She loved it.

She loved him.

She never wanted to leave him.

They still had a lot of things to figure out and had barely talked about the details of their relationship. The only thing she knew for certain was she was not willing to let him go.

She sashayed up to Griffin in her negligee, leaving a small distance between them. She didn't want to be cruel and taunt him with what he couldn't have, but she wanted to torture him. Just a little.

He had his legs spread wide. She stepped between them. She twirled around slowly so he could see all the angles of her barely there outfit.

"So, what do you think? Should we get it?" She smirked.

His expression said it all.

"If you don't get it, I will spank you."

"Is that a promise?" Where did she get her sass from? It was not like her to be so saucy, but he brought it out of her.

"You bet your fine ass it is."

He said with finality, a low growl deepening his voice. His knuckles were white from how tightly he gripped his hands. She knew she was playing with fire. She leaned down and watched as his eyes dropped to her breasts for a moment before flickering up to meet her gaze.

Leaning in, breaths mingling, as she placed a teasing kiss on his eager lips. She moved away quickly before he could get his big paws on her. Smiling deviously as his hands grasped only air.

He let out a disbelieving scoff as she retreated back into the dressing room.

"You'll pay for that."

His dark promise made her shiver with fear and anticipation.

She hoped so.

41

After a day of sightseeing, they stopped at the local grocery store so Griffin could pick up some items for dinner. He had told her he wanted to cook dinner for her tonight, but when the cart started filling up, she became suspicious of his motives.

She kept throwing questioning glances his way as he continued to throw things into the cart. When he went to check out, she tried to ask him why he needed so many things for tonight, but he just gave her a flat look before rolling past her to check out. When she offered to pay, he balked at her, which made her stifle a smile.

Now, she admired the view as he bent halfway into the fridge to put away the cold items. He bought enough food to stock her refrigerator. Quynh tried not to read too much into the gesture, though it was much too late for her heart, which was melting at his thoughtfulness. When he straightened up, Quynh pretended to be busy cleaning the countertop.

They moved around each other in her small kitchen like a synchronized dance, predicting the other's next move. Every time their bodies touched, lightning bolts shot straight through her, making her nerve endings tingle with awareness. She made her way to the small table in the corner and set the table.

Whatever Griffin was cooking smelled delicious. The smells and sounds of Griffin expertly cooking filled the air, making her stomach rumble with hunger. Her mouth watered at the prospect. It had been weeks since her last home-cooked meal. She loved Griffin's meals. He was a natural in the kitchen. Quynh wondered absently if he would have been a chef in another life had he not fallen into the role of being a mechanic.

When it was time to plate the food, Griffin frowned at her when she tried to help him. Griffin looked pointedly at her seat. She bit back a smile and sat down obediently. She missed this side of him. Griffin seemed to enjoy taking care of her.

Who am I to deny him the pleasure?

She tried not to drool as he served the delicious meal he whipped up in her small kitchen. Shrimp scampi. Her favorite meal. She never had it home-cooked before. She waited patiently while he served himself and then sat down before digging in.

"Oh my god, this is so good!" When the flavors hit her tongue, she moaned in appreciation. She twirled the pasta around her fork and brought it to her open mouth for a bite. Pausing with the fork halfway to her mouth, she realized Griffin was quiet. She looked up to see he was staring at her mouth with a hungry expression.

She blushed as she figured out where his wayward thoughts had gone. It didn't help that she was moaning with appreciation over his food. She put the fork down gently and crossed her hands on top of each other on the table.

"Griffin. Eat before your food gets cold," she admonished, though she knew he wouldn't take her tone seriously.

Griffin merely grunted before reaching for his fork. She remained still and watched him as he ate. She watched as the muscles in his forearms flexed when he brought the fork to his mouth. And how his biceps bulged in his white t-shirt. Griffin made eating a sensual experience. From the way he moved effortlessly in the kitchen to the almost erotic way he prepared the meals, down to the way he ate.

She struggled to not squirm in her seat when she watched the way his Adam's apple bobbed when he swallowed. Quynh picked her fork back up and resumed eating, trying to not make any more noises. She really didn't want the meal to go to waste. She knew their self-control was barely there.

After a tense moment of eating, Griffin cleared his

throat. Quynh tried not to tense as she looked up beneath her lashes to meet his expectant gaze.

"We should probably talk about us."

"Us?"

"Yes. What do you want to do about us?"

She paused, grabbed her cup of water, and took a small sip while she mulled over her answer. She didn't know how this was going to go.

"I'm not sure..." she started saying but stopped at his crestfallen expression.

"I don't know how it would work with me being in the city and you in Willowbrook. I've never been in a long-distance relationship before."

"Long distance?"

"Yeah...?" The word came out as a question. She watched as Griffin chewed on a shrimp as he gathered his thoughts.

"Would you consider moving to Willowbrook?"

She tilted her head in consideration. The idea of moving to Willowbrook didn't terrify her like she thought it would. She'd briefly entertained the idea before she fled town to be closer to her father and sister. If anything, she missed the small town with its friendly neighbors and the walkable streets. She would love nothing more than to go back.

But what of my career?

There was no job for her in Willowbrook. At least, none she could find.

What would I do with my time?

"I think...it is a good option. I would love to move back...at some point." She paused. She knew her next words might hurt him, but they needed to be able to talk to each other. About their worries and fears. About their dreams and their future. If they didn't learn how to communicate with each other, they were bound to fail.

"I don't know if I'm ready to leave the city or my job yet. There's no clinic in Willowbrook that I could work at. What would I do there?"

"You could work for me like you have been until you figure it out." His answer came quick, as if he'd been thinking about this for a long time.

"That's true. You do need help around the shop." Her joke fell flat between them.

"What would you have done if you didn't become a nurse?" he asked, the question coming out of nowhere.

"I guess I've never really thought about it," she admitted reluctantly. She finished the rest of her dinner, deep in thought, taking the time to consider what her future would have looked like if she hadn't decided to be practical and become a nurse. Job security was important to her at the time.

"I've been thinking a lot about my parents," she started.

"I used to want to be a writer when I was younger, but it didn't seem like a realistic dream, so I went with the practical one. I love what I do. I love helping people, but...the time and dedication it takes to do my job has taken a toll on me," she finally said. "If I had the time, I guess I'd want to write a book about my parents. Only...I'd like to give them the ending that they should have had. Before...cancer took her."

Tears blurred her vision at the memory of her late mother and her ailing father. She couldn't believe she'd left him behind without even saying a word about her departure.

What kind of daughter leaves their dying parent behind?

She needed to go back and spend whatever time she still had left with him before it was too late. Screw Ruth and her implications. She didn't want money from her father. All she wanted was time. Time was running out the longer she stayed away.

"I need to see my father."

"You can stay at the apartment or at my place. I know Rover has missed you a lot." Griffin rubbed the back of his neck as if he were embarrassed.

"Rover has missed me, huh?" She smiled brightly.

"Yeah. The big oaf hasn't been able to sleep at night without you warming his bed at night."

"Oh, so now I'm warming his bed?" She chuckled.

He stifled a smile and hid it behind his hand. Rubbing his bristly jaw. He shaved it earlier in the day. She mourned the loss of his bristles. She rather liked the feel of them between her thighs.

"I'll think about it. How...How is my father doing?"

"I checked on him before I left. He's hanging in there. He asked when you were coming back. He probably blames me for you leaving."

He wasn't wrong.

"I need to call him or FaceTime him or something." She worried her lower lip. "Have you seen Ruth?"

"She's been in and out around the town. Did something happen between you two?"

Quynh realized with dismay she still hadn't told Griffin about her encounter with Ruth.

"I need to tell you something..."

A frown marred his handsome expression as he gestured for her to continue. Taking a deep breath to calm herself, she launched into the story of how she met with Ruth at the cafe. How the encounter left her reeling as she grappled with her emotions. One of the catalysts that prompted her departure from Willowbrook.

"I really need to call him..." her voice trailed off. There was a churning in her gut at how she had abandoned her last remaining family. Even if Ruth had been awful to her, she was still family. She was ashamed to admit she was no better than her past.

Why do I always run away from my problems?

"I think he'd like that," he agreed softly. "We'll deal

with Ruth later." The grim determination was set in his features. She was grateful to have someone in her corner.

She stood up from the table and grabbed their empty plates. She started doing the dishes and shushed Griffin when he protested.

"You cooked, I'll do the dishes," she stated matter-of-factly. "That's the deal. Got it?"

Griffin smirked at her before grabbing the finger she pointed at his chest in his large hand. He pulled her in close and kissed her on the nose. "You got it, boss."

She smacked his chest. He backed away, moving back into the living room. She heard the sounds of the television turning on. It was getting late. She was exhausted, but the normalcy of the evening made her feel at peace.

While she soaped up the dishes and rinsed them, she ran over their conversation through her mind. They were good together. Fire and ice. Sunshine and her thundercloud. She could spend the rest of her life at Griffin's side and be happy.

So, what do I have to worry about?

Everything else they could figure out together. People changed careers all the time. She didn't need to stay in a career that made her miserable.

She knew it was fear holding her back from making the leap of faith. Fear of failure.

She spent so much money putting herself through school and had all the student loans to show for it. If she changed careers now, all the time and money spent would be wasted.

But what did it matter if I was miserable at the end of the day?

She could throw caution to the wind and move to a small town to be with a man she hardly knew. Wait for a job at the health clinic to open up.

The prospect of returning to work at a soulless health corporation made her break out in a sweat. She washed the dishes a little too roughly and stacked them in the dish rack to dry. Over her shoulder, she caught sight of Griffin reclining on the couch with his feet propped up on the coffee table. Pickles disappeared back into the bedroom after she left his wet food for him but now was lying on Griffin's lap.

She smiled at the sight of the two of them together. Griffin was absentmindedly petting Pickles as they watched Netflix.

She could have this if she wanted it.

Suddenly, she realized what she wanted. No, what she *needed* more than anything.

She needed Griffin.

It didn't mean she needed to move to Willowbrook right away. They'd still have to talk about the details.

There was still the matter of wrapping things up at the apartment. Her lease isn't up for a couple of months.

But the lease was already paid for. It didn't really matter in the grand scheme of things.

She still needed to go back to the office to grab her belongings since everything was considered evidence. The last time she went to the police station to give her statement, she was informed that they would need to go through everything before she could take them home. She received a call earlier in the week to let her know the contents of her office were cleared to be picked up.

She delayed going down to the police station. The thought made her nervous. The last time she was there, she was in complete shock. She gave a statement about what little she knew about her boss. It made her more aware of how she barely knew the man at all. She heard little news about the case, but since she wasn't a suspect, they didn't bother to keep her updated.

Aside from a few loose ends, there really wasn't anything else keeping her in the city. The noise and the smells of the city no longer appealed to her, having experienced peace, quiet, and fresh air. She missed seeing the sun rise over the lake every morning. She missed the quiet of the countryside and taking Rover for walks around the lake.

When she was in Willowbrook, she was relaxed for the first time. It was like being able to take a deep breath after holding it in for years. She felt refreshed and content. Upon her return to the city, she noticed how tensely she held herself in her rigid posture. Almost as if the stress of her environment seeped into her bones. The muscles in her neck and shoulders were more sore recently from constantly being on edge. The sounds of the streets were jarring after weeks spent in the countryside.

She missed small-town living.

Quynh wiped her hands on the dish towel and whirled around. Decision made, she marched up to Griffin, who glanced up when she approached.

"What's up, sunshine?" Griffin asked.

"Is the offer still on the table?"

"What offer?"

"For me to move back to Willowbrook. I can stay at the apartment or..." She yelped as Griffin grabbed her around the waist and yanked her onto his lap, Pickles getting dislodged with a grumble.

"Yes." Griffin planted a firm kiss on her lips before she could reply. She melted into his arms as he deepened the kiss, gripping the back of her head and tilting her so he could delve deeper.

The kiss was a promise for the future. For the first time, Quynh was excited about what was to come.

42

Quynh cursed as she struggled to zip up her suitcase. She found it stuffed in the back of her closet and was determined to fit everything she could into it. She sat on top of it and grunted as she finally zipped it shut. Breathing a sigh of relief at completing her task, she collapsed in a heap on the floor, trying to catch her breath.

It was about a week of trying to wrap up her life in the city. Griffin had stayed until Monday morning but left shortly after making her breakfast. He'd dragged his feet, reluctant to leave her, but he needed to get back to his business. It was a painful goodbye as they tried to avoid the inevitable.

But knowing their future together was about to start soon kept her from falling apart. She barely resisted the urge to fall to her knees and beg him to stay with her just a little longer. They hardly slept the night before. Their lovemaking was frantic and desperate. Kisses lingered, and each touch was torturous, knowing they would be separated again.

It wasn't goodbye. She reminded herself.

They talked on the phone each night, which usually ended with Griffin requesting to FaceTime with her when she was in bed. Things usually got heated after that. Quynh blushed at the memories of them masturbating to each other during a video call.

Modern technology was amazing. She doubted it was why they invented video calls in the first place, but she wasn't complaining. Recalling his hooded look as lust overtook his expression made her tremble with need.

It had been a long week. She missed his touch. She missed the way he seemed to always know what she needed. She missed her grumpy bear.

Aside from naughty video calls, Quynh worked up the courage to talk to her father. Mostly, it was a one-sided conversation, given his difficulties with breathing, but she didn't miss the way his eyes teared up when he finally saw her on the screen. It only made her feel more like a terrible daughter for running scared and leaving him behind.

Ruth was harder to get a hold of. She preferred text messages over talking on the phone, which was fine with Quynh. Though it was hard to read the tone through text, Ruth would take more time to soften. Still, she was looking forward to trying.

Her empty apartment echoed as she walked through to make sure she missed nothing. She donated her furniture to the local women's shelter that provided used furniture to women. It made her happy to know her meager belongings could go to someone who needed them much more than she ever did.

After Griffin left, she'd worked up the courage to take Shelly down to the police station. She was anxious about the trip, though she didn't really know why. The whole situation made her uneasy.

When she finally pulled up to the entrance, she needed a moment to take a deep breath. Walking up to the double doors was intimidating, but she found her way to the front desk without throwing up all over the linoleum floors.

Checking in at the front desk, she was instructed to wait in the waiting area as they retrieved her items. She wasn't prepared for the detective to come out to greet her. She gulped at his approach.

Her palms were sweating. She tried to wipe her hands on her jeans before shaking the detective's proffered hand.

"Ms. Le, nice to see you again. Do you have a moment to step into my office?" Detective Callahan asked casually.

"Oh. Sure." She swallowed nervously before gathering her purse and following the tall detective through the security door. He used his badge to open the doors for them and led her down a brightly lit, narrow hallway. When they approached an open door, the detective gestured for her to enter before closing the door behind them.

"Please, have a seat."

She sat down in the tiny chair across from the desk and watched as he made his way into his office chair, fixing his tie as he sat down. The chair creaked under his weight. Detective Callahan leaned forward to meet her gaze, hands clasped together on his desk.

"I wanted to update you on the case," he started. Her shoulders immediately tensed up again. "After our investigation, we found that Jared Perry had been committing insurance fraud. He was due to be arrested and charged for his crimes. He must have learned about it somehow and took his own life, as you know." Detective Callahan gestured toward her.

Quynh nodded in understanding, though she still wasn't sure why she was brought into the office. This was all mentioned in the article she found.

"Ms. Le, I want to be frank with you. During our investigation, we found evidence that Mr. Perry had been manipulating the charts after you signed off on them for a higher payout. As you are a nurse practitioner, the rate of payout from insurance companies is lower than that of your physician colleagues. Mr. Perry was changing the billing codes after you locked your charts. In doing so, the clinic was paid out more than the services rendered."

Quynh sank back into her chair in shock. She had no idea Jared was changing her charts. It was a violation to alter her notes in such a way. He committed a crime for personal gain at her expense. She wasn't even aware anyone could unlock her notes besides her, but apparently, it was happening for a while.

Detective Callahan cleared his throat.

"We worked extensively with the IT department to determine who had been changing the charts. I want it to be clear that you are not under investigation. I'll escort you down to the evidence room so you can retrieve your belongings." He stood up from his desk, offering her a sympathetic glance.

She mentally shook herself out of her shock and followed Detective Callahan on shaky legs. While she was relieved she was not under investigation, it made rage boil inside of her at the thought of Jared violating her trust. She didn't think it had been worth losing his life over, but it made her wonder how deep his deceit went. She wondered belatedly if he was pocketing the money since the clinic didn't see any of the funds. If anything, he used to complain about how they were barely keeping the lights on and trying to cram more patients in her already jam-packed schedule.

All this time, she was running herself ragged, only to

have Jared steal money from insurance companies and the clinic. Come to think of it, she always wondered how he could afford his luxury condo on the Upper East Side and his fancy car while she struggled to take care of Shelly despite having her apartment fully paid for. Sure, she was probably more frugal than most and kept most of her paychecks in her savings, but she could still never afford to spend it on a car worth more than her entire year's salary.

Whatever the case may be, she was so done with this part of her life. It couldn't have come at a better time. If anything, it only validated her decision to leave all of this behind her. She had so many wonderful things to look forward to in her future.

One of which was a grumpy mechanic who was impatiently waiting for her to get her act together. Suddenly, she was desperate to get back to him.

There was nothing holding her back here anymore. She didn't need to take anything besides the clothes she packed, Pickles, and herself. She planned on getting a good night's sleep and driving back to Willowbrook in the morning but fuck it.

What am I waiting for?

She quickened her steps to match those of the detective and hurriedly signed the paperwork to retrieve her belongings. The box was light and held nothing she absolutely couldn't live without, except her stethoscope and tools.

She thanked Detective Callahan as he walked her back out to the main lobby. Her hurried steps echoed on the linoleum floor as she left the sterile building behind.

Once outside, she took a deep breath of the city air and ran to her car.

She had a long ride ahead of her.

43

Griffin tossed and turned on his bed. A bed which seemed much too large now without Quynh by his side. The anxiety was eating him up inside. By this time tomorrow, he'd have her back in his arms. Once she came back, he would make sure she never had a reason to leave him again. If it meant he had to chain her to his bed, then so be it. He would never let her go for the rest of their lives together.

He'd talked to her on the phone a few hours ago, though she seemed distracted. He chalked it up to her being busy packing up the rest of her apartment for the road trip. Griffin was tempted to fly down there to drive back with her to make sure she didn't have cold feet. Unfortunately, Quynh merely laughed at his suggestion, thinking he was joking.

He was completely serious about needing her back in Willowbrook. Back in bed with him and by his side again.

Every second he spent without her here made him restless. His barely suppressed agitation was obvious to everyone in town who made a more concerted effort to avoid being around him this past week. Even Sean kept to himself, and Julio avoided making any of his usual jokes at Griffin's expense.

He was an insufferable asshole all week. He could at least acknowledge it, but with every passing moment without her being here meant she could change her mind.

He wouldn't be able to handle it if she changed her mind about coming back. He knew she would return eventually to see her father and sister, but it didn't mean she'd come back for him. Even though they loved each other, it didn't make the fear any less real. He could still lose her at any moment.

Growling, Griffin rolled over in bed onto his stomach. He snatched the pillow Quynh typically used and hugged it tightly to his chest. He ignored his semi-hard-on. The damn thing has been unsatisfied with all the times he'd jerked off with Quynh during their video calls. There was no use until he saw her again. Then it would be an act of sheer willpower to not explode as soon as he was buried deep inside her warm pussy again.

Fuck!

He couldn't wait until she was here. Griffin shut his eyes and tried to think of sheep jumping over a fence.

He'd tried every breathing technique he could think of to fall asleep, but none worked. Just when he thought he was in for a long night, he heard Rover stir at the bottom of the bed. Rover had been sleeping in his bed more often since Quynh left. He didn't mind it since it made him less lonely.

"What is it, buddy?" he asked Rover as the dog perked up. Rover's ears twitched as if he heard something before leaping out of bed with his tail wagging.

Frowning, Griffin untangled his legs from the comforter and followed the excited puppy down the hallway, where he sat staring at the front door expectantly.

"Is someone here, buddy?" Griffin asked, voice gruff.

In answer, there was a timid knock at the door. Griffin frowned. He wasn't expecting anyone this late. He padded toward the front door on bare feet and unlocked it. Griffin was not prepared for what greeted him on his front step.

"Hi! I need help. My car broke down, and I was wondering if you could help me out?" The woman on his step bit her lip and looked up at him with her big brown eyes.

Griffin didn't know how to react, but then her words registered. He let loose a grin at the reminder of how they first met before yanking the door open and grabbing her around the waist.

Finally, Quynh was here, back in his arms. She

laughed as he picked her up and brought her inside his house, her hands going around his neck while her legs wrapped around his waist.

"Sunshine," he said in greeting.

"Grumpy bear." She smiled at his mock frown.

"Don't tell me you drove all night to get here."

"Ok, then I won't."

He growled and snapped his teeth at her, which made her giggle. His heart stopped beating in his chest at the sound of her laughter. He buried his face in her hair, breathing in her scent. Griffin hugged her tightly to his chest and relished the way her breath caught in her throat.

"Are you really here?" he murmured against her.

"I'm really here." Her hand moved into his hair, fingernails scratching against his scalp. He bit back on a groan of pleasure as a shiver raced through his body.

"Thank fuck." Griffin lifted his head. Finding her eyes were wet with unshed tears, he frowned.

"What's wrong?" His voice came out rougher than he intended. Quynh offered a small smile before tilting her face up in a silent command for a kiss. He leaned down and met her soft lips with his own. It was a sweet kiss. Gentle. A meeting of two souls as they reunited.

She pulled back and shook her head.

"Nothing's wrong. Everything is right for the first

time in a while." Her smile lit a fire within him, making him aware of every beat of his heart. For the rest of his life, he would make sure she always had a reason to smile at him just like this. Like he was her entire world. He would move heaven and earth to give her everything she might want or need in this lifetime. And the next, if he had anything to say about it.

Griffin never believed in soulmates, but the past few weeks of being separated from Quynh showed him what it was like to exist without his other half. Without her, his soul left his body. She was his in every sense of the word. His soulmate. His better half. The missing piece to his jagged puzzle.

It made him powerful to know a strong woman like her called him her man.

With Quynh tightly wrapped up in his arms, he turned to run up the stairs, only to have her yell.

"Stop! Put me down!" She slapped his shoulder for him to let go of her. When he refused, she sighed. "I need to get Pickles out of the car."

Griffin's grumble was loud, but he let her unwrap her legs around his waist. She made a move to open the front door, but he grabbed her arm and pulled her back. His lips closed around her yelp of surprise, which quickly turned into a groan of pleasure. His cock hardened at the sound. Lips and tongues met in a primal dance for dominance.

He gripped the back of her head, grabbed a fist full of her dark, silky hair, and tugged. Her body went boneless in his arms at his display of dominance. He continued to lead their kiss but pulled back before things became too heated, or he'd fuck her up against the wall.

Pulling back, he untangled his hand from her hair and let her rest against the wall while he ran out to her car, which was parked in his driveway. Pickles was sleeping soundly in his carrier. He gently carried the sleepy cargo inside the house. He put the carrier down on the bench and opened the latch. Pickles took his time to stretch and worked his way out of the crate as if it were a normal occurrence to be back at Griffin's home.

Though Griffin always had a dog for a companion, he admitted it was nice to have Pickles around. Now, they were all united under the same roof. Quynh disappeared into the kitchen. He heard the sounds of her shaking Pickles's dry food out. He watched her as she made sure Pickles was taken care of. She was always thinking of others before herself. A trait he admired, but he knew people would take advantage of her generosity. He'd make it his personal mission to make sure she was never taken advantage of again.

Finally, when Pickles had food and water set up. Quynh straightened up and brushed her hands together. She smiled at him as she slowly walked toward him, her hips swaying side to side with the movement.

There it goes again, his heart stopping in his chest when she aimed her smile at him. She was going to be the death of him. What a way to go. If he died with her eyes on him, he'd die a happy man, knowing the last thing he saw would be her smiling face.

When she finally reached him, she placed both hands on his chest and looked up at him. The moonlight streamed in through the windows, giving her an ethereal glow. She looked like a goddess asking her supplicant for a sacrifice to show his devotion to her. Griffin bent his head down, their lips merely centimeters apart. He grasped her hand above his heart and gave her a small squeeze.

Her pouty lips parted. Her pink tongue peeked out as she licked her lips.

"Take me to bed, Griffin."

At her husky command, Griffin bent at the knees and picked her up. Throwing her over his shoulder as he ran up the stairs. He shut the door before Rover or Pickles could sneak in. He spent the rest of the night showing her how much he'd missed her, whispering promises against her heated skin, wringing out her pleasure with every kiss and touch he knew would make her whimper.

Only when he was satisfied she knew her rightful place was with him did he finally allow himself to come. They fell asleep tangled up together.

The last thing he heard before complete darkness was her whispered words.

"I love you."

I love you, too.

The end.

epilogue

ONE YEAR LATER...

Quynh stood up from her crouched position. She had been cleaning the house all day to distract herself from checking the rankings of her debut novel she just released. It took her most of the past year to work on putting her mother's journals and her father's stories together to form a love story she was proud of. She kept most of their history but rewrote their ending, giving her parents the happily ever after they never got in life. She hoped where they were now, they were able to find each other.

Her father died nearly six months ago now. He lived longer than the doctors predicted, which was a miracle. She suspected it had to do with being able to make amends with his past that gave him a few extra months of life. But in the end, cancer took him, too.

Luckily, Quynh was able to experience having her

father walk her down the aisle a month before he passed. Though she never thought it was possible, she was thrilled when Griffin proposed to her a couple of months after she moved back to town.

Most people would probably say they were rushing things, but they knew what they wanted out of life. There was no other man for her but Griffin. She knew deep in her bones he was the only man she wanted by her side as she navigated life.

Griffin was a major supporter of her dreams of becoming a writer. During the day, she worked at the auto shop to help manage the office, taking care of the administrative side of things. During the downtime, she would work on her book. It took the better part of the last year to finish the first draft of her book. Then came the arduous task of finding an editor.

Several rounds of editing later, her manuscript was ready to publish. Though, instead of trying to find a publisher to take a chance on her, she decided to self-publish. This book was important to her. She wanted it to be her work that was published rather than bending over backwards to make a publisher happy.

So, after her book went live this morning, Quynh started cleaning the house like a madwoman. Every surface in the house sparkled with how fervently she wiped everything down. There was not even a single dust bunny or fur ball to be found. She vacuumed at least three times between this morning and lunchtime.

Her stomach gurgled, reminding her she needed to eat just as her phone rang. Quynh dropped the feather duster she had in her hand and ran to find her phone. She pushed away the disappointment when she realized it wasn't Griffin who was calling, though she smiled brightly as Meg's name flashed across the screen.

She hit the answer button, but before she could finish her greeting, she was met with a pterodactyl scream so loud it made her ears ring.

"GUESS WHO MADE THE AMAZON BESTSELLERS LIST!?"

"Who?" she questioned, though she sensed it was a rhetorical question.

"YOU DID! Oh my god, my best friend is a bestselling author!"

"Whoa, whoa, whoa. What are you talking about? It just came out today!"

"Yeah, I know, and between all of my social media marketing skills and my connections, I was able to launch that bad boy into every corner of every platform. You're a best-selling author, baby!"

Quynh pulled the phone away from her ear as Meg continued to yell excitedly. Her heart was racing. She couldn't believe it. She put Meg on speakerphone and ran to the back of the house where Griffin helped her set up her office so she could write. The best part about her office was the view of the lake through the large double-pane windows. It was a relaxing view when she was stuck on finding the right words or when she had writer's block.

She turned on the laptop as she listened to Meg continue talking about all the reels she made and content pulls, which probably helped sell her book. Quynh didn't know what she was going on about since she didn't manage her social media accounts. Technically, Meg was the one who handled all the nitty-gritty details she couldn't be bothered with, preferring to spend her time writing or with Griffin in the home they made together.

Quynh even made a routine to meet up with Ruth at least once a month at the coffee shop to talk. It took the younger woman some time to warm up to her. Their father left the giant mansion to Ruth and split the rest of his money evenly between the sisters. A fact that was a bitter pill for Ruth to swallow. Unfortunately, they were forever bound together by losing their parents. They only had each other left.

Most evenings, she would sit on the back porch and enjoy the sun as it set across the lake, the beautiful colors making the most majestic canvas of vibrant colors. She'd become friendly with their new neighbors, Ben, Emily, and their six-month-old daughter, Charlotte. On one of their walks around the lake, Griffin and Quynh bumped into the couple as they were pushing Charlotte in the stroller. She discovered Emily was also a nurse, although she was currently staying at home to care for Charlotte.

Quynh and Emily bonded over their shared professions and try to meet up for dinner at least once a month. Though Quynh had no plans to return to her work as a nurse practitioner, she wouldn't completely rule it out. Right now, though, she was happy.

The happiest she had ever been in all of her adult life.

"Quynh, are you even listening to me?" Meg's voice brought her back to reality.

"I'm listening."

"Did you see it yet?"

"I'm pulling it up right now."

With trembling fingers, she typed in the title of her book and sat on her hands as it loaded. Her mouth dropped open in shock at the orange banner listed next to her book.

"Holy. Shit," she gasped out in disbelief.

"I know, right! Congrats, babe! I knew you could do it! Where's that grumpy man of yours?"

"Griffin had to drive into the city to pick up some parts for a car he's working on. He should be back soon."

"Make sure you tell him, or I will," Meg threatened, knowing Quynh would probably try to not make a big deal out of her achievements. "Seriously, babe, you deserve this. I'm so happy for you."

Meg continued her happy chatter as Quynh sat speechless at her book.

Bestselling author. I'm a bestselling author.

It seemed so impossible.

She sat there long after Meg hung up. She needed to make more calls to share the good news.

The sound of Rover barking as he ran into the house brought her back to the present. She got up from her chair and closed the office door behind her. One time, she left the door open only to find Rover had chewed up her office chair. Griffin replaced it, and she got an upgrade. Her new chair had all the bells and whistles, which allowed her to write and fold down the armrest, giving Pickles space to snuggle up next to her. She even had a leg rest if she wanted to sit back and write.

"Hey, you're back early!" she shouted from the hall-way. She stopped short when she almost ran into Griffin's hard chest.

Griffin, who was standing with his hands behind his back and a guilty look on his face.

"What's going on...?" she asked her suspicious husband, worry seeping into her voice.

"I know you didn't want to make a big deal about it, but..." He grimaced as his words trailed off.

"But what?"

"Here."

From behind his back, he handed her two things. A

bouquet of fresh lilies and orchids, her favorite flowers, and a gift-wrapped bag.

"What is this?" she asked as she reached for the items in his hands. She bent her head to smell the fresh floral scent with a small smile.

"Open it," he prompted and gently grabbed the bouquet from her.

Hesitantly, she reached into the heavy bag and found several gift-wrapped items. The first one she opened was a fountain pen with her name engraved on the handle.

"So you have a pen for all the autographs you'll be signing."

The next gift was bigger and heavier. When she opened the package, she gasped.

"Griffin, I can't take this!" Quynh gestured at the brand new laptop she had been drooling over for the past few months.

"As a bestselling author, I think it was time for an upgrade." Griffin's tone was matter-of-fact. She had been complaining about how outdated her laptop was, which meant she couldn't install the latest programs for writing or formatting. It would have made her self-publishing journey so much easier if she had upgraded it, but it was not a necessity. She could get by without it, though it probably took her double the time necessary.

Her eyes watered at his thoughtful gestures.

"There's one more." He pointed to the bag impatiently.

"I don't know if I can handle any more of your surprises," she joked.

"Open it."

At his urging, she placed the laptop down on the nearby counter and grabbed the last item. It was much smaller than the laptop but was elegantly wrapped. She tore the wrapping paper to reveal a leather-bound journal similar to that of her mother's. Across the top was her name, which was hand-sewn into the leather. Her fingers traced the stitching.

Quynh looked up at Griffin with confusion.

"So you can write our story for our kids one day."

She smiled at her husband, touched by his thoughtful gestures and his unwavering support.

Though they talked about the possibility of having children, neither was ready yet. They also talked about adopting, which was most likely what would make the most sense for them, given their family history of cancer and addiction. Neither of them wanted to pass on the genes for either affliction, and there were so many children in need of a loving home.

She hugged the journal to her chest before placing it on top of the laptop. Griffin opened his arms. She flew into his chest.

She squeezed him tightly as she cried, tears of happiness at the life they built together. She rejoiced in the fact that fate brought the unlikely pair together under unlucky circumstances. His arms squeezed her tightly. She leaned back to look up at her husband.

"I love you, husband," she whispered. The words failed to convey the depth of her feelings, but it was the closest she could manage.

"I love you, wife." Griffin leaned down and kissed her softly. She leaned into the kiss and sighed with happiness.

She was no longer down on her luck. Not anymore. She now had everything she could ever hope for. All it took was a string of bad luck to lead her right where she belonged—in the arms of a grumpy mechanic.

*turn the page for
a fun surprise...*

Wow! I can't believe you made it to the very end. My heart is so full with gratitude that you took a chance on an indie author like myself.

If you could, please consider leaving a review. Every review helps but, please, do not tag me in any negative reviews.

Thank you so, so much for reading Quynh and Griffin's story.

join my patreon

Want to read my next book before anyone else? See all the artwork I commissioned and have swag mailed right to your door? Or maybe you want exclusive Patreon editions not available anywhere else?

You should join my Patreon!

http://www.patreon.com/lilyanhnam

want to know what's next?

You can subscribe to my newsletter where I share sneak peeks of my next project!
https://lilyanhnam.myflodesk.com/newsletter

acknowledgments

At the time of publication for Crash, I will have published three times in the span of just a few months. Which is INSANE to me. I did not expect to be writing another acknowledgment so soon after my debut, yet here I am.

None of this would be possible if not for the love and support of my husband, my children, and my feline companions. Earlier this year, I lost my writing buddy and it broke my heart. While he is no longer with us, he lives on in my books. So, when you see cats as a returning element in my stories, know that it's my way to grieve my best friend of over fifteen years.

I want to extend a thank you to my alpha reader, Maria B., and my beta reader, Miriam. Your feedback and GIF reactions gave me life. I love seeing Quynh and Griffin's stories through your eyes.

Thank you to my PA, Paige, who helped me manage life behind-the-scenes so I can get to this point.

To my readers, thank YOU for taking a chance on me. I hope you love this book as much as I do. When I sat down to write Crash, I had no idea that I would be writing differently than my debut. Switching from first person to third person felt so *natural* to me and their story came pouring out. I had so much fun with this story and I really hope you feel the love I sprinkled within the paragraphs and the pages.

From the bottom of my heart, I thank you for reading.

Lily Anh Nam is an Asian American contemporary romance author. She lives in a quiet New England town with her family and her feline writing companions. Her cats are often featured in her stories. Though she grew up on a tropical island, her favorite season is fall. Caramel lattes and mint chocolates keep her running. When not writing, Lily likes to spend time with her family. She rarely leaves the house without bribery.

You can connect with me on:

www.lilyanhnam.com

instagram.com/lilyanhnam

amazon.com/author/lilyanhnam

pinterest.com/lilyanhnam

patreon.com/lilyanhnam